Darkness Be Damned

Ditching Hell Series

Dora Blume

CHAPTER 1

LUCI

It didn't happen very often, a soul getting destroyed, but when it did, it was always a tough decision. Deciding whether someone was a lost soul was my life. Twelve Elites sat around me. The shattering of a glass against the wall pulled me from my reverie. Death was at an all-time high in the human realm. The demons had the illusion that there wouldn't be enough space for all of them. It was heresy, of course. Hell could be as big as I needed it to be. Listening to them argue had been a sport for me at one point in time. Now, I found it bothersome. Had I actually woken up for this nonsense?

"He's been here for too long." Mckenzie, who'd thrown the glass, stood with her hands resting on the conference table. "We've done all we can for him. He doesn't even care about his soul." Ah, she must be the one in charge of his rehabilitation. It can frustrate you when a soul doesn't try.

"We can make him care," Clare said. Her voice was raw with a plea to get them to reconsider. This particular soul was on his third, wait, fourth cycle. I lost track of how many times they'd given this guy a chance. They wouldn't buy into the desperation in the woman's voice. Just like me, always trying to save everyone. I would think it was pathetic if I hadn't felt the same way a time or two. This soul had been famous in his lifetime. Maybe that was the reason we had given him so many chances. My demons had grown fond of his music. When he picked up the guitar, he mesmerized everyone. It may have been a mistake to only choose those with a soul to be part of my Elite team. I wanted them to have compassion for humans. I'd chosen a mix of demons and previously rehabilitated souls, along with a fallen angel or two. It provided a delicate balance for these types of discussions. It was supposed to be difficult to destroy a soul, knowing it would never come back. I would be the final say in this room.

Was a fifth round going to change anything? Very few even got to four. I was considering a fifth. Had I lost my mind? Some days, I wondered if I would feel the same way if I weren't directly involved in making the call. The truth was, I wouldn't. Before my father chose me to help souls find redemption, It didn’t matter how many were being rehabilitated. Now, it was always my decision. The centuries of this job were getting the best of me. I needed a break.

"He must be demolished," Elias said.

I spared him a look. A part of me wanted to know why he wanted to see the soul gone so badly. He had been the one pushing so hard. Glancing around the room, I took notice of all the details others may have missed. Two of the men had their hands gripped into fists. They really didn't want to see this man given another chance. Why? There was something more going on here. I noticed the woman who had been standing up for him. It clicked.

"Who's our best male rehab agent?" I asked.

"What?" Clare asked.

"Clare, were you not the last one to attempt rehabilitation?" My eyebrow rose as I put the pieces together. It was no wonder the men in the room wanted him demolished.

"I was. What does that matter?" She rested back in her chair, her arms folded over her chest. Elias glared at her.

"Because you slept with him. You can't be unbiased in this decision," he spat.

"Show of hands. Who has had sex with the soul in the time he's been in the system?"

Four women and two men raised their hands. My eyebrows rose at the men. An equal opportunity soul. Perfect. "I need the best. Who do we have? Someone who won't be swayed sexually." I focused on Elias since he was in charge of placement. It was probably why he'd been so angry. This guy had gone through half of the Elites. Part of me wanted to meet him personally. I could use a little fun after the discussion in this room today.

Elias' brows furrowed. "He doesn't deserve another chance, Luci. You know this as well as I do."

"Well, I'd say you were correct if he hadn't fucked half the room. I don't think anyone here can be unbiased in this decision." I tapped my finger against my lips. "Randal, he's the best when it comes to unbiased decisions. There's no way he'll be able to sway that guy. If he does, he deserves another round on Earth."

"Fine, who's next?" Elias looked expectantly at Clare.

"Next, we have soul number 6,234,368. It's his second round. He hasn't taken to a single rehabilitation. We believe if he returns to Earth, he will do serious damage. The determination of both agents is that the soul should be demolished." She paused, her chin tilting down. "Any objections?"

I glanced around the room. There was a full-on brawl a moment ago. No one said anything for this soul. "Is there a reason not to give him a third round? Hell, we're about to give the last soul a fifth." I looked around the room. Not one set of eyes met mine.

"It's not advised. Both rehabilitation agents found too many flaws in the soul to determine a need for another round. He's not someone to save, Luci." There was a certain amount of sympathy in the woman's eyes. She was one of the fallen angels. It must hurt her just as much to demolish a soul. Yet, the decisions had to be made.

I nodded. I guess today wouldn't be a good day. I thought we'd made progress with the last guy. They were willing to change the established rules for him, but not this guy. What was the difference, really? Of course, I knew the difference. I wouldn't speak it aloud. Not now, maybe not ever.

I closed my eyes, taking a breath. "Fine. Is there a second to demolish?" I made this seem like a true board, with each member having a vote. The final decision would be mine, but going against the group wasn't in my best interest. One little anger outburst already had me in therapy. You toast a few Elites, and everyone thinks you've got anger issues. The board placated those who thought revolution was a good idea.

"I second," Elias said.

"All in favor, say I."

A chorus of "I's" filled the space.

I nodded, lowering my head. "Then it's settled. The soul will be demolished." I swallowed. Every soul chosen to be demolished felt like a personal failure to my father. You would think after centuries, it would get easier. It didn't. I closed my eyes, taking a moment of silence for the soul. The Elites sat silent. I rubbed my forehead. There was a throbbing just behind my eyes. It showed up when I'd woken, knowing today's meeting was about demolishing souls. It only increased. I wondered if something else was wrong. There was an unfamiliar itch under my skin. Something else was happening. I just didn't know what.

"We understand that this is hard for you." Clare rested her hand on my shoulder. At least someone in here still had a heart. Maybe they'd been doing this work too long. The sweetness in her voice didn't change the heartbreak I felt with every decision to demolish another soul. It was a necessary evil of my role here. A phrase of which my father was quite fond. There were days I could pummel him for his decisions. Today was one of them.

I kept my head low. The hate I felt for those seated at the table grew with each demolition. I didn't want to appear weak in front of the Elites who were kept in my charge. The Elites knew not to undermine my authority but wouldn't hesitate to speak their mind if they believed they needed to.

"We're done for today." I didn't care if there were more souls to go through.

One by one, the Elites cleared out until it was only my best friend standing before me. Checking out after that meeting seemed like the best thing. Kesa wasn't one of my Elites, but she was privy to everything happening. She was my right hand.

"You did everything you could." Kesa rested her hand on my back, rubbing circles.

It was one thing to know something and another to believe it. I willed myself to believe that there wasn't any more I could have done.

It was the double standard that was getting to me. I wanted to speak to my father about my "job." The conversation would end with him telling me there was no other person who could do the job like me. It was the same drivel he had given me every time I asked about my position here.

I didn't exactly like all the stories that had floated around about me. I wasn't the avenging angel who marched an army against my father. I wanted to set the record straight about my real reason for being here. Every single time I tried, my father would insist that it was for the best that everyone believed the stories. It kept more souls from needing to be rehabilitated. They needed to learn their lessons on Earth. It was the best place for them to learn and the only place that offered this particular learning experience. I understood the role I played and its necessity, but I hated it.

"I need a break." I expelled a hard breath. Everything was getting to me. Eliminating souls was always a hard decision, but I shouldn't be reacting this way to every single one. There was no way this could continue. I understood that some souls couldn't go back to Earth. I'd seen firsthand what happened when we sent someone back who wasn't ready. Catastrophic events weren't something I wanted to be responsible for. That was the horsemen's purview. Again, something I didn't want to have a single say over. The heaviness of running hell was enough.

Kesa patted my back fondly. "Then take one."

A hysterical laugh escaped my lips before I could stop it. "Yeah, right, like anyone would actually let me take a break. The dev-il doesn't get a vacation." The thought began to take shape. I sat straighter, a slow smile spreading across my lips. Maybe it was time for me to take a vacation. An actual one where I could frolic among humans with no one bothering me with what I "should" be doing. Oh, the idea sounded like heaven. I sighed. What would they do to me if I took a vacation? Fire me? Ha, I was Lucifer Morningstar! I was, in fact, the boss over every single soul here. The balance couldn't continue without me. Maybe it was time for a salacious vacation with all the fun I could stand.

I clapped my hands together. "Kesa, pack your bags. We're going on vacation to Earth." Kesa gaped at me. I knew her suggestion wasn't a serious one, but I was doing it anyway. Fuck 'em all.

"What? Luci, you can't be serious. Who's going to take over for you here? We can't just leave." Her words ran together in a panic. She was shaking her head back and forth. It had been her suggestion, but now she was freaking out.

"Kesa, it'll be okay. I'll put one of the Elites in charge while I'm gone. It won't be a long trip. Just a night or two away from here will do me some good. I'm sure someone else could handle it for a few days at the most. What's the worst that could happen?"

Kesa blinked at me. "Did you really just say that?"

"Yeah, come on. It's not a big deal." I waved my hand dismissively. "Who's the best on the team? Not one of those jackasses who always want to eliminate souls. It has to be someone who we can trust to do what's in the best interest of everyone." I sat on my settee, pulling my feet up to relax. It'd been a hard day. I wanted to rest for longer than a single night. I wouldn't admit that to anyone.

"It can't be Azazel. He's got the biggest head of the bunch. Maybe one of your brothers?" Kesa suggested.

"I don't know. Michael's still pretty pissed off. I can't imagine Uriel doing me a favor either." I rolled my eyes. Most of my brothers were super overdramatic about my role in scripture. I ended up with worshipers on Earth, and it peeved them.

"So, one of the fallen here, then?" Kesa tapped her pen on her notebook. I swore she took that thing everywhere. I never understood her incessant need to write everything, but I also appreciated it when she always had the answers I needed.

I thought about all the angels whom I could ask to take over for a bit. I thought about the few my father insisted on checking up on me here. One would think he didn't trust me to rehabilitate souls. He always seemed to think my pride would get the better of me. So far, I'd proven him wrong. I'd been nothing but a faithful servant, helping to rehabilitate souls who could be and making the difficult decisions when they couldn't. I was my father's daughter, after all. Loving souls ran deep, but I knew when to make the hard choices. Closing my eyes, I ran through the angel's faces. "Sariel, I believe he's the most trusted of those here. Is he out collecting souls?" He was the one who was in charge of all the angels of death. He could easily take over the responsibility of deciding who could be redeemed, at least for a little while. His operation ran like a well-oiled machine. He would also be the most likely to consider all options before making any harsh decisions. He was the most level-headed of the lot.

"Oh, yeah, he would be a good choice. Can he step away from his own role, though?" Kesa made a note.

"I think he could. Will you call him in to see me?" I wanted some time before I spoke with Sariel. I needed to look my best when I went out tonight. When Sariel said yes, I wanted to leave for Earth immediately.

"Aren't you supposed to be in therapy?" Kesa narrowed her eyes at me. She knew my apprehension about seeing the therapist. The Elites demanded it after I'd smoked a few too many.

"Fuck, what time is it?"

"Time for you to get your ass to therapy. Respectfully." She smirked.

"Yeah, yeah, I'm going." I rolled my eyes and portaled to my therapist's office.

I focused on the flowers that elongated from the vase on the table. I wasn't avoiding the conversation, per se. Being here, in this office, and talking to a therapist wasn't my favorite thing to do. After I'd lost my temper on an Elite, the others demanded therapy as my penance. Like, I would really kill another one. It wasn't my fault he'd been an asshat one too many times for my liking. They were in my realm, after all. You'd think they'd pay me a little more respect some days. His head had gotten too big. He'd said the wrong thing, and I'd gotten a little mad. The fire was out in a matter of minutes. Not that big of a deal, really. The flowers that transfixed me were an elegant blue with leaves shaped like tiny stars. They seemed to lean towards the light pouring in from the window. It wasn't just the flowers. The white vase that held them looked elegant, too. I'd concluded, like I did every time I sat across from my therapist and looked at the flowers, that she had very sophisticated tastes. I wondered if she'd been the same before coming here. Maybe that was what brought her here. Vanity got the best of so many human souls. It got worse with each new piece of technology. Everyone was looking for their fifteen seconds of fame.

The flowers weren't the only interesting décor in the room. There were paintings of all sorts. Famous paintings, but I knew they were only replicas because the originals were on Earth. Framed quotations filled any open spaces on the walls. I noted a particular one in every meeting that read, "What we think, we become." If only more humans knew how true that one was for what happened after death. They might actually spend time creating their reality instead of complaining about it.

My therapist kept her eyes fixated on me, but I pretended not to notice. I knew I was stalling. Had I mentioned how much I didn't want to be in this office, talking about my feelings or whatever I was supposed to be doing? There was a notepad on her lap. The red-soled pumps she was sporting let me know vanity was definitely her vice. I bet she'd traded sessions putting up with me to get them to get her all the designer things she liked. Her tailored suits certainly weren't cheap in her human realm. At least having to study me paid her well. Even if none of those things actually mattered here.

Sometimes, I suspected she wasn't a very good therapist in her human life. Her rehabilitation had been to fix me. So far, that was going swimmingly. I could feel her impatience growing with each tick of the clock. In the human realm, these sessions were an hour. That was one saving grace. My therapist liked her routine. An hour was all the time I had to waste looking at the flowers and upbeat messages on the wall.

"Luci?" The rise in her tone had me biting my lip.

I finally pulled my eyes away from the flower arrangement to my therapist's waiting gaze. She was a slim woman with bronzed skin. It shimmered slightly under the fluorescent lighting she'd chosen. I wondered if she used some sort of cream to get that effect. The therapist's ebony-colored hair was in a low bun, and I was sure I'd never seen her wear it in another style. She attempted a reassuring smile that felt as fake as the Jimmy Choo handbag resting at her feet.

I shook my head to rid myself of my straying thoughts. I was given a chance to talk about whatever was on my mind. The woman had sworn a blood oath that nothing I said would leave these walls. If she were to betray that oath, she would instantly become dust. I still didn't think she took that oath as seriously as she should. The insistent way she said that she'd sworn an oath to client confidentiality always. I would like to believe her. But I was Satan. It wasn't in my nature. I liked to have a little extra protection. She had little choice.

The only sentence stuck in my head was the same one that had been nestling there for what felt like forever. What would happen if I left Hell? I'd put the motions into place, but what would really happen when I left? Was it even possible? Questions raced in my head, along with all the things that could go wrong when I left. It was an anxiety train, and I was all aboard whether I liked it or not. I regarded the woman again; her patience was uncanny. I knew her annoyance was festering below the surface, but she kept it in check nicely. I almost wanted to commend her for it. I would've lost my shit if I was being so blatantly ignored.

"I'm doing all right," I finally spoke. It was an immediate lie. Nothing about today had been all right. I was about to lose another soul. I would get reamed if my father ever found out I'd given so many opportunities for rehabilitation. It was unheard of to give a soul so many chances. Of course, he would say I wasn't taking my responsibility seriously again. I was so tired of hearing how I failed him. The one disappointment in a shining collection of miraculous feats.

There wasn't much I wanted to say to this woman. I looked away from my therapist, well aware that the woman's gaze wasn't wavering. Every time she looked at me like that, I found myself oversharing. My oversharing could certainly get me in trouble. I considered leaving hell. The thought wasn't daunting; it was the repercussions of the position I held. It was more of the fact my father was God. If I walked away now, I would just be another disappointment. Maybe I needed to spin that in my favor. What was the line in that song? If I could be anything, I'd be a disappointment, am I right? Maybe being the constant disappointment made for better branding. That's how they portrayed me in the human world. Might as well live up to their expectations.

Ugh, I didn't want to have that conversation when he found out I left.

The therapist worked closely with those in hell. I wasn't the only one having a hard time. Even if it wasn't about the demolition of souls, the other demons had what bugged them, and that was why the therapist was essential. Those in heaven didn't need a therapist. What did they have to be sad about? The place was a literal paradise that breathed nothing but life. Rehabilitation of whatever ailed you in your human life didn't just magically disappear after you died. You still had to work through whatever shit landed you here. So, I may have recruited a therapist or a thousand to work with those who'd ended up in my humble abode. It was brilliant. Therapists were literally the worst sometimes. So many of them ended up here. It made sense that I recruited them to help the other souls, too.

"Are you sure you're all right? You've been working impossibly hard lately. You know they aren't all your responsibility, right?" Her voice was light despite the heavy content she delivered.

"They're all my responsibility, which is why I was chosen for this." Didn't she understand? Each soul here was in my world. It was my responsibility to rehabilitate the souls who came here. Everything here was on me. No one else. I shifted under the weight of my responsibility. You can't offer salvation to someone who doesn't want it. There had to be some way to get them to want it. To entice them into thinking there was something better. Hope was the destruction of the masses, even here.

"You can't take that all on yourself. It will eat you up inside. You need to find the balance." I heard the soothing words, but they never registered. I felt like we'd had this same conversation hundreds of times. Nothing changed. Nothing would change. It was why I needed to take a break so desperately. The weight of everything would crush me if I didn't seek my salvation.

"I'm thinking about taking a break." I'd said it. I didn't care. I needed to say it to someone besides Kesa. She'd seen me at my worst. Kesa was as honest as they came, but hearing another opinion wouldn't hurt.

"Running away from your feelings doesn't help at all. You know that already."

Well, shit, I wasn't expecting that.

"Do you feel overly stressed?" Her head cocked to the side slightly. Had this woman ever really listened to me? There had to be hundreds of reasons for me to be stressed, penciled in that damn notebook. Yet here we were. The stupidity of her words left me flabbergasted.

Closing my eyes, I could hear the souls screaming. Rehabilitation wasn't always pleasant. I could hear them when I was particularly vulnerable. Most of the time, I shut them out. Hearing voices was usually frowned upon. Telling anyone you could hear the screams of tormented souls. Yeah, not something you want to share in polite conversation.

"I think I just need to take some time away from here. Get my head together. Take a vacation. That's what people do when everything gets too much, right? They take a break. The only way I'll be able to do that is if I leave. I think I need to leave." My words ran together. I wasn't sure who I was spilling all this for, her or me. I needed more convincing than anyone. Could I leave the rehabilitation of souls and Hell in someone else's hands? Could I trust anyone that much? I doubted it. But I needed to get away.

The therapist nodded like she understood what I was going through. If she did, then she was an amazing therapist. No one would ever understand her. I rolled my eyes. An existential crisis in the therapist's office. How fitting.

"It's no secret that you care about the souls, and everyone has seen you working hard to help all the souls that are sent here. It's not an easy feat to get not just one but four cycles for a human soul. You did that." There was a level of pride in her tone. I wasn't aware that she knew what happened with the souls and the Elites.

"Yes, I did."

"Aren't you at all happy about what you accomplished today? I heard it's never been done, but you made it happen. You need to celebrate the wins more often. I think it would really help you." She leaned forward, one heel slipping behind the other. I recognized that look. Our time was almost up, and she would leave me with some last piece of advice. Maybe that worked with her normal patients, but I wasn't normal.

I blinked when she stood and went to her desk. She pulled out a piece of paper from inside the desk. Where was the advice? Had she written it down so she'd remember?

"Let's go over the steps for rehabilitation together. You need to see the accomplishment you've made today." She held the parchment in front of her, poised to read.

I remembered the day my father told me I was taking over hell. I'd read and memorized the steps he'd given me for his ideas about rehabilitation. Then, I assumed it would be the easiest job in the world. Humans needed saving, and when they knew that if they didn't get it right in hell, they would never get another chance. It was the end of the road for them, and there was no option to turn back. I promised I would do my best for the good of all souls.

"I know you will, Luci. You were always my morning star." He'd called me that throughout my childhood. I didn't want to disappoint him. I'd never wanted to disappoint him. It just came so naturally to me sometimes.

The steps were easy. I had done it so many times I didn't need to look through them. When a soul got sent to Hell, the first thing to do was orient them. That was necessary. Get the complete shock of being dead out of the way. You didn't want the souls thinking that their arrival to Hell was for all eternity. Although, it was a fun prank to play on some of the trickster souls sometimes. Hey, we needed entertainment here. It was Hell. Our amusement was to see how each soul spent quite some time begging my father for another chance at life. They never got it. He wasn't even listening once they'd entered Hell. People needed to atone for their sins.

The next step was to review their life with them. It would surprise many people to know that most people who got sent to Hell were clueless about the acts that sent them there. Begging was always involved in this process somewhere. I should have written about the stages of grief. Seriously, I saw them enough times.

They received their penance and assigned an agent. Penance was never fixed, though. The agent assigned had full discretion to change and vary the rehabilitation process at will. The purpose of the demons in Hell was to make sure that everyone who got sent there was being rehabilitated properly. Agents needed to be kept in line, too.

Those who were convinced always surprised me that they were there because God didn't like them. Like that was actually a thing. It took a while to convince them to get on with the rehab. Leaving Hell wasn't an option until a soul was determined to be completely ready.

If they weren't ready, they would be given another round as determined by the Elites. A new agent would be assigned. We had a special group for those who needed more than one round. It wasn't exactly a regular thing, but some were just harder to crack than others. We referred to them as special cases. When more than one attempt failed, we discussed demolition. Those were the conversations I despised. They were necessary but so depressing. Once demolished, a soul was gone. Their energy was dissipated into the aether. It was the literal end.

"Is there a reason you're not celebrating? Does that list suggest multiple rounds are normal for a soul?" she asked.

"No, of course, it's not normal. But what the hell is here? Just because one guy was saved while another was demolished makes nothing better. We still lost a soul today. We lose souls every day. Don't you understand? That's why I need a break." Frustration filled me. I didn't want to celebrate. One soul was still here, but so many were not.

"I know it isn't easy to come to terms with the fact a soul was demolished today. You can't save those who have no interest in being saved. All the people who made it to paradise are those who did their penance like they were told to do. Souls who get demolished are those who refuse to be better. There's nothing you can do about that." The therapist was trying to make me feel better, but it wasn't working. It never did.

"I get that it's your job to make me feel better about what I do here. But please stop. I don't feel good about demolishing a soul. It's not supposed to feel good. It's supposed to hurt Every. Time. That's why I was chosen for this role. I'm not supposed to take it lightly. Death, it's supposed to hurt. Grieving their souls was my penance. It's what makes me who I am. So, please stop trying to spin the losses to be something they're not. It doesn't help anyone." I closed my eyes, quieting the subtle rage building inside me.

"Good, now we're getting somewhere." She folded her arms over her chest. There was a sense of accomplishment in her squared shoulders.

"What the hell?" I glared at her.

"Anger is one step closer to acceptance." She beamed.

I shook my head. "Time's up." I stormed out of the room. That woman felt some level of accomplishment at my pain. I was so sick of being here. After my meeting with Sariel, I would go. He wouldn't let me down. I was sure of it. At this point, I wasn't sure I cared. Maybe the place needed to see what it was like without me for a bit. Maybe they would appreciate what they had with me as their leader. What was the saying, absence makes the heart grow fonder? Well, in this case, I needed them to appreciate that I kept this place running. I was the reason everything went off without a hitch. The damn Elites thought they could fight me on decisions. Maybe they needed to see what it would be like without me around for a while. Dammit, I was leaving. I'd made my decision. I would ditch Hell. *Human realm, here I come.*

CHAPTER 2

Luci

I left the therapist's office with a sense of purpose. Leaving Hell, if only for a little while, was just the thing I needed to get my groove back, or so Stella says. I may have lost a soul today, but there were still so many to save. The day was bright, but I knew everyone believed that Hell would be a dark and fiery place. The jokes people made about hell and the heat were quite amusing, considering Hell was nothing like the sauna Earth was on any given summer day. I rolled my eyes. Like they didn't know they were doing it to themselves.

Hell was beautiful. My little paradise to do with as I chose. Most saw the rows of houses much like they did in the human realm. We mirrored it after what the souls were used to so as not to cause too much of a shock. I'd learned early that a soul finding out they were in Hell was enough of a shock without all the devilish ambiance to accompany it. I was more interested in color, anyway. I didn't want to be surrounded by jutting rocks, flames, and doom. Yuck! What a way to spend eternity.

My schedule for today wasn't daunting. I was supposed to see the therapist and show up to meet the new recruits. I loved meeting the ones who would rehabilitate the souls. We got too large of an influx of souls on any given day for me to greet any of them, but the ones who were there to rehabilitate the new souls were the ones I wanted to meet. Some were fallen angels, some new demons, and others were simply selected from various supernatural communities. Those who'd been shifters or vampires on Earth had a talent for rehabilitating souls in the afterlife. It was probably because they'd lived several lifetimes on Earth. There was something to be said for that kind of wisdom. It certainly wasn't anything one could learn without the cruelest of teachers. Time.

"There you are," a familiar voice said from behind me. I turned around to greet one of my favorite Fallen. I turned around to greet Izzy, who had woven strips of red leather down her long, black hair. Her all-leather attire matched her less-than-pleasant attitude. She always looked and acted like she was ready to spring on anything that pissed her off. We'd become fast friends. Izzy's signature sardonic smile made me almost giddy to see her. I had seen the simple curve of her lips drive humans and demons mad with lust. Meeting Izzy as a fallen angel hadn't surprised me in the least. I wondered what she had done to gain my father's favor in the first place. Pissing him off made sense, but to be liked by him was what confused me. Izzy was pretty tight-lipped about her status or what happened before she ended up in my beautiful realm.

"Izzy, my love, what do I owe the pleasure of your company?"

"Girl, I've been looking for you everywhere. Don't act like you aren't happy to see me. If you're not now, you certainly will be."

"I'm sure I will be. So, what's up?" Izzy did nothing without purpose. She liked to move between here and the human realm as often as she could. I couldn't begrudge her for wanting to have fun. I heard the stories of all the fun she got to have there. It made me more than a little envious.

"It still feels as depressing as the last time I was here," Izzy shuddered.

"And yet, here you are." I waved my hands out. "I know, I know, you don't like colors that aren't black or red. God forbid I use a little color to liven the place up a bit. You can't say you don't enjoy the radiance of a purple and pink sky."

"Ugh, why are you so, you?" She rolled her eyes. "Okay, focus. I'm only here to do you a favor. Trust me, you want me to do it." She waved her hand with such an air of confidence it was hard to refuse.

"Is that right?" I couldn't say I wasn't more than a little interested.

"You don't know how exceptional of a favor it is. Seriously, you're going to be so happy I found you today." She stopped walking and turned to face me. I stopped and gave her my full attention, which seemed to be what she was demanding.

"Don't play with me, Izzy. What's it?"

"The horsemen." Izzy leaned close, her eyes shifting around us. She had to know I liked my privacy. No one bothered me after the therapist. Not unless they wanted me to take out on them whatever issue I was dealing with. Izzy was lucky it was a relatively pleasant visit.

"Yeah, what about them? Aren't they locked away in some pocket realm where my father likes to keep them until whatever doomsday prophecy he cooks up and brings them back again? He's quite childish when it comes to them." I rolled my eyes. Some days, I thought the all-knowing God could be a child. He used them to keep his followers in check. It was never an actual threat, only something to remind them of his power.

"They're loose." Izzy pressed her lips together. I stared at her for several long minutes, trying to comprehend what that meant exactly.

"What?" My brows rose. "What are you talking about? That's impossible. My father always tells us before he releases them because of the influx of souls. I would know if they were free." I blinked. My father had always told me when they were going to the human realm. It was common courtesy to warn me so I could prepare my team. He wouldn't just let them loose, would he?

"Girl, you know I wouldn't lie to you about something like this?" Izzy cocked her head like it appalled her. I would even suggest such a thing.

"Shit, who fucked that up?"

Izzy winked. "Probably one of your incompetent brothers." Izzy had real issues with the other angels. Most likely because she was a fallen. I didn't pry.

I pulled my hand through my curls. The horsemen loose were a problem. More souls would come to Hell. My crew needed to know about this. I needed to find out what the hell was going on.

"Are you sure? Like one-hundred percent positive, it's the horsemen that are out? You didn't just get drunk and someone told you he was a horseman or something. It's impossible. It's not their time. I would know."

Izzy nodded, no sign of annoyance on her face. "No, you know I would have vetted information as important as this. Besides, they're the foundation of the four supernatural breeds. Every vampire, shifter, fae, and witch knows when they're on Earth." She held her hand to her chest in mock annoyance. "Aren't you happy I found you today? Aren't you grateful I shared this with you as soon as I found out?" She fluttered her lashes, her hand still resting over her heart.

"Yes, I am. Let me guess, you want something from me."

"Well, I heard through the grapevine that you might take a trip."

"How in the hell did you hear that?" I balked. Kesa was the only person I'd talked to about it. Well, Kesa and my therapist.

"Okay, Kesa mentioned it. So, do you need a friend to be your tour director? It's been a few years since you ventured there, and things have certainly changed. I know you're going to need someone to show you around." She scraped her bottom lip with her teeth.

"Let me guess, it would honor you to be that someone?" I rolled my eyes.

"Well, of course, I would. I'm so glad you asked." She skipped a step. "Okay, Love, gotta jet. Let me know as soon as you're packed. We have some debauchery to get to." She winked and whisked off, a skip in her step as she went.

Izzy would either be a damn good time or a whole lot of trouble. I wasn't exactly sure which. Either way, she always made things interesting. It was time to go home. My day just got complicated with a whole new level of fuckery.

"How do we know she's not lying?" Kesa stood stock still as I broke the news.

"Izzy may be a lot of things, but a liar isn't one of them."

Kesa nodded, but there were still traces of doubt in her eyes. To be frank, the four horsemen weren't exactly easy to picture frolicking on Earth. I couldn't ignore the information. The four horsemen had awoken, and they would wreak havoc on Earth.

I resisted the urge to scream. Going to Earth was supposed to be a vacation. A way for me to get away from the stresses of Hell. Now it would be a damned job. One that only I could handle. There was no way I was sending someone else to handle something this catastrophic. There would be no argument. I would be the one to go to Earth and figure out what the hell was actually going on.

"We're going to Earth to find the horsemen."

"Are you serious?" Kesa's tone let me know just how thrilled she was with the change. I imagined her jumping and squealing when I told her we would go to Earth. My best friend acted like it was the last thing she wanted to hear. All the while, her eyes were wide as saucers. Kesa had the prettiest dark eyes I had ever seen.

"I expected more excitement." I poked Kesa's side lightly.

"I wasn't exactly expecting our trip to be a hunting expedition." Kesa laughed a little. She looked down at her hands like the admission embarrassed her. I patted her shoulder.

"The plan is simple. We're going to get the horsemen and put them back before proceeding to have a damn good time. Are you okay with that?" I smirked. No one said we couldn't have a little fun on our adventure. With Izzy as our tour guide, it would be quite the time. Honestly, I couldn't wait. We just had to deal with the little nuisance of someone starting the apocalypse. No big deal, right?

Chapter 3

Luci

The human realm wasn't the same. The air felt different. It was thicker, heavier, and more humid than usual. The sky was a hazy gray, and the setting sun hid behind thick clouds. A strange, rotting smell filled the air. The birds stopped singing, and the only sound was the wind rustling through the trees. I felt uneasy, like something bad was about to happen. I looked around, trying to figure out what was going on. This time of the year, spirits should be high. People were supposed to be getting ready for summer. The expectation was shorts and tanks and lots of visible skin. People wore clothes meant for winter. There was a man in a straggly coat to my right, coughing and heaving violently. The street lights enhanced the deep lines on his face as he wretched onto the street.

Glancing up, there was a crowd of people in front of a large, lighted building. A hospital. People huddled together, wrapped in wool blankets. The temperature had to be around sixty. Why were they shivering on the street? Where the hell was Izzy? It made little sense that we landed in front of an overcrowded hospital.

"This is what the human realm is all about?" Kesa paled as she took in the scene. "No offense, but it really isn't worth all the hype."

I couldn't blame her. This wasn't the Earth I had wanted to introduce her to. The Earth I imagined when I made promises to all the beautiful places and people was nothing like the current state of the world. The Earth I promised Kesa had more laughter, and death didn't hang heavy in the air. There was supposed to be light, and the air was supposed to be breathable, not thick with sorrow.

In the distance, a woman let out a piercing scream. Both of our heads snapped towards the sound. A nurse bent towards the woman. Her scrubs clung to her, and dark circles rimmed her eyes. "He's gone." She closed the man's eyes.

The woman clutched him tight against her chest. "No," she screamed. "You can't leave me. You can't leave me alone."

I looked up and then to the door of the hospital. There were at least forty people out here. I walked closer to the body, even though Kesa held her hand out to stop me. The man looked pallid; his skin stretched over his defined bones. Black patches were around his eyes and mouth. The nurse came back with two men covered in thick, white suits. Those outside shook their heads in pity but said nothing. The men slid a body bag under the man.

One of my brother's reapers showed up and hovered over the body as it was being zipped into the body bag. He should have been here upon death. He waved his hand, and the soul stood next to him, looking down at himself. The reaper bowed in recognition, and they both disappeared before my eyes. Reapers weren't much for conversation.

Pestilence had started his work.

"What's going on?" Kesa asked.

"The apocalypse has begun." Looking at all the people who were suffering when it wasn't even time stirred something inside me. Maybe I should have told my father and allowed him to take charge of whatever was happening. There should be no reason for me to handle this much of a shit show. My father should know the horsemen were on Earth. He was the almighty, after all. None of the chaos and pain around me should be happening. Unless he was the reason for it and didn't tell anyone.

I planned to rip Pestilence apart and show him the human definition of hell. If it wasn't time for them to be woken up, and I was certain they knew it wasn't, why did they start? There was no excuse for this torment.

The rate at which the illness had spread proved that Pestilence hadn't just gotten here like Izzy led me to believe. Why hadn't Izzy told me sooner? No way this just started. I whisked Kesa into the nearest bar. The news played across the television screen above the bar. Several patrons were drinking as they watched indifferently.

The number of deaths doubled every day. Chances of surviving were slim. The reporter explained how scientists were doing their best to create a vaccine. Those who didn't have it appeared to be taking extra precautions. They reported several countries had gone into lockdown. They were threatening the same all over the world as the virus spread rapidly. The newscaster promised it would only be a short time before a vaccine was available.

It was false hope. Humans thrived on hope. It was the destruction of more lives than I could count. I was sure that no one was close to making a discovery of either a vaccine or a cure. The disease

Pestilence created wouldn't be that easy. It was the sole reason for his existence.

I ran my hand through my hair. I was at a loss for where to start. The best place would be to find the horsemen before they got the chance to unleash something worse. It was only a matter of time before we saw evidence of the second or third horseman.

If the white horsemen were in the human realm, without a doubt, the other horsemen were here. They were certainly scheming something worse. The epidemic was only the beginning.

Like an answer to a prayer, Pestilence appeared on the screen. I felt his power was like a beacon to mine. His strong jawline contrasted with his round glasses. Intrigue went through me as I watched his commanding presence. How could no one else see it? He was wearing a white coat, a clear indication he was a doctor.

"He's a doctor." The bartender pointed. "He'll be able to tell us what's going on."

Cade White, the name read beneath him. I waited, my hands curling into fists. He spread his lips into what was supposed to be a reassuring smile. "Thank you, Robert." He glanced to the side where I assumed the anchor was sitting. "I'm here to dispel any fears about the virus. Doctors with the CDC have partnered with the World Health Organization to find a vaccine. The virus seems to spread rapidly through secretions when breathing. We recommend wearing masks in public to curb the spread. Every effort is being made to slow the spread and get a vaccine rolled out as soon as possible. Until then, take the necessary precautions to keep your family safe." His voice was soft, almost calming. It was no wonder they chose him to represent the CDC. He had a knack for keeping his voice smooth and calm.

I scoffed at his audacity. How could he be the reason people were suffering and the one who offered them hope? It was cruel. He was a monster, a smile on his lips while he furthered humanity's torment. His meek appearance was a façade. The power pouring out of him was an aphrodisiac for someone as powerful as me. I couldn't help but notice how attractive he was. If I weren't here to stop him from destroying humanity, there could be something there.

I listened to him continue to reassure the public that every effort was being made to ensure their safety. He spoke with such eloquence. His speech pulled attention from the small crowd in the bar. They watched the screen with bated breath. I sighed, watching the desperation in their eyes. It was false hope. Not that they needed to panic, but it was only the beginning. No one here would understand.

"Is that him?" Kesa asked.

"The one and only, Pestilence in the flesh."

"He doesn't look like the source of all magic. So, what's the plan?"

I pulled my gaze from the charismatic man on the screen. "Yeah, he's keeping up quite the façade. We're going to the conference tomorrow." I pointed at the screen. It gave the address for what appeared to be a press conference with up-to-date information on the situation. It was the perfect opportunity to fetch him and possibly the others who may be around. I doubted they would be in the same place, but one could hope.

"What are we going to do until then?"

"Now, we have a little fun while we wait."

I slid the new deep-burgundy lipstick across my lips, pressing them together with a pop. Tight black leather hugged my body as I finished preparing for a night in Sin City. The thrill was the same regardless of how many times I'd been to Earth. I teased my brown hair into a twist with curls that bounced around the top.

Kesa exuded strength and poise in a black corset over a plum dress. Her light-bronze skin shimmered with a fresh coat of lotion. Her hair fell loose around her shoulders. Silver chains glittered around her neck. Kesa booked a place for us to stay while we hunted for the horsemen. They were a problem for tomorrow. Tonight was filled with promise.

A knock sounded. Izzy strode through what should have been a locked door.

"Since when do you knock?"

"I thought I'd at least give you the courtesy of knocking before barging in." Izzy was in silver platform shoes. Her blue and purple glitter bodycon dress hugged every curve. She was a sight with platinum-blond hair in large, pinned rolls around her head. There was so much glitter.

"I appreciate the courtesy." I smirked.

"Wasn't Vegas the perfect place to start?" She beamed. "There's so much fun to be had in a wonderful city like this one." She clapped her hands together and looked at us expectantly. "I assume you're ready."

"Lead the way." I held my arm out towards the door. Choosing Izzy as our guide would either be the best decision ever or the worst.

The air was surprisingly chilly for the desert. The cold didn't bother me. As we bounded down the street, my eyes fell on those who were all bundled up. Some of them wore masks, as suggested by the newscast. A horseman gave them that advice to stop the spread. You'd think he'd want it to spread faster. It was curious indeed. Another question for tomorrow.

Kesa tugged on my arm. "Are you all right?"

I nodded. "Yeah, just thinking about things."

"Well, stop it. We're going to have fun tonight. The horsemen are tomorrow's problem."

My thoughts drifted to the increase in fallen angels. Currently, the number of angels who had lost their dignified position wasn't enough to cause worry, but it made many people wonder what was going on. I couldn't help but wonder if it was all connected.

Izzy led them to a club that looked more than a little sketchy from the street. It was perfect. I always enjoyed a little danger with my nightlife. Izzy was a girl after my own heart. It wasn't a good time if there wasn't a strong possibility of a fight. Clubs weren't the place to find a life partner. Bodies bumping against each other as the beat pulled them into motion. Quickies in the bathroom with someone you would never see again. Drinking until oblivion was a close companion to the cold linoleum. The anticipation was enticing. I wanted every second of it.

"Are you ready for a damn good time?" Izzy winked as she strode past the people standing in line.

"Should my stomach feel weird?" Kesa leaned closer to me.

"Just a little nerves. Don't worry; we'll take good care of you."

Kesa laughed. "Sure, you will."

"Why would I lie to you?" I smirked.

Izzy paused at the door, side-eying the bouncer when he didn't immediately move to assist her in entering the club. He shook his head. "No trouble tonight, Iz. You know how the boss gets when you cause trouble." He moved the rope to the side.

"Trouble? Moi?" She held her fingers against her chest. "I wouldn't even think of causing trouble." She fluttered her lashes as she passed. We followed close behind. Izzy must frequent this place often.

I pulled Kesa along as we wove our way around the many bodies here tonight. "Let's get a drink before we dance." The heat from the packed club hit me. Bodies filled in all the open spaces. Crowds lined the bar, hands waving cash in the air to get the bartender's attention. "How are we going to get a drink in this place?" I looked skeptically at Izzy.

"Oh, ye of little faith. Come on, we're going upstairs." She led us past another guard and up the stairs to a private section. She smiled at a man standing near the entrance. "Hey lover, you have quite the crowd tonight." She leaned in to kiss each of his cheeks. His hand lingered on her hips, pulling her closer to his body.

"To what do I owe the pleasure, Iz?" Something about him changed in her presence.

"I just wanted to show a friend of mine a good time. I couldn't think of a better place than your fabulous club." She ran her hand down his arm, toying with the cufflink on his sleeve. "You don't mind, do you?"

He blinked. "Of course not. You're always welcome here." His eyes smoldered down at her. "Please introduce me to your friends. You know any friends of yours are friends of mine."

"This is Luci and Kesa." She held her hand out to each of us when she said our names. "They're in dire need of a drink. It was such a long walk over here." Izzy kept her arms tucked in the man's elbow. I wondered at her immediate possession of him. Izzy was a free spirit, but there was something about how she held him close to her that was telling.

"It's a pleasure to meet you." He bowed slightly. "I'm Marcus. Welcome to my club."

"It's quite the place you have here." Kesa's eyes were wide as she took in everything.

"Marcus caters to an interesting collection of clientele." Izzy winked.

My eyebrows rose. "Oh?"

"I do. Most everyone here is involved in the supernatural community. It's why Izzy is so fond of it here." He glanced sideways at his companion. She hadn't detached from his arm. I wondered if they were in some sort of relationship. Izzy's definition of it may be a little looser than most.

I glanced around, only now noticing the demons present. Some of them gave me a quick, respectful nod. The whispers started. They wondered what exactly I was doing here. Fear sparked on some of their faces. I smiled widely at the many faces I recognized. "Interesting, indeed."

Marcus snapped his fingers in the air, and a woman with a tray stepped in front of them. "Yes, sir. How can I help you?"

"Get these ladies anything they desire. I expect them to leave more than a little satisfied." He leaned over and kissed Izzy's cheek. "I have some calls to make. I'll check back with you later." He paused, narrowing his eyes. "No trouble." He held a finger in front of her.

She bit it in a flash. "No promises."

He shook his head. "Have a good time."

"So, mind telling us what that was about?" Kesa asked.

"Just a friend."

"Friend? Yeah, sure." Kesa smirked. I knew Izzy would never be a one-man woman. Her attraction to him was obvious. I couldn't fault her taste. The man was devastatingly handsome. Maybe she'd be willing to share later.

Izzy pulled them to a high-top table. "Three cosmos and keep 'em coming."

"Oh, we're sophisticated ladies tonight?" I tapped the server's arm before she walked away. "I'll take a whiskey, neat, please."

"Come now, have a little fun," Kesa chided.

"Oh, I plan to. I also plan on drinking whiskey. Those aren't mutually exclusive." I rolled my eyes. Those two could drink whatever they wanted. I'm a whiskey girl.

"So, what's on the menu tonight?" Izzy focused on me as I scanned the crowd.

"Besides your beau?" I turned back to focus on Izzy.

"I told you, he's just a friend." Izzy rolled her eyes.

"I certainly don't mind the selection at this club. What do you think, Kesa?"

"I think we should dance." Kesa pulled Izzy's and my hands.

"Oh, I love to dance." Izzy squealed as we all made our way to the dance floor.

We danced together for what felt like minutes but had actually been hours. A warm body pressed up against my back, and two hands rested lightly on my hips. Whoever this was, they were being rather forward. Not a soul had laid a hand on me the entire time I'd been here. Being that most were supernatural, I wasn't surprised. "Interesting seeing you here, Lucifer." Hot breath whispered in my ear. I felt an electric current run up my body from where his fingers grazed my bare skin. A lick of magic followed the trail he'd left behind.

I was lost in the sensation for a split second before rationality caught up to me. Another warm body pressed against my chest. Shifter, my brain processed.

"Hey," Izzy belted.

"What the—" Kesa was cut off as four tall, burly men surrounded me. I recognized one of them as the doctor I'd seen on television. There was an intensity coming from each one of them. It lit me up from the inside. What was this?

"I hear you may be here for us, Kitten," the doctor purred. His pale white locks were a striking contrast to the two blue jewels behind his steely glare. The radiant blue marked him as a magic wielder.

I narrowed my eyes on him. "Maybe I am. Maybe I'm just trying to have a bit of fun."

"Fun? Oh, Darling. We're here to have fun." The man to my right, his mouth curved into a devious smile. His jet-black hair was a sharp contrast to his bright smile. The brunette, with a surly frown, elbowed him in the ribs.

"We're not going back," he said, his dark eyebrows slanted down. His thin lips pressed together into an unmistakable frown.

"You're not continuing here, either." I rested my fist on my cocked hip. "I don't know who let you out, but you aren't supposed to be here." I tapped my finger on my lips. "What's that line from the song? You don't have to go home, but you can't stay here. Yeah, something like that." I smirked. "I'm not forcing you back to your realm, but you aren't supposed to be on Earth. I don't care where you go, as long as it's not here."

Cade snickered. A devilishly handsome smile spread across his lips. "You aren't our leader, Lucifer. We don't answer to you."

I hated his immediate dismissal of my power. My eyes blazed red. "Is that so?" I froze every person in the room except for myself and the four gentlemen.

The man with the thin lips and chestnut hair growled, "We're not leaving."

"Agreed. We're not leaving. We're having too much fun." He clapped his hands together. A strand of black hair fell out of where it was slicked back from the movement.

"Huxley," Cade cursed.

"What? We're having fun." He held his hand out to me. "She said she was here to have fun." His eyes lit with the excitement of a child at a birthday party. I wouldn't mind having fun with him.

The final man shook his head. "I'm betting our fun isn't exactly what she's looking for, or is it?" His dark eyes focused intently on me. I could feel the coolness of him. His pale skin and black eyes marked him as the leader of the vampires. He was death incarnate.

"And which one are you?" I took a step towards him. There was something so alluring about him. I couldn't help but be drawn into his orbit. It was the reason vampires made such good predators.

"Thane." He took my hand and placed the gentlest of kisses on my knuckles. "Delighted." A surge of desire coursed through my body at the touch of his lips. I shouldn't be feeling desire. I shouldn't be feeling anything beyond a sense of duty. What the hell?

"I would say it's nice to meet you all . . ." I took a step back from the alluring men, "but you need to stop. If you won't stop willingly, I'll have to use force." I pressed my lips together. These men didn't seem like the type to obey anyone, including my father. I was the devil and was more powerful than each of them. I hadn't considered having to take them all at once. I also didn't expect to meet them all on my first night here. It was my lucky night.

All the men held matching smirks. "No can do." The shifter shook his head.

Huxley chuckled. "Catch us if you can." Four colors appeared as they disappeared from the bar. I was left blinking at where the four men had just been. What the hell was that?

Chapter 4

Cade

My cocksure grin vanished when we reached my penthouse in Las Vegas. There was much to do, and none of us wanted to be caged in that wasteland again. The reason for our release was irrelevant. It was time to go to work. The death count from the first release of my virus was nearing thirty thousand. I took great pride in my selection this round. The advancements in biologicals, combined with my magic, made it far too easy to pick a virus that spread fast with no cure in sight. Entire countries were locked down, but they weren't fast enough to stop my beauty from infecting thousands more every day. It was magnificent. I beamed in triumph.

"You brought the reapers here too quickly, Cade." The glare Ryder gave me could torch a city. The temper on him rivaled any archangel or demon in existence. If his anger got too out of control, I'd be staring down a wolf instead of a surly man.

I walked casually over to the bar cabinet. Pouring out a bit of bourbon, I faced my brothers. "Just doing my part, little brother." Ryder hated being the youngest of our group. We thought of each other as brothers, but we were only bound by purpose. The destruction of the world as we knew it. The apocalypse was our purpose, although something about our current release felt off. We were the balance of the supernatural world. If God thought any of our breeds got out of hand, we were released to bring order back to the world.

Ryder lunged at me. Thane and Huxley gripped him before he could get far. Too bad. It had been a few centuries since my last good brawl with Ryder. Vexing him was a favorite pastime.

"Cade, do you think you could be a little less of an asshole?" Thane dropped his hand from Ryder.

"I could certainly try." I sat in my favorite brown leather chesterfield and waited for the next one of them to deduce whatever they believed our next steps should be.

"Did you feel it?" Huxley asked, his voice soft, uncharacteristic of our fae trickster.

"You mean with the woman?" Thane turned his attention to Huxley.

"Come now, you know we're talking about the woman. Lucifer herself, coming to round up the four bad boys of the apocalypse." I rolled my eyes. "How cliché."

"Yeah, except she shouldn't be trying to stop us. She's well aware of the grand design and the part we play in it. So, what's she doing here?" Thane questioned.

"You should ask why she thought she needed to stop us. We're the servants of the Creator, her father. Once released, we have specific orders to follow." I took another drink of my bourbon. "I didn't perceive any gratitude for the assistance we are providing her. She's certainly received more willing servants in the last few months." I scratched my chin, contemplating what her being here meant for us.

"Okay, but did you feel it?" Huxley plopped down on my sofa now that Ryder's breathing had evened out. The sound of my sofa under his weight, as he fell more than sat, grated on my nerves.

"Feel what?" My brow quirked. I knew exactly what he was referring to, but I hadn't wanted to speak it aloud. The attraction I felt for our little she-devil was intoxicating. Our next encounter should be quite an exhilarating experience. I planned to bed her before any of the others had a chance. Remaining oblivious provided me with the much-needed time to plan my seduction.

"The desire." Huxley trembled as he said the words.

"I felt it. What about you, Ryder?" Thane's gaze zeroed in on me. "Cade?"

"Hmph." Ryder crossed his arms over his chest.

Thane chuckled. "So, that's a yes from Ryder."

"Such eloquent execution, Ryder. Can we focus on the matter at hand? I have a press conference in the morning. The public's trust is paramount to my endeavor." I paused, looking at the three men. "Meaning, I certainly can't look like an unkempt heathen in the morning. Rest is a vital part of my appearance." I rolled my eyes at the group when not a single one moved.

"Your evasiveness says what your words don't. We all felt a level of attraction for the girl." Thane paced the room. He was obviously having one of his contemplative moments. I hoped, for my sake, he got on with it.

"Girl," Huxley chuckled. "Not the word I would use."

"This changes nothing. I'm moving forward as planned." I relaxed back, crossing my legs. Having a brief fling with the devil wouldn't deter me from my mission on Earth. Bedding women was what we did. My current conquest of being the devil changed nothing, as far as I was concerned. I would continue with my plans despite any interference.

"Cade, this changes everything. Lucifer is here for us. There's no way we should be together. It's too dangerous. We need to decide how to handle this situation. You need to quit passing this off as though it's no big deal. It is, and you know it is. She shouldn't be here." Thane blew out a frustrated breath. He worked himself into quite a tizzy. I hadn't seen him in such a state in quite some time. Not much rattled our level-headed Thane.

"Careful, Thane, you don't want to have an aneurysm." I stood to refill my glass.

"I think having her around is going to be fun." Huxley clapped his hands together.

"You would." Ryder's fists were clenched at his sides. "Divide and conquer?"

"Ah, yes, War, ever our savior. When are you leaving? Soon?" I looked between the men who'd made themselves far too comfortable in my penthouse. I had important things to attend to. None of those things involved them.

"Cade, we need to figure out a plan of action. We can't just go on as if we hadn't seen or felt the desire for her. You know we can't. Why are you insisting on blowing this off?"

"It's what Cade does." Ryder said my name with venom.

"I thought blowing things was your role?" I winked at War. He gripped the chair, his knuckles turning white. I smirked back at him, knowing he was close to the edge.

"Cade, be serious." Thane crossed his arms over his chest, shifting his weight as his eyes bore down on me like the disappointed father I never asked for or needed.

"I get that you all want to talk out your feelings or whatever. My role here hasn't changed. I plan on attending my press conference tomorrow, ensuring the people that the CDC has this virus well under control. It's so easy when those in office are basically my puppets. Imbeciles." I shook my head as I thought about the puppet in office. Humans deserve the apocalypse. Being here made so much sense after I had to listen to that man's drivel. My God, they gave him power over the free world. I wish I could say it astonished me, but little did when it came to humans. It was far too easy to decimate them. They did it to themselves.

"We're going to talk about this further. For now, the best plan of action would be to separate. I don't think we should make it easy for Lucifer to find us, especially not all of us together. We'd made our point at the club. Are we agreed?" Thane turned his attention to me.

"Agreed on what, exactly?" He hadn't spelled out his request. I planned to bed the devil. None of them would stop me. I wanted to beat them to the punch. Each of us felt the desire, which none of us wanted to admit was the mating bond. I felt it in them as much as I felt it within my bones. She was ours. I just wanted to make her mine first. It would be a fun little game of cat and mouse. One I planned to win.

"None of us will make contact with the woman until we meet again. Can we agree?"

"Woman? You could be less formal for once. She has a name." I rolled my eyes and sipped my drink casually.

"Fine, none of us will contact Lucifer until we meet to confer on our plans. Agreed?" I could hear his aggravation. He wanted us all to agree. I knew, for one, I had no intention of leaving our little devil alone. I planned to give her a reason to chase me. Hell, I'd be on every television set in the world tomorrow. I'd call out our girl so she'd want to come find me.

"I'm not agreeing to jack shit until that asshole does." Ryder pointed a finger at me.

"Tsk, tsk, Ryder. Don't get those panties in a bunch. I won't attempt to contact her until we have our little therapy session to work out our feelings. I mean, we should work out who gets that juicy little mouth of hers before we see her again. Ryder, you've always struck me as an ass man." I cocked my head. "Or am I wrong?" Ryder lunged. No one stopped him this time. His blow struck my face so hard I felt the bones crack beneath. Huxley and Thane just stared. I didn't move to strike him back. I'd already have to use some serious mojo to get my face looking camera-worthy tomorrow.

"Cade!" Thane gasped.

"Seriously, you just had to go for the face." I wiped away the blood oozing from my now-broken nose. "Come on?"

"You deserve worse, you fucking bastard." Ryder stalked across the room. It looked like he needed the space to stop himself from shifting and attacking me. His body vibrated with pent-up rage. My magic would clean up any mess he left behind. It'd been ages since I had this much fun with him.

"So, I agree to the terms." Huxley held up a finger.

"As do I." Thane bowed his head.

"Can we count a punch as an agreement? From what I saw, I believe Ryder is in full agreement. At least, he is about not contacting

Luci. You two are going to have to figure out your hostility in your own time. I'd rather not be a part of that therapy session." Huxley shook his head, upbeat after the altercation. Though Ryder and I fighting wasn't anything new, I enjoyed irking him as much as he enjoyed hitting me. It was a game we liked to play. He made it so fucking easy. It helped him learn to restrain himself, or so I told myself.

"Cade?" I could feel Thane's penetrating gaze on me. "Do you agree to the terms?"

"I already agreed. Now, if you don't mind. My press conference is in the morning. I would prefer to spend the rest of my evening alone." I went back to the bottle on the counter and poured myself another two fingers of liquor.

"You may want to cut back on the bourbon if you're going to keep up with the charade that you need to be presentable tomorrow." Thane flicked a glance down at my glass.

"Maybe I wouldn't need it if you'd left me in peace. I don't care that Lucifer came to scold us. There's nothing she can do to stop me. My plans are already in motion." I returned to the brown leather chair that brought me such peace. I'd positioned it so I could look out the massive windows high above the city. Nothing like this had ever been available at any other time we'd been here. I loved the new lights and technology offered by this time period. It was too bad the humans made their destruction simple. I wouldn't mind spending a lifetime here.

"Fine, we'll go. I'll be back to check on you after your little show-and-tell tomorrow. We all know how much you like to put on a performance." There was an edge to his voice that wasn't lost on me. My gaze hadn't strayed from the window overlooking the city.

The city lights shone back at me in their brilliance. I heard the door click and knew my brothers were gone. I finished my bourbon in one gulp. Each one of us had a dark history. We'd lost so much each time we came here. I'd made the dreadful mistake of falling in love once. I wouldn't make that mistake again. I felt the pull as well as the others, but I'd already learned that lesson. I had no intention of learning it again, especially not with the devil. That wasn't the punishment I fancied. I may want to play with the devil, but I wouldn't allow any more than a simple tryst. The challenge she presented was far too tempting.

The next morning, I rolled my eyes as Carol, the media spokes-woman, reassured everyone in the crowd that the United States was doing everything in its power to stop the spread of the virus. The public was naïve enough to believe her. I tuned out most of what she was saying. When she turned to me, it took me a second to realize she was waiting for me to step forward. I plastered on my charming smile, intent on reassuring the public that everything was fine. There were reporters from every news station and newspaper house in the country at the White House. Some wore masks, but not enough. They crowded together as if there weren't a deadly virus infecting people around the world. Typical. The reach of the conference would be im-peccable. Being a scientist in the United States had been the perfect mark to keep a close eye on what was happening with my baby.

I was the official leader of a group of scientists that had gotten together to take on the epidemic sweeping through the country. I loved that they trusted me so much with their lives. I took the podi-um, and the reporters went crazy. Taking pictures and trying to get my attention.

"Mr. Cade, over here," one reporter shouted over the others.

"Doctor," I corrected.

"My apologies, Dr. Cade." She held her arm out towards the podium.

I didn't look anywhere in particular. If they wanted a picture of me, I was more than willing to pose after the press conference was over. Shaking the hands of the press while knowing I was behind the virus made me feel fantastic.

"I would like to start by thanking you all for being here. The steps that the president and Mrs. Dirx explained are aggressive actions necessary to get ahead of the curve. These actions will remove the constraints so that people at the state and the local level—the individual physician all the way up through the federal government—will have as many constraints as possible removed for them to do everything they possibly can so that we can implement the containment and the mitigation of this virus.

"The steps taken today will be important in slowing the curve. We still have a long way to go. There will be many more cases, but we'll take care of that. And ultimately, as the president and Mrs. Dirx said, the virus will be stopped, and we will be stronger after." I turned and bowed my head slightly to the president and Mrs. Dirx. Then I glimpsed Lucifer standing in the back corner, her mouth turned up slightly at the corner. Was she impressed by my speech, or was she marveling at the brilliance of my plan? I had infiltrated the CDC. I was the face of their savior, providing them all the information they needed to keep the American people safe from my wicked little virus. I stepped back to allow the next speaker to take the podium. My eyes caught hers across the room. Another striking woman stood beside her. It was the woman who'd been on the dance floor with her at the club the night before. I could sense her demonic presence. Then

I realized I hadn't felt Lucifer when she'd come in? The strong desire I'd felt when I'd seen her the night before was a faded memory. How was she able to cloak herself from me? I didn't have long to ponder that as the conference ended. They ushered me backstage with the rest of the experts. The president was particular about what we said in front of the reporters. He didn't want us in front of them any longer than absolutely necessary.

Luci strutted behind the curtain. With her eyes slanted down and a laser focus on me, I couldn't wait to see what she was about to fire on my way. I imagined all the words that would fall from her red-painted lips. Everyone said she had a soft spot for the humans, but was it enough reason to leave her place of residence to see what I was doing to them? Didn't she have demons to rehabilitate through punishment or something? The devil must have a lot of free time. It was interesting to see her. It excited me that she took the time out of her schedule to show up at my press conference. After last night, seeing her again was inevitable. Why did she seek me first? Not that I minded being her top priority.

"What the hell are you doing?" Luci pushed me off to the side, away from the others. How in the hell had she even gotten back here? I'd watched her glide right past the Secret Service. That was quite the skill. I marveled at it.

"My job. How did you get back here?" I glanced over her shoulder to the two Secret Service men who had flanked the doors. She shouldn't have been able to walk past the president without at least a few questions. She came to a stop inches from me. Her scent unsettled me. Who knew fire and brimstone could be so damn sexy? I wanted to breathe her in. She looked me dead in the eyes.

"You don't belong here," she growled.

"Don't I?"

"No, you don't. It's not your time. I don't know how you got out of your little world, but you absolutely need to go back to it now."

"If you're going to rake me over the coals, can we at least do it over a nice meal, maybe a drink or two?" I paused, my eyes scanning down her body. "Maybe a little dessert." Her black leathers fit in all the right places. The tight red tank showed me what I was missing beneath. Even the chains from her leather jacket intrigued me. I understood why people might be so shocked to meet her only to find out she was the devil. Humans have a fixed idea of what the devil was and what he was supposed to look like.

For starters, the devil could never be a woman. There was something about the devil being feminine that would never enter their imagination. Women were the epitome of goodness. They'd sooner accept God was a woman than they would the devil. It was their own fault with all that angel of the house bullshit they'd used for centuries to keep women out of the spotlight and taking care of men. More importantly, they had the wrong idea about Hell. It was, to them, a place where souls–bad souls–went to spend eternity gnashing their teeth and blaspheming. That part was truly laughable. I would like to know where they got that idea. For all I knew, Luci had started it to throw them off. Could she be that cunning? The thought intrigued me. I wanted to know more about her. But first, I wanted to feed her. It was a primal need coming from deep within me. The mate bond most likely sparked, making me want to take care of my mate.

Luci glanced back over her shoulder, realizing the same thing I had. There were too many people here for this conversation. "Fine, but we're talking about you leaving."

"Grand, I know just the place." I grabbed her hand and felt a rush of heat from the contact. I couldn't decide whether it was because she was the devil or it was because of the connection between us. The president was already looking for any reason to get rid of me. Having an outsider around who hadn't been thoroughly vetted wouldn't bode well for my future. I could make up something for the neanderthal, but I didn't want to have to waste my time with the effort. I ducked us into a dark hallway and transported us just outside my room at the Bellagio. The cutest line formed between Luci's brows.

"Where are we?" Not like this hallway would look any different from any other generic hotel hallway, but it was the Bellagio, so it should.

"The Bellagio penthouse. I thought you'd like to have this conversation in private. Besides, I can have anything delivered. The world certainly has made everything much more convenient than my last visit." I bowed as I held the door open to my luxurious suite. I had to admit, I enjoyed the extravagance of everything at this new time.

"You brought me to your hotel room? Rather bold of you, don't you think?" She whirled on me, her arms crossing over her chest. She reminded me of a Siamese kitten— all claws and sharp teeth. I would enjoy playing on the wild side with this kitty cat.

"Bold? Hardly. We needed somewhere private to discuss our little misunderstanding. This room is soundproof for just such conversations. Not that I think anyone in this world would need to have a private conversation with the devil herself, yet here we are." I waved my arm out again. "Excuse me while I order us something decadent and sinful. You seem like you might be up for something scrumptious." I winked at the devil before I made my way to the bedroom. Phone in hand, I ordered from room service. A decanter of mimosas, along with one of everything from their brunch menu, would be a grand start to seducing the kitten in the other room. I wanted the opportunity to spend time with her. I didn't believe her story about the horsemen being here too soon. That wasn't possible.

She turned upon my entrance. "So, you want to tell me who let you out early?"

"Early?" I shook my head. "You're a determined little thing when there's something you want. You should make yourself comfortable. Food will be here shortly. I'd prefer conversations over a meal. It makes others more amenable, wouldn't you agree?" I added a little extra charm to my tone as I made my way over to the davenport. I held my hand out, indicating she should join me.

Luci's weight shifted from one hip to the other. Her indecisiveness was cute. "You do know I'm your boss, right? You should be more than willing to answer my questions."

"Kitten, you may be the devil, but no one is my boss. Besides, I'd hardly suggest that anything you ask of me will be simple. I'm actually looking forward to the challenge. Now, will you please have a seat? Your glare is giving me tingles and not the good kind."

Her eyebrow lifted. "Oh, are you intimidated?" She strutted over, lowering herself down to the chair slowly, deliberately, before crossing one leg over the other. Both of her wrists rested on the armchair. It was an intoxicating power position. She knew how to use her assets to her advantage. I involuntarily licked my lips. She would make this all the more challenging, and I reveled in it.

Chapter 5

Luci

I rolled my eyes. My body language was having the desired effect on Cade. Not that he wasn't absolutely scrumptious, but I had a job to do. Cade and the others needed to be more cooperative. Not that I was at all surprised Cade was being more than a little difficult. He struck me as the type to make things interesting. At least my time with him wouldn't be boring.

"So," Cade started, "what are your favorite things about the human world? I hear you used to be here every other day."

I rolled my eyes. "For the record, I wasn't here every other day. I used to be here every day. It would be nice if people got their facts right, especially since they decide to speak of me so often."

"I have a feeling you fed them some of their information." He smirked.

"Now, why would I do that?" I ran my finger over the arm of the chair, not meeting the gaze I could feel on me. The attraction heightened now that we were alone in his hotel room. I should have made him take me somewhere public. Kesa had joined me at the press conference. I hadn't gotten the chance to tell her I was leaving. Where had she gone? Would she be looking for me since I vanished?

"Oh, Kitten, you certainly are fun." His eyebrows waggled at me.

"Oh? Why's that?" I quirked a brow at him.

The corner of his mouth lifted. "I've heard the stories, ones that you most certainly have fed the humans. Unless, of course, the stories are true."

"When are the stories ever true?"

"Oh, Kitten, I have a feeling when it comes to you, all the stories are true."

I ignored his comment as I studied the surrounding room. I had to admit that I was in awe of the decadence of the penthouse. The décor was so much more refined than I'd expected. It was a far cry from the club from last night. It surprised me he didn't have anyone waiting for him back at his humble abode. The horsemen were well known for their exploits while they were here. I should have boned up on their previous visits before I came rushing down here to greet them. When I glanced up at him, I noticed a small smirk on his face as if he were reading my thoughts. He was an insufferable man. I'd have to be careful. My biggest weakness was a charismatic man with eyes I could get lost in for days. There was something alluring about him, and it wasn't the obvious attraction I'd felt from the night before. It was something more. Based on the look he gave me now, he knew exactly what was on my mind. I wanted to reach across the room and slap his smug face. I needed to find my center. The sexy devil-goddess in me certainly wanted a taste, but the rational part knew I should absolutely not mix business with pleasure. Wait . . .

"—Business? We have to discuss business." I was here for a reason. I furrowed my brows, trying to concentrate on anything but my racing heart. How was he able to have this effect on me with only a look and the husky smoothness to his voice? He was sexy, charming, and infuriating. A sure recipe for a cocktail of regret that included a headache and an empty feeling in the pit of my stomach the next morning. Not that I regretted any conquest. I enjoyed pleasure for its sake alone. But I had a feeling that with him, it would be more than the physical act to satiate the need deep within my body. He would be a heartache for me. I didn't have time to be wrapped up in something I couldn't control. I needed to complete my business, send the horsemen back, and return to Hell before the others discovered I was gone. I didn't know how Cade had gotten out, but I wouldn't lose my head to a sexy smile and six-pack abs. No matter how charming I thought he was.

"Business? What business do you think we have to discuss, Kitten?" he asked. He darted those blue eyes up as his lips curved into a salacious smile. He was clearly enjoying my discomfort.

"Why don't we start with you telling me how you got out of your realm before your scheduled time?" I raised an eyebrow.

A knock sounded at the door. "Saved by the bell." He was up and at the door in one fluid movement. Holding the door open, a gangly young man wheeled in the cart piled with silver lids. The plates he unveiled had an assortment of breakfast foods like fruit-topped french toast, pancakes, eggs, bacon, sausage, and more. A basket was filled with various pastries and muffins. What was he expecting, to feed an army?

"Is there anything else I can get you?" the server asked in a surprisingly deep voice.

"No, thank you." Cade handed him a bill and led him out of the door.

"Fucking ridiculous," I mumbled. This was obviously a show.

"What?"

I shook my head. "Nothing."

"Oh, please, patronize me all you want, Kitten. It clearly makes you happy." Cade's voice dripped with sarcasm. "I could hear your stomach growling across the room at my press conference. Don't act like you don't want to devour all of this." He popped a raspberry into his mouth and smirked.

"You're infuriating, you know that?" I tapped my foot against the floor, watching him as he poured two glasses of the mimosas he'd ordered. If he were any other man, I would have stormed off; consequences be damned. But he wasn't just any man. He was a horseman. There were answers I needed only he could provide. And I hated him for it. This was supposed to be a vacation away from all the stresses of Hell. Now, I was on a mission I hadn't asked for, cleaning up a mess that wasn't mine. The smug look on his face was the cherry on top of an already unpleasant situation. My plan was to come down to Earth, have a little fun, then head back to Hell with no one being the wiser. Now, because of this infuriating asshole, I have to figure out who thought it was a good fucking idea to start the apocalypse early.

He held out a glass, and I glared down at it.

"Are you trying to starve yourself to bother me? Fine, do whatever you want. I told you I wasn't talking until we'd eaten. Civilized people enjoy having conversations over a meal, or so I've been told." He flicked a heated glance down the length of my body. "Would you like to take the less civilized route? Will there be torture involved? I do enjoy a good whipping every now and again." He gave me one of those smirks, followed by an even more infuriating wink.

"Are you waiting for me to beg for answers? Maybe kiss your feet?" I crossed my arms over my chest. I lifted the glass he'd left on the cart and downed the sweet liquid in one gulp. This would be more difficult than I'd expected.

"That wouldn't be so bad. I mean . . ." His eyes scanned down my body again. The heat in his gaze made my heart skip a beat in my chest. I wouldn't. I couldn't. Not until I had the answers I sought. Instead, I glared at him.

"Damn, Kitten, you're adorable when you're angry. I'm having a hard time keeping my hands to myself." His mocking tone grated on my nerves. "Listen, grab whatever you want to eat. We can talk about what I know about our release as you eat. Although I don't know that much. None of us had any inkling that we weren't supposed to be here. That was until last night when you appeared and said as much." He held his arm out to the place across from him at the table.

"Is this your peace offering?" I narrowed my eyes at him, untrusting.

"Despite how fucking adorable you are when you're angry, yes. I don't want to fight with you. Other things," his eyebrows rose, "yes. Fight, no. I believe we have more pressing things to discuss. Plus, I'd like your belly to stop growling so loudly at me. It's distracting, and I can't help but want to feed you. So please . . ." This time, he got up and moved to pull my chair out. My eyebrows hit the ceiling. What the hell?

"Are you actually being a gentleman?" I took the seat, more out of shock than anything.

He bent so his lips were next to my ear. "Don't get used to it." A low grumble reverberated down my spine. The spicy scent of his cologne hit my nose. Nothing should smell that intoxicating. The way his shirt clung to his chest had me licking my lips, wanting a taste of the defined muscles I could see beneath. He smelled like a mixture of citrus, spice, and ocean.

He placed the plate of French toast and berries in front of me. I furrowed my brow, my stomach growling in response to the smell. "How did you know?"

"I saw the interest in your eyes when he lifted the lids. Those were the first things your eyes gravitated towards. Was it the sweetness of the berries or the savory-sweet brioche that caught your attention?" I didn't like how much he noticed about me.

"Why does that matter?" I cocked my head, studying the man who'd been elusive just moments ago. He was being far too forthcoming now. What changed?

"Would it surprise you that I simply want to know you better?" There was a level of sincerity in his tone that I hadn't expected. The façade of earlier was gone, replaced by a measure of vulnerability.

"I don't understand." I leaned back against my chair, unsure of what to say. I could feel the kernel of desire deep within my soul, but I'd been doing an excellent job at ignoring the little twitch. I didn't want to admit I wanted to get to know him, too. That was the problem. I couldn't know him. My mission was to send him back to a realm I couldn't go to. He needed to go back to stasis. I needed to go back to my duties in Hell. I couldn't even entertain the idea of knowing him. Getting close to him was a means to an end, nothing more. So, why did I want to? Why did I want to lean across the table and see if the berry tasted just as sweet on his lips? Why couldn't he just be a regular asshole? "What did you mean earlier about not knowing how you got out? How is that possible?" I didn't believe for a second that he was as oblivious as he seemed. The cocky bastard enjoyed being the smartest person in the room at the press conference. The sharp cut of his glare when that reporter hadn't used doctor to address him was telling. He had information. Getting him to tell me that would be a challenge.

A smile softened his features. "You're a puzzle, Kitten. I want to figure you out. If this is what it takes to have a civil conversation, so be it. I'll play your games as long as you're willing to play mine."

"So, you're not just a narcissist who thinks the world revolves around him?" I raised an eyebrow. I'd been thinking he'd been putting on an act. A man like that would be far too cocky to care what I thought, but something in his tone was different. There was no way he was being kind to me for no reason. He wanted something from me.

"I'm a man who knows what he wants." His voice fell to a husky whisper. Those blue eyes heated as he moved to sit next to me. "I believe I've made that more than clear." His eyes stayed locked on mine.

Once again, I was backed into a corner. There was nothing about the feeling that I liked. I could do this. We could have our meal, and I could return to Hell with a little more information. I could find one of the others who would be more willing to talk without such drastic measures. But I knew he was feeling the same inclination as I was. It was below the surface of all his talk. He felt it as much as I did. The problem was I didn't understand what it meant. I'd felt it once before in my life. A time I hadn't thought about in a long, long time. I'd been fighting it, but it was more difficult being so close to him. I knew from the past that it would only get stronger the longer we spent time together. Bonding wasn't in the cards. With his ego, it wasn't hard to ignore the instinct as desire pushed at me. I got up from the table, walking to the window as I thought about exactly how to play this.

"How about a little tit for tat? You tell me what you know." I turn my heated gaze on him, knowing exactly which of his buttons to press. "And I'll decide if I should reward or punish you for the information." I ran my finger over the hem of my low-cut top.

"Mmm." The sound reverberated through my body despite his distance. "I like how you think, Kitten." He licked his sultry lips, eyes focused intently on me. "Ask one question. I'll give you an answer. You will have to decide for yourself if you can trust that what I'm saying is the truth. I'm far too intrigued by being punished by the famed punisher herself."

"I already know. I can't trust you." I rolled my eyes, moving to sit next to him.

"Then why are you here?" His dark eyes studied me.

"You know why I'm here." I narrowed my eyes on him.

"Oh? I don't think you know why you're here. But I'll play." His thumb stroked over my knuckles. My stomach growled, breaking the sizzling heat between us.

He sat back. "Eat," he ordered. "We've got more than enough time for games as soon as you're well-fed." I watched as he took a sip from his mimosa, moving it from where he'd been seated earlier. He was staying close. I couldn't trust him, could I? One minute, he was being a narcissist; the next, he was letting his guard down and making sure I was fed. I studied him for too long. He reached his hand to push the plate closer to me. I was the devil. I didn't need to eat, or at least I thought I didn't. The raw emptiness in the pit of my stomach after the night of drinking made me well aware my stomach had a different plan. It wouldn't hurt to eat a little. I could ask my questions as soon as I was satiated.

I took a bite of the french toast and let out a soft moan. "This is delicious." The food was heavenly. He watched as I savored every bite, occasionally taking a bite of the crisp bacon from his plate. "So, can I trust you?" I asked, setting the fork down on my empty plate.

He chuckled, but there was a certain seriousness in his tone. "I'd say yes, but would you believe me?" I hated that he thought he knew me already.

"Probably not."

"Exactly, so it looks like we're at an impasse. I can tell you what I know, but you won't believe it's all I know. Not that knowing will matter much, anyway. We're already here. There's nothing you can do to stop the apocalypse. It's well underway."

"How about if you tell me what you know, and I'll decide if it's important?" I glared at him.

"What happened to a little tit for tat?"

I ground my teeth. "What do you want?"

"Hmm . . ." He tapped his finger against his lips. "What could I ask of the devil herself?"

"Don't get too excited, even I have limits." I rolled my eyes.

"I want to stay here. I doubt you're willing to entertain that notion."

"No, I'm not. You're not supposed to be here. I don't know how you were released, but I intend to find out. You have to leave." Of course, he would ask for the one thing I couldn't give him.

"Not even a little more time?" Cade's eyes were downcast. I realized how harsh I'd been a moment ago, but he absolutely could not stay on Earth.

"I don't have the power to make that kind of decision. Few do. That's why it's so important I figure out who could release you before your time." I hated admitting to limitations, but I also didn't want him to think I was choosing not to let him stay because I just didn't want to.

"I don't believe you couldn't let me stay longer if you wanted to do so." He glared at me.

"Listen, whoever released you was fucking with the whole grand design. What they've done could end everything, not just Earth, but Heaven and Hell, too. They're playing with fire. I can't let your desire to be on Earth destroy the world and everything in it. You get that, right?" I cocked my head. I thought he was selfish, but end the entire world selfish? I didn't know.

"So dramatic." He looked up at the sky. "Fine, how about I tell you what I know in exchange for staying as long as it takes you to investigate whatever is going on?" I began to speak, but he put a finger over my lips. "Wait, just listen." I nodded, and he dropped his hand. "You're going to need my help to figure this out." I scoffed. "Fine, you need someone's help. It might as well be me. I'm a direct link to my brothers as well as having the power to assist you should you need it."

"I won't."

"Fine, maybe you could just use some company. I could be your guide of sorts. You need someone at your back either way. Everyone needs someone protecting their six. I can be that person for you while we figure the puzzle out together. I certainly don't want to be a part of destroying everything." He pressed his lips together.

"You're such a liar. You were created to start the apocalypse."

"Yeah, but you never asked if we enjoyed it. Not like I've ever stuck around long enough to see the end, anyway. We're the balance. As long as my mages are on Earth, I will wait for when your father believes my people have gotten out of hand." He rolled his eyes up to the sky again.

"Fine, you tell me what you know, and I'll keep you around until it's necessary to send you back." I waited for him to agree. It was the best I would give.

"Oh, I'm going to be a kept man. How exciting." He cocked his head. "I think you can do better than that. I know wording is everything when it comes to making a deal with you."

"Okay, what do you want, exactly?"

"You agree to keeping me on Earth until you find whoever is responsible for releasing us and trying to end the world early. Besides, whoever it is must be powerful. You're going to need reinforcements." His tone was level. I studied him. I didn't trust him.

"I don't need anyone's help."

He refilled his glass. "Everyone needs help, even you, Lucifer Morningstar. " The way he punctuated my name sent a thrill to my core. Dammit.

"Fine, you tell me what you know and help me find the person responsible for your release. You can stay here on Earth until we find them." I held my hand out to shake.

"Don't you usually do a blood oath for these types of deals?"

"Do you want to give me your soul at the end of our deal?" His mouth fell open.

"I thought that was a myth?" He paused, his hand scratching his chin. "Although it might be preferable to being in stasis again. Loneliness in another realm is sometimes worse than death." His voice was pitched low. So low I wasn't sure if I was supposed to hear him.

I pressed my lips together. "It's a myth. I'm not in the soul-collecting business. That's the reaper's job. I rehabilitate those souls before they're recycled into the system." My joke didn't exactly land when he talked about loneliness. It seemed cruel to send him back. I thought he would be with the angels in between. It didn't dawn on me they'd be alone. Plus, I thought stasis was like sleeping without memory. I couldn't imagine living forever while also not being able to actually live your life. Angels, demons, they have roles to play and purpose. The horsemen's purpose only came around when they were needed. I'd never actually thought about what happened to them when they weren't doing their job.

"What exactly did you do between apocalypses?" I couldn't help my curiosity.

He sighed. "That's complicated." He got up and strode over to the picturesque window, his gaze drifting over the city skyline.

"Isn't everything?"

"I don't know you, Kitten. Not enough to share all my secrets." He turned to look at me. "Besides, we have more pressing issues, wouldn't you agree?"

I nodded, knowing I wasn't exactly one who willingly shared my secrets. "Yeah, I guess we do. So, what do you know about how you're here?"

"Not just anyone could have let us out. Only your father and a few of his select angels would have been able to break the barrier, let alone release us onto Earth." He shook his head, his gaze still fixed out over the skyline. "They would have needed powerful blood from each supernatural breed. It's not just breaking the barrier; it's a complicated process to release us. Your father made it difficult for a reason."

I leaned forward, desperate for more information. "Do you have any idea who it could have been?"

He shook his head. "No. I wasn't all that interested in finding out. We come here with one role: to start the apocalypse. You may be under the impression that it's not our time to be here. I've been here for two years, working closely with my magical community. It certainly seems like our time." He paused, shaking his head as he stared at the world below. "I know that whoever it was, they wanted us free. Otherwise, we wouldn't be here." He turned to face me. I could feel his sincerity.

I nodded, contemplating what he'd said. It made sense. Someone wanted them out to begin the apocalypse, but why? That was the question I had to answer. "What normally happens when you're set free? Have you been given instructions previously?" It seemed odd that they would just be placed on Earth and expected to know what to do.

He chuckled. "Kitten, we don't need instructions. That's why we're so good at what we do." He walked back to refill his glass. The cockiness from earlier was back. It felt as though I'd insulted him.

"Seriously, not once has my father been like, here are the instructions for how to start the apocalypse. The humans certainly wrote his instructions down." I took a drink from my freshly refilled glass. He may have been insulted, but he still poured me another drink.

"Not to point out the obvious, but I'm far from human."

"That wasn't an answer to my question."

He huffed and sat back in the chair next to me. "What do you think? Your father sat down with us at a chess table and told us how to destroy the world for him." He chuckled. "No, this is his pride and joy. You think he actually wants to see anything befall it? I'm pretty sure humans are his favorites. Good luck getting him to admit that." He took a slow sip, his eyes far away.

"Good point." I knew my father. There had been a design, and he'd said at some point, humans and supernaturals would need to be thinned out for the good of all. He never relished having those conversations. Speaking of which, anytime the horsemen had been released in the past, he was routinely absent.

He nodded. "Your father is always gone when it's time to start the apocalypse. He's never given us a direct order. We understand that something has gone amiss with our breed. Our first order of business is to make sure everything is as it should be. Then we begin." He paused and looked into the distance. "We're here to start the apocalypse and make sure it runs its course. There were never specifics, just that it has to happen, and we must do it in the proper way. We're the masters of destruction. Every living creature on Earth has a chance to stop us. It's part of the grand design. So far, they've succeeded. Not all the seals have been broken. Humans, usually with the help of supernaturals, have stopped us. We know when they've done what was necessary to send us away." He paused, the muscles in his jaw working. "We rarely see that coming, either. One minute, we're here; the next, we're not. Again, with no choice." He spoke through clenched teeth. I could feel the bitterness through his words.

"You want to talk about it?" There was obviously more to what he was saying, something from his past that had caused such bitterness.

"No." He stood from his chair and went to the windows again. The silence was deafening. I wasn't sure what it would be like to not have any choice in your life. To not be able to choose when you appeared on Earth and when you were locked away. Wait, I knew a little something about that. My father had chosen his favorite daughter to rule hell. Not once was I asked if I wanted to punish souls for all eternity. Yet here I was. Stuck in a life chosen for me by someone else. Someone who swore he knew what was best for me.

"You know, not getting to choose your life path is pretty standard for all of us. If you wanted to talk about it, I might be one of the few people who could understand." My voice softened. I wanted to extend a lifeline.

He turned away from the window, his face a mix of emotions. He sighed heavily before finally speaking. "It's not something I talk about. Having no control over my life, over what I do and when, it's not something you get used to. It's easier to focus on our job here." He gritted his teeth, his fists clenching. "But I understand what you're saying." He squared his shoulders, gathering his composure. A strength shined in his eyes.

He stepped closer to me, his gaze never wavering. At this moment, I saw something else, something more than just the horsemen of Pestilence. I saw the man that had been locked away. The one who was tired of being manipulated and controlled. The one who was willing to fight against anyone or anything that threatened his freedom.

"I understand," I said, my voice barely above a whisper. I felt a kinship with him I hadn't felt with anyone else. Here was a man who was just as broken as I was yet still had the strength to fight for his freedom.

"My past is my own, and I should be the one to tell it. Maybe one day. I will." He turned away from me, his eyes back on the city. "But not today."

"Why not?"

"Because today I have other plans."

"Oh?"

"I believe you offered to punish me if my answers to your questions weren't to your satisfaction. I'd hate to miss out on an opportunity like that." The mask was back. The moment of vulnerability gone. "I believe I've been more than cooperative enough for an afternoon. Since it doesn't look like I'll be getting punished, Kitten, I have others I'd like to entertain for the day. If you don't mind—" He stood before the open door. My cue to leave.

"What? That's it? You're kicking me out?"

"Were my answers not sufficient?" His face was unreadable.

"You told me some, but I don't know who let you out." I shook my head. What the hell was happening?

"As I've established, neither do I. You agreed I was forthcoming with you as well as honest. Now, be on your way." He wrapped an arm around my shoulders and literally led me out of the room. I turned to face him, only to meet the wood of the door closing in my face. What the hell was that? Who dared throw out the devil? I blinked in shock.

Cade. Fucking Cade.

CHAPTER 6

Luci

"Another meat-packing plant closed. Maybe it's time to cut your losses with Pestilence and move on to famine." Was that pity in Kesa's voice or annoyance? I never could tell with her. She kept her feelings close to the vest.

I'd been stewing over my interaction with Cade for the entire day. How dare he throw me out? I went over every nuance of the conversation. Had I been too forward? One minute, there was an intense attraction between us; the next, he was kicking me out. There was something in his past. Something I was determined to find out. But for now, I had a job to do. Plague was wreaking havoc, and I had to stop it. None of the horsemen should be here. Humans shouldn't be hurt because of someone starting the apocalypse early. I sat back at the table of our rental. Kesa was excellent at getting exactly what she needed. This place was perfect for their operation here. There wasn't much I could do about the virus. It's already taken hold. It was up to the people to do their part to stop it. Kesa was right. I needed to shift focus.

Kesa cleared her throat. "You know, the longer you wait, the more damage they can do. Maybe it's time to move on to the next horseman."

I nodded and stood, my mind turning to famine. "I know." I'd been able to find them once before, and I would do it again. Determination drove me to find out who freed the horsemen and to prevent the apocalypse.

I sighed and stared into the glass of whiskey I'd poured, swirling the golden liquid. I knew I shouldn't be thinking about Cade right now. The future of the world was in my hands. The only problem was I didn't know where to start. I could use some advice. But there wasn't anyone I could turn to for help.

"What can I do?" Kesa sat across from me.

"I don't know." Honesty was the best policy. I felt out of my depths.

"You're letting that man get to you." She shook her head. "Stop that shit right now. You are Lucifer fucking Morningstar, ruler of Hell. Despite everything you think, your father gave you this role for a reason. You care about what happens to them." She jerked her head towards the bustling world outside of our rental.

"Sometimes I wish I didn't care so much. I'm the only one investigating. Doesn't that seem strange? Where are all the angels when shit's going down?" I pressed my lips together. I didn't know what was causing my current funk.

"Okay, snap out of it." She stood, resting her hand on her cocked hip. "You have another horseman to interrogate or seduce. Your choice." She winked. "Besides, your brother is helping you by taking over Hell so you can figure out what's happening. Maybe the others just don't know, yet." She shrugged as if that was the simplest explanation.

"Oh, they know. Angels can't keep a secret for the life of them. They also can't stay away from humans, even if they think they're beneath them." I rolled my eyes. It begged the question, why was no one else looking into the horsemen being on Earth? Not that I thought the angels would question anything my father chose to do, but not one of my family thought something might be off. It made little sense. I needed to shift my focus.

Huxley— he would be my next mark. Maybe he knew more than Cade. Maybe he would at least be more forthcoming than Cade. Although Cade was honest about what he'd said. When it came to talking about the past, he wasn't interested. I would need to find out what happened and if it applies to what's going on now.

I stood, determined. I knew what I had to do. I would find Huxley and get the answers I needed. It was time to work. I closed my eyes and focused. Now that I knew what it felt like to be in their presence, I could focus on them easily.

My power flowed through me. I opened my eyes. A campfire burned before me in the dark. Hadn't it been daytime in the city? Where the hell was I now?

"Sorry for the disruption of your portaling," a voice spoke from the flames.

"What the hell?" I blinked.

Izzy stepped forward, a smirk playing on her lips. "That was fun!"

"Iz, seriously? Did you have to go all Moses on me? I was at the house Kesa rented for us. You could have just stopped by." I shook my head. Izzy's theatrics could be annoying sometimes.

"No, I couldn't. I needed to make sure you were alone."

"Why? Kesa is my friend. You can trust her." I studied her.

"You shouldn't trust anyone. The more I look into the horsemen, the less I trust a single soul. You should heed the warning. Something bigger is going on here, Luci. It's more than just the horsemen being here before their time. The others are being distracted. Anyone on either side who is asking questions just disappears." She looked over her shoulder like she was wondering if the same would happen to her any second.

"What? How are they being distracted?" I couldn't fathom what would have both sides too busy to figure out that something was seriously wrong. My Elites certainly would keep things running well without me. Not to mention my brother helping out.

"More souls are showing up, but they're being sent to the wrong places. People who are supposed to go down are going up, and vice versa. It's chaos."

"What? I need to get back there right away." I took a step.

Izzy's hands were on me. "No, you can't. Whoever is behind this doesn't want anyone to know what's going on. Your brother has it handled for now. It's why I'm here. He said you need to figure this shit out like yesterday. It seems bigger than we initially thought. It certainly isn't just about the horsemen. Someone is fucking with the whole cosmic order."

"Why? Who gains from the chaos?" I tapped my finger against my lips. Per usual, I had more questions had answers.

"I don't know. I'll find out what I can under the radar. Disappearing isn't in my day planner." She shivered.

"Be careful, Iz. I will find out who's behind this. I swear."

She nodded. "I know. I just don't want to be caught in the crossfire."

"I know. Iz?"

"Yeah, Boss?" She smiled. I hated it when she referred to me as boss.

"Don't let them destroy any souls while I'm gone. I don't want them to make those kinds of decisions when we don't know where the souls should actually be. It might be a distraction to get rid of someone. Keep an eye out, okay?"

"Got it. You be careful, Luci."

"You too."

Izzy stepped back into the flames. It was weird to watch her blink out into the fire. She had always been one for the dramatics.

Huxley, focusing on him, was my priority. Closing my eyes, I let my power flow through me to focus on his energy that I'd felt the night before. I relaxed and let my body lead me straight to him. The heat from the fire disappeared, replaced by a chill. I blinked my eyes open.

There he was, standing amidst the chaos that unfolded before me.

The tire building roared with furious flames, billowing black smoke that tainted the air with an acrid stench. Its fiery grip tightened, devouring the structure with an insatiable hunger. The crackling heat licked at Huxley's skin, causing his muscles to tense and beads of sweat to form on his forehead. Bemusement danced across his face, mingling with a sense of accomplishment at his creation before him. My stomach rolled at the sight of him.

Amidst the chaos, a woman sprinted out from Target, a shopping cart clattering behind her. Within its metal confines, a massive fifty-five-inch television teetered precariously, threatening to topple at any moment. Her eyes gleamed with a disturbing blend of madness and exhilaration, a twisted form of glee etched upon her face. With each hurried step, she distanced herself from the building, her stolen prize symbolizing a desperate grasp at a tumultuous world.

But she wasn't alone in her frenzied escape. A torrent of figures streamed out from the store, their arms burdened with bundles of clothing, towels, and bedding. The air reverberated with the frantic beat of their footfalls, a dissonant symphony of desperation and greed. Their faces, distorted by a mixture of fear and reckless abandon, mirrored the woman's maniacal expression as if the chaos swirling around them had unleashed an untamed euphoria.

In stark contrast to the frenzy, a solitary man perched atop a weathered bench just outside the inferno. Clutching an orange juice carton, he watched the scene unfold with a heavy shake of his head, his gaze filled with a mix of resignation and disdain. The chaos seemed to roll off him like water on an impermeable surface as he sought solace in the simple act of taking another sip. The tangy citrus flavor mingled with the bitterness of the situation, a bittersweet reminder of a world turned upside down.

For me, the spectacle triggered a surge of memories that stretched back to 1992. Though I hadn't witnessed the events firsthand, the tales recounted afterwards had etched themselves deep within my consciousness. Now, as I stood on the fringes of this frenetic display, the echoes of the past mingled with the present chaos, magnifying the surreal nature of the scene. It was as if time itself had looped, and I found myself caught in a disturbing yet strangely familiar tapestry of destruction and pandemonium.

I stepped forward and walked towards him, a sense of foreboding washing over me. He wrote furiously on a notepad as chaos ensued around him. His power seeped into the people around us. Huxley fueled their rage. A smile crept up his face as another woman exited the store with a cart full of baby things. He took advantage of their desperation. Every part of me wanted to stop what was happening, stop them from hurting themselves, stop them from feeling the rage. But I couldn't. Not with him still here. It was time to handle business.

"What the hell do you think you're doing?" I rested my hand on my cocked hip.

"My job. What does it look like?" Huxley didn't even glance over.

An insatiable rage surged through me, a fiery desire to engulf his entire being in flames. He was a parasite, feasting on the vulnerability of those around him. Standing there, his presence exuded a tangible aura of power, drawing people in like moths to a deadly flame. His seductive allure was infuriatingly captivating as if his indifference to the chaos unfolding before him only intensified his irresistible charm. Damn, he knew exactly how to play the role, effortlessly embodying a seductive charm that made my heart skip a beat.

Despite the turmoil engulfing our surroundings, it was as if we existed in a surreal vacuum, shielded from the destruction and madness that engulfed everyone else. Time slowed to a crawl, and the cacophony of chaos faded into a mere background murmur. As I narrowed my eyes, a profound recognition pulsed within me, an ancient instinct awakening from its dormant slumber. It was the unmistakable call of a mate, a connection that defied my very nature.

I, who bore the name Lucifer, had never entertained the notion of a mate, let alone two. My existence revolved around embracing the depths of desire and pleasure, never restricting myself to the confines of a monogamous bond. Commitment was an alien concept in my world, an idea I had long rejected. I would forever be a wanderer, a lover of countless souls, unbound by the shackles of fidelity. Such was my essence, an eternal rebel against the notion of being a one-woman man. Period.

When he finally looked over at me, a sly smile spread up his lips. "Well, hello, beautiful. I've been waiting centuries to meet you."

"Centuries?" I scoffed. "Right."

The scene unfolded in a dizzying whirlwind of chaos and violence. My eyes fixated on the pandemonium that unfolded before me. A horde of desperate individuals streamed out from the store, their frenzied footsteps pounding against the pavement. Amidst the bedlam, two men were locked in a vicious struggle, their primal instincts unleashed as they fought tooth and nail over a coveted laptop. Their grunts and curses mingled with the crackling tension that hung in the air, a palpable reminder of the depths to which humanity could sink.

Suddenly, the serenity of the moment shattered as the sharp report of gunshots shattered the peace, reverberating through the streets like thunder. Instinctively, I flinched, my body tensing, but I darted my gaze to Huxley, who stood there, immovable and unflinching amidst the erupting violence. The deafening echoes of danger barely registered in his realm of indifference, as if he were a statue carved from unyielding granite.

The juxtaposition between the chaotic frenzy and Huxley's stoic composure sent shivers down my spine, a dissonance that clawed at the fabric of my senses. It was a visceral reminder of the fragility of our existence, the thin thread that separated order from anarchy. At that moment, the world teetered on the edge of oblivion, and Huxley, an enigma carved from indifference, seemed to be the embodiment of that precarious balance.

"Do you feel the energy between us? You could enjoy the brilliance of what's happening before us. The world will never be the same after today." He stepped closer to me, his eyes searching mine. It was hard not to notice his strong jawline, full lips, and intense dark eyes. Focusing on him should be impossible with everything happening around us, yet it wasn't. His fingers grazed down my bare arm, and goosebumps rose over the trail of his fingers. "Interesting."

"What I find interesting is why you think this was a good idea?" A surge of frustration twisted within me, a visceral force that compelled my words to cut through the tumultuous air like a knife. I gestured wildly, my arm slashing through the chaotic scene that unfolded before us. The air vibrated with the aggressive cacophony of men's voices, their desperate shouts tearing through the atmosphere like primal roars. The acrid scent of fear lingered, mingling with the metallic tang of blood that stained the streets. Yet, amid this savage symphony, the piercing wail of sirens remained conspicuously absent, a chilling silence that echoed the abandonment of justice.

As my eyes scanned the heart of the looting and madness, a sense of dread gripped my very core. Lives hung precariously in the balance, their fates intertwined with the whims of Huxley, a catalyst for the chaos that threatened to consume everything. I knew, deep within the depths of my being, that today would be marked by tragedy and loss, lives extinguished in the wake of this maelstrom.

A knot of anguish coiled within my stomach, its tendrils constricting my insides, a physical manifestation of the pain and urgency that clawed at my soul. The plea tore from my lips, laced with desperation, demanding an end to this madness that spiraled out of control. "Stop this," I implored, each word resonating with a fervor born from the realization that the stakes had never been higher.

"Why? This is what we do. You're well aware of our place in the balance of the universe." He squinted at me. "Why are you so bothered? We've sent you so many souls. Isn't that what you want? More of your little minions feigning over your every move." His eyes shifted from the chaos to me.

"No, as I told you last night, you aren't supposed to be here. Someone let you out early, and I need to find out who before you idiots end the damn world." I crossed my arms.

Huxley raised one eyebrow. "What?" He chuckled low in his throat. "That's not possible. Only your father and a few others even have the power to release us from our world. There's no way we're here before our time. You know this as well as I do."

I shrugged. "All I know is that you aren't supposed to be here. I plan to find out who sent you to Earth early. Now, stop this chaos."

Huxley shook his head. "Well, you see, I don't take orders from anyone. Including you, Princess." He stepped closer to me, his body heat radiating over my skin, making me shiver. "Although I may make an exception under the right circumstances." His tongue flicked out and ran over his lip.

I rolled my eyes and stepped back. "That won't work on me. I'm not here to play games. I'm here to get you and the other horsemen back where you belong."

Huxley sighed. "There's no way someone has enough power to let us out." He looked around before turning back to me. "But for argument's sake, maybe I'll tag along. I'm certainly curious."

"Great, now can you stop this war zone you have going on here?"

"Oh, I didn't do this. I was just here to watch and influence. Unjust actions by those in power are the only things that could get people this riled. Now everyone is pissed. I've been helping them channel their anger." His apathy gnawed at my core, igniting a fire of frustration within. To him, this chaos was merely routine, another mundane day at the office. Gunshots shattered the air, each explosion reverberating through my bones, while the screech of tires clawed at my eardrums, leaving a trail of anxiety in its wake.

"Wouldn't that be War or Death's job?" I wanted to irk him. Make him feel something.

"Yeah, I was closing down a plant nearby. Since the virus is making my job easier, I looked into what was happening here. Death and War were both tied up when this started."

"Where are the others?" I asked.

"Ah, Honey, I'm not that easy. We may both want to know who let us out, but I don't agree that we're not supposed to be here. Until you can prove otherwise, we have a job to do." Huxley folded his arms over his chest. His muscles bulged under his tank top.

"Why would you want to help if you think you're supposed to be here?" Wouldn't he want to stop me? Maybe that was his plan.

"Because, beautiful, haven't you ever heard the phrase, the truth will set you free? I'd like to know the truth. Once I know, I can decide for myself whether we should move forward as planned or if we should hunt down the arrogant asshole who thought he had more power than God."

"Fair enough." I nodded.

"So, my place or yours?" Huxley winked.

"Mine." I grabbed his hand and blinked us out of the chaos.

Chapter 7

Cade

"Cade, I believe we had an agreement," Thane chided.

"She met me at the press conference. What was I supposed to do?"

"Not bring her back to your penthouse, for starters."

"Why? It's not like we did anything scandalous."

"Cade, it's dangerous for all of us if you continue to pursue her."

"Who said I had any intention of pursuing the devil?"

"Cade, I've spent centuries with you." He crossed his arms. "Every one of us knew the moment she appeared, you perceived her as a challenge."

I shrugged, a smirk crossing my lips. Thane was right, as usual. My attraction to the devil wasn't just a challenge; it was an obsession. There was something about her that drew me in, like a moth to a flame. Maybe it was her fierce independence or the way she challenged me at every turn. I couldn't quite put my finger on it, but I knew I had to have her.

Thane let out a heavy sigh. "Cade, we can't afford distractions right now. The apocalypse is looming, and we need to focus on our mission."

"I am focused," I said, my tone defensive.

"Are you? Because from where I'm standing, it looks like you're more focused on bedding the devil than starting the end of the world."

I bristled at Thane's words. "I take my duties as a horseman seriously. Just because I have other interests doesn't mean I'm not committed to our cause."

Thane stepped closer to me, his eyes boring into me. "I hope, for your sake, that's true. Because if you continue to pursue the devil, you'll be putting all of us in danger."

I opened his mouth to defend myself, but Thane held up a hand to silence him.

"Think about what I'm saying, Cade. We have a job to do, and there can be no distractions. Least of all from the devil herself."

"My mission is already well underway. There isn't much anyone can do to stop the beauty I created." I relaxed back in my brown Chesterfield. Thane was being all fatherly like usual. I knew I could handle one woman. "I need something to do since my part here is done." My rub on Thane was obvious, but I didn't care. He could mind his own business.

"Oh? You're finished?" Thane shook his head disapprovingly.

"As I said, nothing is stopping my beauty from spreading across the Earth. My virus is perfect."

"We agreed that you would continue to monitor the situation from the White House. It's why you posed as the doctor to be at the front lines. Your virus may have started, but it's your responsibility to see it through." He paused. "Unless you've sided with Lucifer? I can't imagine another reason why you'd abandon your post. Remember what happened the last time a woman distracted you?"

"That was low, even for you, Thane." My fists clenched at my sides.

"Just a reminder of what can happen when your head isn't in the game, Cade. I will say whatever I need to keep everyone focused on why we're here."

"Do vampires have hearts?" I asked. He was always too cool when it came to emotions. It made me wonder if he had any emotions at all.

"No." His response was matter of fact. "Can we get back to business?"

"Of course, you were the one who insisted we discuss Lucifer. I would much rather hear about all the important details of what you've accomplished," I chided.

"Were you aware that Lilith is on Earth?" Thane strode to the windows, peering out over the city.

"Oh? Isn't she aligned with Lucifer? What would make her come to Earth now?" I couldn't imagine the mother of demons coming to Earth for fun. Although she did like to have a bit of fun.

"I think they may disagree with the state of their arrangement. You know how she likes to entertain herself with my vampires. I've received word that not only is she here, but she's looking for Pandora's box."

"What? Why would she need the box? It's the fifth seal. We've been searching it out since we arrived here. What could she possibly want with it?" I was shocked. Lilith wasn't one to help us. She enjoyed the arrangement she'd made with Lucifer far too much. Her demons enjoyed their time in Hell. Lucifer kept them happy in their new home. What could have changed?

"I believe there's a power play happening before our very eyes." Thane looked at me over his shoulder. Thane had been the studier of history while we waited for our release. If anyone knew strategic moves, it was him.

I contemplated what he meant by that. Who would want power over Earth? God certainly wouldn't let that happen. "Do you think Lucifer is right? We were let out before it was our time?" I couldn't fathom it, but Luci had been dead set on the idea.

"Rumors spread that God has been absent from his precious creation. There's even speculation that he's abandoned Earth to its own devices." Thane strode over to relax on my couch. He always believed formal conversations should happen while seated. It was this belief that had me pushing Luci to eat with me. After a few centuries together, he'd rubbed off on me.

"When the cat's away, the mice will play. Any idea who's behind it? I believe Lucifer discovered the same thing." I was intrigued. Who had the power and wherewithal to attempt a coup against God?

"There are whispers of a powerful being, one who has been hiding in the shadows and gathering power for centuries. They call him the Dark One." Thane's expression turned thoughtfully grim. "I fear that Lilith may be seeking out Pandora's box on his behalf."

"The Dark One? I've never heard of him." My brow furrowed, and a feeling of unease settled in my stomach. If there was someone out there who could challenge God, we were all in trouble.

"He's a legend among the supernatural community. Some say he's a demon; others believe he's a fallen angel," Thane explained. "But one thing is certain— he's not someone to be trifled with."

"Well, we can't let Lilith or anyone else get their hands on the box," I said firmly. "That's our mission, and we'll see it through."

Thane nodded in agreement. "We'll need to act fast. I'll send word to the others to keep an eye out for any signs of Lilith or the Dark One."

"Wouldn't it be in our best interest to work with Lucifer to find the box? She wants the same thing we do." I knew Thane wouldn't agree with me. I needed to say it aloud since I'd already agreed to assist her in the pursuit of who let us out early. Not that I had actually believed her at the time. With the new information, it was hard not to. If God was absent, and Lilith was looking for Pandora's box, all bets were off on the grand design being enacted this time around. She had been right all along.

"We don't have the same interest, Cade. Lucifer wants to stop the apocalypse. We do not." He peered at me through slitted eyes. "You've fallen for her already."

"Of course not. I just think it would be in our best interest to work with her since we're after the same thing. We can always cut ties once we've retrieved the box." It seemed simple enough to me.

"No, we don't need the devil's assistance. We'll find the box ourselves." Thane's tone left no room for argument.

I rested back. "Okay, great leader, what's our next move?"

"I have a lead," Thane said mysteriously, standing up and brushing off his pants. "A contact in the underworld who may have information on the location of the box."

"The underworld?" I raised an eyebrow. "Since when do we associate with the devil's minions? You certainly didn't want to associate with the devil herself. Why use one of her own people?"

"Since we don't have much of a choice," Thane said grimly. "Time is running out, Cade. We need to act fast."

I sighed heavily, knowing Thane was right. We didn't have time to waste on morals and personal vendettas. The fate of the world was at stake. "But you won't work with Lucifer?" My eyes narrowed. "You're worried about the attraction you felt for her. You believe you will act on that attraction as much as the rest of us? Oh, Thane, you do have a heart after all." I couldn't help but goad him. He was acting superior when he didn't think he could handle his own attraction to her.

"Being bonded certainly complicates things," he said, his tone harsh.

I'd hit a nerve. "Fine, if you don't think you're strong enough to resist the devil, by all means, let's go chat with one of her people. I'm sure she wouldn't know the same as her own minions would." I chuckled. It was uncharacteristic of Thane to show an ounce of weakness. I was enjoying this far too much.

"I have zero interest in getting distracted. I am not you." I knew he meant it as an insult, but I appreciated the compliment.

I couldn't deny that I had a reputation for getting distracted when it came to women, but this wasn't about me. This was about finding Pandora's box and stopping whoever was behind the power play. "We'll do it your way then," I said with a shrug. "Lead the way, oh great leader."

Thane rolled his eyes but didn't say anything in response. Instead, he headed towards the door and motioned for me to follow. As we walked down the stairs and towards the street, I couldn't shake the feeling of unease that had settled in my stomach. The idea of whoever this Dark One was and Lilith working together to gain power over Earth was daunting to think about.

But I pushed those thoughts aside as we made our way through the city streets, our destination unknown to me. Thane had always been cryptic when it came to his sources of information. All I knew was that this contact of his was a powerful figure in the underworld and had connections to all sorts of supernatural beings.

As we approached an unmarked door in a dimly lit alleyway, Thane knocked three times in a specific pattern. After a few moments, the door creaked open, and we were greeted by a tall, menacing figure with red eyes and sharp claws. It was a demon, one of Lucifer's minions, no doubt.

"What do you want?" the demon growled, looking us up and down with suspicion.

"We're here to speak with your boss," Thane said calmly, not even flinching at the demon's aggressive stance. "Tell her it's Thane and Cade."

"Izzy's expecting you." He moved to allow us entrance.

We followed him inside, stepping over puddles of questionable liquid on the ground as we made our way down a dimly lit hallway. The walls were lined with doors; some closed, and others opened to reveal sordid scenes taking place behind them.

"Classy joint," I muttered under my breath, not entirely sure I wanted to know what sort of business was conducted within these walls.

We arrived at a door at the end of the hall, marked with a sign that read, 'The Devil's Den.' The demon opened the door for us, and we stepped inside.

A figure sat at a desk in the corner, their face hidden behind shadow. "What brings you two here?" a sultry voice echoed from the darkness.

"We're looking for information," Thane said coolly. "The location of Pandora's box."

Silence filled the room for a moment before the figure spoke again, "That's not exactly common knowledge."

"We're willing to pay," I added, stepping forward. "We'll offer you whatever you want."

The figure chuckled, standing and revealing themselves to be a beautiful woman with long, black hair and a sardonic smile. I knew her. She'd been with Luci the night before at the club. Was this where Thane was getting his information? Did he know this was Luci's close friend and demon?

"I bet you are, Cade. I do appreciate a man willing to do anything." The sardonic smile stretched further across her lips. Should I call her out?

But before I could say anything, Thane stepped forward. "We're not here to play games, Isabelle. Give us what we want, and we'll be on our way."

Her expression hardened when he'd said her name. "You should watch your tone, Thane," she warned. "I may be willing to help you, but that doesn't mean I have to put up with your disrespect."

Thane shrugged. "I'm simply being direct. We don't have time for games."

She narrowed her eyes before finally speaking. "Fine. I may have some information about the box. But it's going to cost you."

"Name your price," I said eagerly, already reaching for my wallet.

Isabelle shook her head. "Money won't cut it this time. I need something more . . . valuable." Her gaze flickered to Thane, and suddenly, I knew what she wanted.

"No," Thane said firmly, his body tense.

She smirked. "What's the matter, Thane? Afraid to give in to temptation?" Her hand reached out to brush against his arm.

I could see the struggle in his eyes, but he remained steadfast. "No deals involving bonded individuals. That's final."

Izzy sighed dramatically as she withdrew her hand. "Such a shame." She paused for a moment before turning her focus on me. "You're not the only one I could make a deal with. Now, are you, Thane?" Her eyes sparked with delight.

I narrowed my eyes. "You're not the only one with valuable information. Does Lucifer know the games you're playing?" They seemed like friends at the club.

Izzy leaned forward, her eyes glittering in the dim light. "Are you trying to blackmail me, Cade?" She bit her lip, giving me a seductive smile. She was playing a dangerous game.

"It doesn't have to be a threat unless there's a reason you don't want Lucifer to know."

"I'm the reason she's down here." Izzy rolled her eyes like that should be obvious. "I'm only asking for a simple request, and I'll give you all the information you need to find Pandora's elusive box. You know it moves if it feels like it's being threatened."

"What are your terms?" I asked. Thane had stayed uncharacteristically silent during our exchange. He'd stopped bargaining the minute she suggested he bond with the devil.

"You bond with Lucifer, keeping her thoroughly distracted for a short time, and I'll give you what you need to find the box." She leaned back against the front of her desk. "To be honest, you're getting the better end of the deal." She fluttered her lashes. "Luci is a minx in the bedroom, and you'd be so lucky to get one night with her, let alone a lifetime."

"How were you able to bond us to the devil?" There was no way she had enough power to accomplish such a feat.

"Oh, I didn't. I only want you to complete the bonding. I had nothing to do with making it possible." She held her hand to her chest. She wasn't lying, although Huxley would be able to tell for sure. Thane could probably read her heartbeat and breathing to know for sure as well.

"Then who did?" I asked.

"One of the fates, probably. I don't know for sure. I'm here to repay a favor. Someone wants you to bond with Lucifer pretty damn bad. To be honest, it's in her best interest, too. She's trying to save the world with no one at her back." It sounded like Izzy actually cared for Lucifer while stabbing her in the back.

"Aren't you supposed to be one of the people who has her back?"

"Yes, but I value my life. Besides, would bonding with her really be that bad for you?" She rested her fist on her cocked hip. "No, it wouldn't. Do we have a deal?"

It looked like she was as impatient as Thane. "We have a deal." I didn't see the harm. Having sex with her would be a fun challenge, but getting her to complete the bond with me, the additional venture intrigued me.

"Good, now give me your hand." Izzy sliced down her hand and held the blade out to me. I took it and did the same. I took her hand in mine, sealing the pact.

"If either of us should break our pact, as it was done to you, it shall be magnified ten times ten in retribution upon you," Izzy said. I knew the scripture well enough.

"As will you." I let go of her hand. It was done. Now, all I had to do was bond with the devil. This should be interesting.

CHAPTER 8

Luci

Kesa squeaked at our sudden appearance in the living room. "Could you not." She tossed her hair over her shoulder and continued to the kitchen. Both she and Izzy could be divas at the weirdest of moments.

"What?" I shrugged and followed after her.

"The other one is upstairs." She waved her hand as if we were an annoyance.

"What other one?" I questioned.

"The guy from the press conference yesterday. I didn't want him down here, so I sent him upstairs." The annoyance in her tone was palpable.

"What? You left him alone up there?" I whipped around.

"It's not like there's anything up there. We haven't even been here that long."

"Kesa, seriously?" I ran up the stairs.

"What's the big deal? It's not like he'll find anything. It's a rental." I could still hear her at the bottom of the stairs. She shouldn't have left anyone in the house, let alone one of the horsemen.

I flew into the first bedroom where Kesa had slept the night before. The soft lavender room was empty, the comforter still tossed aside from the morning. It had been a wild night, but Kesa had gone to bed before me. I didn't need sleep. I liked the feeling, but it wasn't necessary. I'd stayed up after the club to try to figure out my first move with Cade. I'd left notes out about what I'd learned the night before with Cade. Kesa basically left him upstairs with my notes and plan.

I burst through the door of my room. Cade sat at my makeshift desk, one of my notes in his hand. He turned his smug, unapologetic face to me. "What the hell are you doing?"

"Ah, Hux, I should have known you'd be her next target. Didn't even put up a fight, did you, Brother?" Cade tsked.

"Why fight the inevitable?" Huxley stepped closer to me. "Besides, I'm as curious as you are, Brother." There was an edge to the way he'd said *brother*. I knew they weren't actually related, but was it a jibe they used against each other?

"Inevitable? Hardly, you should know better than that."

"Obviously, I don't. I want to know the truth. It seems the only way to do that is 'to work with her." Huxley shrugged. I wasn't sure I liked his 'if you can't beat 'em, join 'em' attitude,' but I could let that slide as long as they were working with me.

Cade grumbled before turning back to me. "I see you've won him over. Do you have a plan other than investigating me?" He held up one of the papers.

I took a deep breath, gathering my thoughts. I hated that he'd read my notes from the night before. I should know better than to write anything down, but it was helping me process what I'd learned so far. "We need to figure out who let you out early and why. After that, we can talk about you going back to your world."

Cade chuckled. "You make it sound so easy. What if we're not interested in going back to that barren place? It's certainly more fun here."

I ignored the second question altogether. "It won't be easy. You didn't even ask questions when you were released from your world. You just started the apocalypse. Maybe if you'd been a bit more inquisitive, you could be of some help." I narrowed my eyes on him. Not once had he wondered about being free. Nope. Instead, he created a virus that was well on its way to killing hundreds of thousands. I wasn't even sure I could slow down what they'd started, let alone stop it. Not that I would ever admit that to anyone.

"Careful, Kitten. You may not get my help."

"I'm not sure I need it." I glared at him. I hated the attraction I felt towards him. It made me angry every time we interacted. Taking it out on him would be my new hobby. I turned my attention to Huxley. At least he hadn't been a complete asshole from the moment we met. "Do you know anything about who let you out? Cade was less than forthcoming about the details of your release."

Huxley's gaze rested on Cade. "What did you tell her?" He walked over and sat on the end of my bed. How could he look so damn sexy just sitting there? Ugh. Dammit. Focus.

"I told her what I knew, nothing." Cade shrugged.

Huxley rolled his eyes. "Cade, did you at least tell her about the note?"

"No, what bearing would that have? None of us know who left it or why we each got one." Cade crossed one leg over the other, looking far too superior.

"You told me you woke up here. That was it. I asked if you were given instructions. You said you've never been given them before. You lied to me."

"It was a simple omission." Cade tried to brush it off.

"Oh? I asked specifically about it. There was nothing simple about your purposeful omission. I don't tolerate liars." My eyes blazed red as my hands clenched at my sides.

"Whoa." Huxley stepped in front of me. "Luci, Cade can be an asshole sometimes, but you can't hurt him." Huxley glared over his shoulder. "He enjoys making people angry and looks for a fight at every turn. Don't give him the satisfaction." He turned to face Cade. "You're going to share everything from now on, right, Cade?"

"Come now, Kitten. You're not going to hurt me." He leaned back in the chair, looking as superior as ever. "You need me to find out what's going on. Besides, the damage has already been done. It's not like I can roll back a pandemic when it's already infected so many people. There's nothing you can do now but watch how it all plays out." His smug tone made me want to show him what I did to demons who tried to defy me.

My gaze homed in on him, a mischievous glint dancing in my eyes. A wicked smile crept across my lips, a playful anticipation tingling through my veins. With a mere twitch of my finger, an invisible vice closed around Cade's throat, his desperate gasps echoing through the air. I effortlessly pressed him against the wall, his hands clawing at the unseen force that held him captive. Flames flickered hungrily beneath the gleaming black soles of his shoes as if the ground itself hungered for his torment. Huxley's eyes widened in shock and horror, captivated by the spectacle before him, as Cade's gasps and futile kicks against the unyielding wall created a twisted ballet of pain.

"I believe we established earlier that I am, in fact, more powerful than you. You may have the power of one horseman, but I hold more power in one finger than you do in your entire body. I believe, at the very least, you should be giving me the respect I deserve." I looked down at my nails, secretly delighted at the gasping whimpers escaping Cade's mouth.

"Luci, I know he's an asshole, but can you not barbeque him? It smells like burning rubber. I can taste it." Huxley coughed as he turned his face away, tucking his nose beneath his shirt, trying to get away from the stench of Cade's burning shoes. "Please."

I let out an exasperated sigh and released my hold on Cade. He had a point about the stench; I certainly didn't want my bedroom reeking of burning rubber. Although, it did evoke memories of the pit, where I once reveled in tormenting those resistant to rehabilitation. Some of them truly relished their bad-boy personas, giving me the perfect opportunity to indulge in a variety of playful and twisted games until they saw the error of their ways. Oh, how I missed those wickedly delightful encounters.

"Fine, but I expect better behavior. No lying to me." I glared at him.

Cade choked and gasped on the floor. "Noted," he croaked.

"Good boy. Now, is there anything else you didn't share with me? I need every piece of information you have. I would also like to see the note left for you. There might still be a lingering trace of whoever left it behind."

Cade recovered enough to lean back against the wall. He'd pulled his knees up and rested his elbows on his knees. I hoped he learned his lesson. Not that I thought he wouldn't test my boundaries again, but at least he knew what he was up against. "Mine's in my penthouse in Las Vegas." His voice was still hoarse when he spoke. Not the elegant, charming, manipulative man from a few moments ago. It pleased me more than I could say.

"Huxley?"

"I tossed mine. I didn't think I would need it." He shrugged nonchalantly, seemingly unconcerned. "This time hasn't been different from the past. There was a note, nothing catastrophic." He paused as though only now showing interest. "Although Cade is right. We don't typically get instructions. It's basically, surprise, you're on Earth. Now, do your thing." He ran his hand over his chin. "Sometimes we have a little fun before we go to it. We've all enjoyed our time here. The faster we begin, the less time we have to enjoy all that Earth has to offer . . ."

I sat on my bed next to Huxley, resting my hands behind me. "So, what made you get started right away this time?"

"The note, I suppose," Huxley began, his voice tinged with a hint of uncertainty. "Cade took an unconventional approach, diving straight into virus research. Normally, we'd focus on warfare, but Cade had a different idea. We decided to unleash Pestilence as our primary weapon this time. Surprisingly, our plan came together swiftly."

"Full-proof?" I interjected, glancing between the two men.

Cade chuckled softly, his voice oozing with a devil-may-care charm. "You see, there's an overwhelming lack of population control out there. Introducing a lethal virus seemed like the simplest solution. Just take a look at the unsanitary state of public spaces. The ease with which diseases spread among people was staggering. Our notion was to unleash the virus in a specific country, setting the stage for a blame game that would eventually escalate into all-out warfare with others." Cade's voice, cool and nonchalant, echoed with a hint of mischief as he described their sinister plan to destroy the world and end countless lives.

I gritted my teeth to stop from beating the shit out of both of them. They weren't the real problem. "You know you're talking about killing thousands of people, right?"

"It's what we're resurrected here for, Kitten." Cade finally stood up from the floor, his jaw set. He paced the floor, his self-assured swagger back in full force. "Though, we agreed to start immediately. The note being the reason for all of us." He rubbed his thumb over his bottom lip. "The note wasn't really an order. It simply stated— *it has begun*. I'm still not sure why we thought that meant we needed to begin without our normal indulgences. I'm not convinced it referred to the apocalypse at all. What it could be referring to perplexes me. Quite the mystery you've decided to embark on, Kitten." He leaned back, adopting a relaxed and casual posture.

"What else could it be referring to?" Huxley asked. His brows furrowed as though Cade stumbled across a confusing math problem. I found it kind of adorable.

"I'm not certain, but I would love to find out." Cade turned to me. "Care to join me in my penthouse, Kitten?" The words were like a caress against my skin. How was he having such an effect on me? I could feel a deep need to bond with him below the surface of my skin. It lingered as a constant reminder of a desire I couldn't satiate with either of these men. Someone was behind this. I needed to focus. A mating bond wasn't something I intended to follow through on, no matter how much my body hungered for them.

"Couldn't you just bring the note back here?" Huxley complained.

"Worried I'll make my move while you're not around, Brother?"

"No, it just seems like a wasted trip. Luci and I could investigate more here."

"No, I want to see this note as soon as possible. This isn't some mystery to solve for fun." I glanced pointedly at Cade. "We're discussing someone with immense power. Who knows what they have planned next." I pursed my lips. "Let's go. You two aren't leaving my sight until I know who's behind this." I pointed at the two horsemen. "I'm not taking any chances. I don't want either of you running off and doing something stupid."

"Yes, ma'am," Cade said with a mock salute.

We made our way out of my room with Cade and Huxley in front of me. I followed them at a distance, keeping a close eye on them. I had a feeling this was only the beginning of something much bigger than we expected.

Cade held a hand out to me when we reached the landing. "Your car or mine?" The sly smile on his face was as infuriating as it was intoxicating.

"Driving to Las Vegas? Uh, I'm not sure we have time for that."

"We've got nothing but time." Cade pulled me against him in one swift movement.

My breath hitched as air swished around me. One second, we were in the living room of my rented house; the next, we were somewhere else entirely. Lights glimmered on the other side of the floor-to-ceiling windows. Cade kept taking me back to his penthouse. I wouldn't have thought a horseman would take such gratification in a home that wasn't his own. I felt Cade's gaze lock on me as I took in the familiar room. Everything had hard lines and modern touches. It seemed Cade liked everything to be pristine. A brown chair was a sharp contrast to the white leather couch. The windows showed the lights from the city below. Of course, he would want to be as close as possible to all the excitement the city had to offer. Cade hadn't let me go. I heard the race of his heart against me. The deep feeling inside me grew restless at the closeness.

"Show off." I heard Huxley curse. "You know she could have gotten herself here."

"Jealous?" Cade's eyes smoldered as he looked down at me. Our bodies flush against each other, neither of us making a move to separate.

"Very." Huxley stepped next to us.

That snapped my attention to him. There was an edge to his voice. My heart skipped in my chest. The desire in the room was palpable. I wanted to taste both of these men. I shook my head. "Where's the note?" I managed to say.

"Are you sure that's what you desire, Kitten?" Cade looked at me like he could read the need on my face.

"That's why we're here." My eyes bore into his, challenging him to question me.

"All work and no play make a dull little devil. From the stories I've heard, you're not dull, Kitten." He winked at me, oozing self-confidence. His confidence irked and delighted me at the same time.

Two could play that game. I darted my tongue out to lick my bottom lip. I watched as Cade tracked the movement. "So, where is it?

I'd like to have some inkling of who may have thought it was a good idea to start the apocalypse."

"My bedroom," Cade said as he turned and walked away.

I glanced at Huxley. "As usual, he expects us to follow his lead."

"Is he always so expectant?"

"Yes," he sighed as he held his arm out for me to go first.

Cade's bedroom exuded a stark simplicity, mirroring the rest of the house. The bed, adorned with gunmetal gray bedding, stood at the center, an island of monotony. A black square tray rested on the white dresser, eagerly awaiting Cade's adornments. Two matching white nightstands flanked the bed, their pristine surfaces void of any personal touch. In the corner, a slightly ajar door beckoned with an air of mystery.

My attention was drawn to Cade, who was hunched over one of the nightstands, his body contorted in anticipation. A flicker of anticipation danced in his eyes as he retrieved a slip of paper, clutching it in his hand. Our gazes locked as he strode purposefully towards me, extending the enigmatic note. I accepted it, feeling a jolt of curiosity surge through me.

Closing my eyes, I focused on the paper, my fingertips tracing its delicate texture. A subtle, lingering, magical essence clung to its surface, teasing but elusive, like a whisper in the dark. It held a trace of enchantment, a tantalizing clue, yet insufficient to unravel the identity of its sender. The desire to delve into its secrets overwhelmed me, urging me to examine it meticulously, piece by piece until its hidden message would be revealed.

"Anything?" Huxley stood beside me.

"There's a subtle signature, but I can't discern who it may belong to. I'll need to keep it."

"I told you it wouldn't be much help. We do have some power, you know. I tried to sense who left the note without success." Cade's voice was more annoyed than anything. His constant need to be superior grated on me.

"Impressive as your efforts may be, I'll do better," I declared with unwavering determination. In the blink of an eye, I vanished from the room, leaving behind a trail of lingering annoyance. Ah, the solace of my infernal abode, where comfort embraced me with a familiar intensity. The very essence of home in the depths of Hell cocooned me, the walls exuding a sense of familiarity, the scent of ash enveloping my senses. The sight of well-worn books adorning the shelf ignited a sense of belonging, wrapping me in an embrace, radiating warmth and contentment. Nothing felt quite like home. "Iz?" I sent my power to call her to me.

Izzy blinked into the room. Her body was poised to spring at anyone who dared to disrupt whatever the hell it was she'd been doing. Her brows furrowed, and her hand rested on her cocked hip as she glared at me. "You know I could have been in the middle of something."

"You could have." I held the paper out to her. "I need your prowess to discover who left this note for the horsemen. I can sense a slight signature, but I need you to do better."

"Oh? Where did you get this?" The curiosity in her tone erased any annoyance.

"The horsemen; someone left this note for them after they'd released them on Earth."

"Making nice with the horsemen?" Izzy's eyebrow rose.

"Only out of necessity." I folded my arms over my chest. "Come find me when you have something." Perched upon the crimson expanse of my worn leather couch, I sought solace within the confines of my thoughts. A moment of rest to delve into the depths of contemplation. I knew I should return to the men waiting on Earth. Yet I yearned for solitude, a momentary escape from the tumultuous mystery I left behind.

I pondered the perplexing mystery in the depths of my mind. Who, in their audacity, dared challenge the authority of my father? The very idea shook me to my core. For it was he, the Almighty, who held the power to unleash the horsemen upon the world. An act of cataclysmic consequence that should remain solely within his control.

"The Elites are managing quite well without you," Izzy grumbled, her tone laced with a rebellious edge. "Surprisingly, they've been keeping your absence hush-hush." A mischievous smile danced upon her lips, her playful nature shining through.

"Well, I suppose that's good news," I replied, my voice tinged with skepticism. Izzy's timing seemed off, and I couldn't help but wonder why she was sharing this with me now.

"Yeah, figured you could use a bit of positivity," Izzy muttered, her gaze cast downward, a hint of vulnerability in her eyes.

"Why? What's going on?" I probed, knowing Izzy well enough to understand that she wouldn't simply offer good news for the sake of it.

"Well, it turns out the only ones who possess the power to release the horsemen are those similar to you," Izzy confessed, her lips pressed together, avoiding direct eye contact.

"What does that mean?" Frustration tinged my voice. I disliked when Izzy chose to be cryptic. I needed information, and I needed it fast.

"It means, Luce, that it's likely only someone in your own family holds the potential to awaken the horsemen," Izzy admitted, her voice laced with worry.

"Someone in my family?" I furrowed my brows, my mind racing. "Why would anyone in my family want to kickstart the apocalypse without my father's express permission? Not that we've heard from him in ages, but still." I paced the room, my thoughts spinning in a whirlwind of possibilities.

"Well, off to work I go," Izzy declared, vanishing from the room. It was clear she didn't want to hear what I might have discovered during my contemplation of her revelation. I trusted Izzy with my life, but what was she trying to convey? There had to be more to it than just the involvement of my family. They always seemed to have their fingers in every pie.

It was good to know that Hell was moving along without me despite the chaos of Izzy's last bit of information. Someone must assume I was still in Hell. Souls going to the wrong place would keep everyone busy on both sides. Why bother with the distraction? Wasn't starting the apocalypse enough? A part of me was petrified at the state of my rehabilitated souls. How many would be caught in the crossfire of this disaster? I had to believe the Elites would continue my legacy and make sure no one was destroyed without serious consideration. They knew what was at stake for each soul.

What was with my father, who, for reasons only known to him, had yet to intervene in the chaos ensuing? Why was he sitting back and letting the horsemen run amok when the lives of those whom he created were on the verge of being wiped out? That was the part I didn't understand. Surely, he didn't mean for the horsemen to see their task through.

A weighty sense of responsibility settled upon me as I realized I had left two men in the wake of my sudden departure. Regret seeped into my thoughts, knowing that I shouldn't have abandoned them. Though, in all honesty, how much more harm could they have inflicted? Despite their actions, there remained a crucial conversation that lingered between us, one I had been avoiding since that surge of desire ignited within me at the club.

It was a desperate need, a yearning that stretched far beyond mere physicality. As the devil herself, I was well-acquainted with the intricate facets of desire, but this was different—something I couldn't quite articulate with words alone. Every fiber of my being resonated with an undeniable claim, binding myself to them. The magnitude of it all overwhelmed me, urging me to explore the depths of what it meant for us.

And so, my journey began, starting with those two souls patiently awaiting my return in the vibrant city of Las Vegas. There, amidst the dazzling lights and intoxicating allure, I would seek answers and unravel the enigma that intertwined our destinies. What lay ahead was uncertain, and yet, the insatiable curiosity within me propelled me forward, driving the need to discover the true extent of our connection.

Little did I know that this reunion would only be the beginning, a mere whisper of the tumultuous journey that awaited us. In the midst of Las Vegas' intoxicating haze, the tantalizing web of desire and destiny would entangle us further, unveiling secrets and unleashing forces that could shake both Heaven and Hell to their very cores.

Chapter 9

Luci

The two men stood in Cade's penthouse kitchen, heads bent in conversation. The level of comfort I felt at the sight of them unnerved me. I was here to deter them from their role in the cosmic design. The apocalypse couldn't continue, and it was my job to make sure they went back to their world before further chaos ensued. Yet, I couldn't help but feel a sense of contentment being in their presence. I strode over to them, my heart pounding as they watched me intently.

"Have a pleasant trip, Kitten?" Cade's eyes were dangerously enticing. Maybe it was because I came here knowing it was time to have a talk with them.

"I did. One of my people is looking further into the note left for you." I tucked a strand of hair behind my ears. I wasn't sure why I was suddenly nervous. Nothing made me nervous. I was the damned devil. Yet, here I was, hands trembling slightly and butterflies in my stomach at the thought of asking them about the desire I felt for them.

"Oh, so one of your demons is going to accomplish what we couldn't." Cade's scoff had my blood boiling. Any nervousness forgotten.

"Please, you didn't even try."

"Cade, you need to hold your tongue before she barbeques you."

Cade's eyes flamed as if the idea intrigued him. "You're so unbelievable. Can we have one civil conversation before you ruin it with your damn mouth?" I rolled my eyes.

"Do you think your demon will find out more information?" Huxley asked.

"She's the best." I paused. "She mentioned something else." I glanced down at the floor, interlacing my fingers.

"Yeah? Did she find something else out?" Huxley took a step towards me. I wondered for a moment if he could feel my tension.

"Yeah, it may have been one of the archangels who let you out early." I didn't want to meet their eyes. Knowing it was one of the others who let them out had me on edge. I couldn't fathom why an archangel would want to harm humans. They knew our father's love for them. Yet here we were. The apocalypse was already well underway.

"That's not news, Kitten. It had to be someone pretty damn powerful to enter our world, let alone free us." Cade's tone was harsh and condescending like he was scolding a petulant child.

"Careful, I may decide I don't need you for a damn thing if you keep speaking to me in that tone." My eyes blazed red again. I needed to get my temper under control before I took it out on the unsuspecting public or the asshole in front of me.

"Now that we know it's a celestial being, it narrows it down considerably." Huxley gave me a reassuring smile. I wondered how often he stepped in to cover for Cade.

"Not really," Cade scoffed.

I glared at him. "I'm still not sure I believe it's one of them. Other powerful beings could be responsible. We can't know for sure if it was one of them." I knew I was grasping at straws, but I needed to, for now. I wasn't ready to face one of my family's blatantly killing humans. We had our issues, but murdering humans wasn't one of them. Archangels were their protectors.

"It's not like you can do anything. The apocalypse is well underway. I doubt there's even a champion born to stop us. If your father hadn't planned our release, nothing is as it should be." Cade made some valid points, and I hated him for it.

"I will stop this." I ground out.

"Sure, Kitten." Cade remained as unyielding as he was when I first met him.

"What's your problem? Why are you such an asshole all the time?"

"He's just angry. He's actually feeling a connection to someone on Earth. The last time he had any feelings, it didn't go well." Huxley explained so casually that I just stared blankly at him.

"What? What does that even mean?" My eyes shifted from Huxley to Cade.

"Hux, she doesn't need to know our business. Damn, are you going to just tell her whatever she wants to know? You realize she's here to send us back to our world. The faster she does that, the better for her." Cade's jaw set, his cheeks reddening with suppressed anger.

Huxley took a step back. "Are you just trying to get rid of us?"

I blinked. "Yeah, I don't want the world to end. Is that wrong?"

"Well, no, but I didn't think that was all you wanted. Especially since . . ." He trailed off.

The elephant in the room. "Come now, you can't deny the feeling you have for us. I saw the change in your face the moment we walked into the club." Cade cut right to the point.

"Of course, I feel it. Understanding how it's even possible is another thing entirely. Being that I've never had a bonded, I don't get how I know it's the mate calling. Have you ever had a mate in your previous lives?"

"Not once," Huxley stated.

"We've certainly enjoyed all the pleasures available to us while here." The desire laced in Cade's voice had me glancing over at him.

"What does that mean?" The words were out of my mouth before I'd even thought.

Cade's dark chuckle sent a thrill through me. "Kitten, I think you know exactly what that means." He took a step closer to me. "Although I wouldn't mind providing you with a thorough demonstration."

Huxley cleared his throat. "We haven't experienced this before now. Who would have the power to affect the grand design? The Virtues are the only ones I can think of who would have that kind of power over the actual design of the universe. I thought bonding only happened between certain supernatural groups."

"Yeah, shifters, mages, and a few others have what are considered life mates. Archangels certainly don't. Demons definitely don't. This is a first for me. I was sure I knew everything that was possible in this world." I moved away from the two and paced the living room. What would it mean if archangels had bonded mates? There's no way we could fulfill our purpose with such a distraction. So, who was doing this now and why?

"You can't know everything," Cade drawled.

I wanted to smack him. "I make it my business to know everything. Who do you think has to do clean-up when shit gets fucked up? Yeah, me. Who ends up with more souls to rehabilitate with each new terrifying world event? Yep, me again. I need to know what the hell is going on at all times."

"Is there anyone else with that kind of power beyond the Virtues? Anyone above them would have that power, correct?" Huxley was back to figuring out the complex problem.

"No one else has the power to rewrite the natural laws of the universe. Mates fall under the Virtues' purview, yes, but I doubt anyone else could manipulate a natural law." It baffled me that they would even bother. "We're not high on the totem pole. Why would they risk it?"

"Kitten, we bring about the end of the world. Don't you think that has some bearing on why they might have made an executive decision? Can't you just ask your father to intervene and make everything right again?"

I rolled my eyes. I didn't exactly want to admit that no one has spoken to him in a century. "No, I can't just call him up to fix it. Nothing works like that."

"We've never seen him. One day, we just end up on Earth. Starting the apocalypse is a part of us. That's all we know." Huxley relaxed back in his seat.

"Oh? So, you definitely shouldn't be mated to anyone because you aren't on Earth long." I threw up my arms. This was a mess.

"We've been here a few years. We usually get at least seven years before anyone catches up to us. Even then, there has to be a champion to stop all that we've done. No champion, no chance of ending the apocalypse." Huxley was the reasonable one.

As I listened to him speak, I couldn't help but feel overwhelmed by the weight of their existence. The revelation that they brought about the end of the world was enough to make my head spin, but the fact they were my mates made the situation even more complicated. I couldn't deny the pull I felt towards them, no matter how hard I tried to fight it. It was like a magnetic force that I couldn't resist.

But I couldn't give in to them, not when the fate of the world was at stake. I needed to stay focused on finding out who was behind the bonding. It was a puzzle I needed to solve, and I couldn't afford to be distracted.

"You're right. We need to figure out who's doing this and why," I said firmly. I stopped pacing to face them. "But we can't do that if we're constantly being pulled towards each other. We need to focus on the task at hand."

Cade smirked at me, his eyes glinting mischievously. "Oh, I think we can do both. We can work together to solve the puzzle and explore our connection at the same time."

Huxley shook his head, a small smile tugging at the corners of his lips. "As much as I agree with Cade, I understand your point, Luci. We need to be careful. We don't know what kind of power our bond holds."

I nodded, grateful for Huxley's level-headedness. "Exactly. We need to keep our focus on figuring out who would have the power and means to accomplish such a feat. I think we need to have a conversation with the virtues, and I know just where to find one."

My lips curved into a wicked smile. I'd heard from Kesa on more than one occasion about the scandalous things Lydia had been up to when she wasn't supposed to be on Earth. Word had gotten around that my father was MIA, so his children certainly liked to play. It was surprising to me that one of the top tiers of the Kingdom of Heaven would gallivant on Earth, but right now, I was grateful.

Cade smirked. "So, we won't be distracting ourselves with some fun activities while we're here? Damn, I was hoping for a taste of sin herself." He winked at me.

I glared at him. "I'm serious, Cade."

"So am I, Kitten. Any investigation we undertake together will have all of us distracted."

"Cade, you can't keep your mind off of sex for five minutes?" Huxley sighed.

"I'm just stating the obvious, Brother. I know you feel the same thing. How will we go anywhere when we could be taken over by our needs at any moment?" He shrugged.

"Get your head in the game. We've got a club to visit." I smirked, enjoying the pained look on Cade's face as I whisked all of us to one of the most prestigious and well-hidden sex clubs in Nevada.

The air in the club hung heavy with pulsating beats, its rhythm intertwining with the raw energy that surged through the writhing bodies on the dance floor. The cacophony of moans and the intoxicating symphony of skin meeting skin reverberated through the space, igniting an undeniable sensual charge that electrified the atmosphere. It was a fusion of passion, desire, and unbridled hedonism, each heartbeat synchronizing with the primal pulse of the music.

Every corner of the club was an invitation to indulgence. Bodies pressed against bodies, their movements blending into a feverish dance of seduction and abandonment. The air buzzed with a palpable heat as if the collective yearning of the crowd had set the very atmosphere ablaze. Sweat glistened upon exposed skin, a testament to the fervor consuming the room. The mingling scents of perfume, musk, and desire wafted through the air, creating an intoxicating brew that revitalized the senses.

Amidst this sensual symphony, my gaze was drawn to the two figures waiting for me. Their anticipation was palpable, their eyes aflame with a mix of longing and uncertainty. The allure of the club heightened the tension between us, each moment heavy with unspoken possibilities. In this sanctuary of temptation, we stood on the precipice of exploration, our desires entwined and poised to ignite. The world melted away as we prepared to dive into a realm where pleasure reigned supreme, bound by a connection that defied comprehension. A pleasure that indulging in would distract all of us. The purpose of the mating bond. I cursed the being who created this damn bond.

Cade's eyes lit with delight. "Well, Kitten, you're full of surprises. If you wanted to take our little rendezvous public, you should have just said so." The sexy growl in his voice had my core clenching. Who knew just a slight rumble could make me wet in a second?

I ignored Cade's suggestive comment and scanned the room, searching for the Virtue I needed to speak to. It didn't take long to spot Lydia. Her flaming-red hair and striking features made her stand out even in a room full of beautiful people. She was in the midst of a heated threesome, her body writhing with pleasure as she moaned in ecstasy.

I cleared my throat, trying to get her attention without interrupting her fun. It didn't work.

Cade chuckled, his eyes glinting with amusement. "Looks like the Virtue of Chastity is taking her job seriously."

"Or not seriously enough," Huxley added, his gaze fixed on Lydia's body.

I rolled my eyes, pushing past them and making my way towards Lydia. "Lydia," I called out, hoping to get her attention. "We need to talk."

She finally noticed me, a frown forming on her face as she disentangled herself from her partners. "Lucifer," she said, her voice laced with annoyance. "It's been a while." She paused, taking a moment to right herself. "This better be important."

I ignored her tone, getting straight to the point. "Yeah, I'd say it's important. Someone thought it would be a good idea to bond me to the four horsemen. You wouldn't happen to know anything about that, would you?"

Lydia's expression turned serious, the annoyance fading from her eyes. "Bonding the horsemen? That's a serious accusation, Lucifer. Who would do such a thing?" Her tone told me she was exactly the person who would do such a thing.

"That's what we're trying to figure out," I replied, my own frustration growing with each passing moment. I didn't buy her façade. If something was happening on Earth, especially if it had to do with bonding, Lydia knew about it. "Lydia, I need you to tell me the truth right now. I don't have time for games."

Her eyes sparkled. "Excuse me, you're the one who barged into my club, throwing around accusations. You better have some pretty damn good evidence to accuse me of something like that. I'm at the top of the hierarchy, and you know it."

I rolled my eyes. She may be near the top, but she didn't have the same power I had. "Maybe we should take this somewhere more private."

One man who'd been with Lydia strode over with a baby-pink silk robe. He held it open so she could slip her arms through it. When she finished yanking the rope closed, she glared at me with malice. "Yes, maybe we should." She strode down a hallway in the back, her heels clicking against the black-tiled floor. You'd think they'd choose something that didn't show off everything under the strobe lights. One thing was for certain: I wasn't sitting or touching anything in this place.

When she entered an elaborate office, the man who'd followed closed the door behind us. Lydia sat behind the desk, her man taking up a foreboding stance next to her.

"What are you doing, Lydia?" I narrowed my eyes at her.

"Well, I was enjoying myself. I thought that was pretty obvious." She smirked. I wanted to rip the smile from her face. The way she avoided every question irked me. I wasn't called the lie detector for nothing.

"No, you're avoiding my questions, which means you know something. Tell me, now, before I lose my patience." I crossed my arms over my chest. I wasn't playing her games.

"Are you sure you want to continue to throw accusations around? It won't be welcomed nor tolerated. Besides, your boys look like they'd like to enjoy some time in my club. I won't let them if you make me angry." Her eyes flicked between the two men flanking me.

"Lydia, stop evading."

"Lucifer, you'd think you would enjoy yourself. It's not like you've ever settled down with anyone, let alone four handsome men. I think you should relish the opportunity you've been given. Isn't that what you wanted after all this time? To settle down with someone who would love you like you deserve. You should be grateful. You got exactly what you wanted." She crossed one leg over the other, looking far too comfortable for my liking.

It took a second for what she'd said to register. "How could you possibly know what I want?" I breathed. She wasn't wrong. It wasn't just a break I was looking for in my life. I wanted more. I had a divine purpose but no one to share my life with. Living eternity with shallow lovers whenever I desired was long past old. I wanted something more, something meaningful. But how in the hell would she know that?

"Darling, I know everyone's desires. How do you think I manipulate fate so well?" She leaned forward. "I also know you're not as upset about this predicament as you purport to be. Like I said, why don't you just enjoy it?" She licked her lips, looking between the two men behind me again. "If you're not going to, I may take advantage of you bringing them here to me."

My eyes blazed red. "No." My voice came from deep within me.

"Ah, there she is. I was wondering where your possessive streak went. You forget, I know you. Whether you want me to or not. This isn't a bad thing. One could even say I did this for you, Luci." She sat back in the chair, folding her arms over her chest. The man next to her took a subtle step closer to her. I could tell he was supernatural, but I wasn't sure what exactly. I didn't like not knowing what I was up against.

"Not that I'm not enjoying your little banter here, but could you tell us who put you up to this so we can go?" Cade cut in. I could hear the annoyance in his voice. He knew she was evading as much as I did.

"Who says anyone did? I was just giving our devil here what she wanted. The least I could get is a thank you." She flipped her hair over her shoulder, the light making the pink stand out against her dark skin.

"I know someone put you up to this. You can't think I'm that naïve, Lydia. Start talking. My patience has run out."

"Not today, darling. I value my life more than you obviously do. I'll say that the idea was presented to me, but I figured you wouldn't mind. Especially with you taking a hiatus from hell and all. Why don't you just take advantage of this gift I've given you?"

I glared at her. "Who?"

"I have no interest in ending my place here. Let's just say that someone wanted you to be distracted while they enacted their plan. I won't tell you any more than that. I've already overstepped. They can end us both. Now, if you don't mind." She stood, pointing to the door.

My eyes narrowed, and I threw her up against the wall behind her, the picture crashing to the ground and shattering next to her. "You're giving me a name before I leave here." My magic tightened around her throat. She blinked in surprise, then she stood next to her desk, brushing her hands down over her robe. "No, I won't. Now, I asked you to leave nicely. I won't ask again." She snapped her fingers, and I could feel the air whoosh around us.

Chapter 10

Luci

I blinked, looking down at the dark-brown water. We hit the surface, the air leaving my body on impact. I gulped down the murky water before it engulfed me. I coughed, only taking more water into my lungs. I felt a hand wrap around my arm, yanking me towards the moonlight.

As I struggled and was yanked to the surface, my mind raced with thoughts of who could have possibly put Lydia up to this. I knew I had enemies, but someone who wanted to distract me while they enacted their plan? It could only mean one thing, and that was trouble. Serious trouble.

Finally breaking the surface, I took a deep breath of fresh air and hacked up the water I'd swallowed. I looked around to assess my situation. The crescent moon shone above us in the night sky. It was hard to see beyond that. A few lights indicated some houses were in the distance. Certainly, too far to swim. My lungs burned with the rawness of expelling the water. I was immortal, but I still felt pain.

One of my father's little gifts to make sure we'd be amenable to doing what we were supposed to do. Wouldn't want us to stray from his divine mission.

Cade and Huxley emerged from the water beside me, looking just as confused as I felt. "What the hell just happened?" Cade demanded. His arm left mine and raked through his wet, tousled hair.

"I don't know," I admitted, still trying to shake off the shock of being transported into the water. I cursed Lydia for dropping us just above the water with no time to react. "But we need to get out of here and fast. Lydia gave us enough to know that someone is planning something big, and we can't afford to be distracted."

Huxley wrapped his arm around my waist, helping me stay afloat. "We need to find out who's behind this. Before it's too late."

I nodded, feeling a sense of dread settling in my stomach. The fact that someone was using me as a pawn in their game meant that something big was happening. And if we didn't figure it out soon, it could mean the end of everything.

"We need to regroup," I said, pushing my wet hair out of my face. "Figure out our next move."

Cade nodded in agreement. "Let's get out of here first. This place gives me the creeps."

Huxley chuckled, his hand rubbing circles on my back. "You're just afraid someone might see you not looking your best. God forbid someone were to see you in a dripping-wet suit."

The corner of his mouth twitched. "Shut up, Huxley."

"Is this Lake Mead?" Huxley glanced around the beach.

"That bitch has a sense of humor. I'll give her that." Cade twisted the bottom of his shirt, deciding to shuck the jacket. His white button-up did nothing to hide the hard lines of muscle beneath. I licked my lips, wanting a taste but remembering that it wasn't Lake Mead I wanted a taste of. "See something you like, Kitten?" His eyes darkened as he looked at me through his lashes.

"We need to get cleaned up." I blinked out of my gawking.

"I couldn't agree more." Cade took my hand, and the familiar feel of the air as we portaled enveloped me. I stared at myself in the mirror, taking a second to adjust to my surroundings. White marble counter, rich gray cabinets beneath, and a huge shower that could easily fit four people. The stone floor was a nice touch. Two giant rain showerheads were in the middle, with full-body sprayers along the wall on all four sides. Cade obviously had a thing for being clean.

"The bathroom? Really?" I shook my head at Cade.

A second later, the air blurred, and Huxley stood inside the shower. He shook his head. "Cade, you need to stop doing that."

"What? You have the same power to portal as I do." He smirked, his eyes full of mischief.

"Yeah, but when you do that, I have to concentrate to figure out where the hell you went. The only reason I can is because of the bond." He shook his head, opening the large glass door to the shower.

"Maybe I wanted her all to myself." He stepped closer. "Would you like to get cleaned up, Kitten?" His eyes darkened with desire.

Damn, yes, yes, I do. Wait. They were meant as a distraction. "I think I can handle a shower on my own."

He stepped closer, erasing any distance between us until I could feel his wet shirt against mine. "But why would you want to when you could be worshiped? Come now, Kitten. I want to hear you scream with desire. I want to see you come all over my cock."

My core clenched. I needed to say no to this man. Someone did this on purpose to distract me from stopping them. His hand skimmed down my arm, over the swell of my hips, stopping to grip my ass and pull me against his hard cock, pushing desperately to be free of the constricting pants. Damn, a little play time couldn't hurt.

I pushed him back against the glass door, my mouth crushing against his in an instant. The gasp when he opened his mouth sent a giddy shiver down my back. I loved that I'd surprised him. I bit his bottom lip when he lifted me to wrap my legs around his waist. "Fuck," I heard both men curse.

I ground my hips against him, hating the heaviness of the wet clothing between us. Cade's mouth dipped, nipping at my throat. "Do you want both of us worshiping every inch of you?"

I felt Huxley move closer to us. Cade dropped me to my feet, turning me to face Huxley. "This one is going to need your express permission, Kitten. He won't touch you otherwise."

I furrowed my brow. There was a story behind that I intended to find out later. "I want you," I spoke the words in a breathless pant as Cade sucked on the side of my neck, his hands exploring every inch through my wet clothes.

"Good girl," Cade bit my earlobe.

My pussy clenched at his words. Huxley grabbed for the hem of my shirt, lifting it over my head in a second. He took in my body like I was the answer to every prayer he'd ever said. His mouth closed around my nipple, biting through the lace fabric. "Mine," he growled, and I felt it all the way down my body.

Cade had reached around, undoing my pants and slowly sliding the wet fabric down my long legs, his fingers tracing a line with his nails down my inner thigh to my calves. He lifted each of my feet to get my pants free. "More, I need more."

"Someone's impatient. Don't worry, Kitten. We're going to take very good care of you." He spun me in a swift movement, his hands cupping my sex. I wanted to feel him inside me. In answer, he slid two fingers beyond my panties to rub inside me. I felt the exact moment he'd found what he was looking for when my legs weakened, and I grabbed Cade's shoulder to keep my balance. Huxley pulled my panties down my legs. Not waiting for Cade to move before barring me to them both. I heard him curse behind me as I felt his pants rustle to the floor.

"Fucking lake water," he cursed.

I let out a laugh. "Lydia sure is a bitch for that one."

"I plan on letting her know what I think of her little joke next time I see her." He bent to my neck, placing kisses and running his tongue along my neck and shoulder. My head fell back against him as Cade's mouth closed around my clit, sucking it hard between his lips. I gasped.

His tongue flicked out and hummed out at an impossible pace as air hit my sensitive lips. I wanted to know how in the hell he was doing that when Huxley's fingers cupped my breast before pinching my nipples between his two fingers. Another gasp escaped, edging me closer. He yanked the bra from my chest.

I felt the climax building between my legs as Cade worked his tongue at an impossible pace. I dug my nails into his shoulder as Huxley pinched my nipples. I cried out, throwing my head back against Huxley. His hands braced my thighs against him as my body shook with my first orgasm. Cade stood, plunging deep inside me. My pussy clenched around his thick cock as I rode out my orgasm. I could feel my wetness dripping down my thighs.

"Damn, how?" Cade kissed me in response, and I could taste myself on his tongue. He sucked and bit my lips, worshiping my mouth as he'd done my pussy.

I felt Huxley's fingers on my thigh, soaking up my juices with his fingers. "Remember how you said you wanted both of us?" Cade's brow rose. I recognized his mischievous grin.

" I do," I managed to say before Huxley's fingers entered my ass. "Oh, Fuck." I leaned forward as Cade pumped a few times inside me. His brother stretched my ass with his fingers. Damn, having them both inside me sent a surge of delight through me. I clenched my lips around Cade, and he growled.

"Our girl likes that. I told you I would make you scream at my cock." Cade lifted me, stepping into the shower. "I also remember promising to get you clean in the process." He turned on the shower. It was cold for a split second before the heat hit me.

"Sorry, Love," Huxley murmured in my ear.

"What?" I gasped as his length pushed inside me slowly. He backed out before pushing a little further, backing out again. The last time, he thrust hard, his length filling me to the brink. I braced myself against Cade, even though I knew he already held my thighs in a punishing grip. They both stilled, letting me adjust to both of them, filling me completely. There was something delicious about feeling them both buried deep. I claimed them as much as they were claiming me. I lowered my head, biting Cade's shoulder, and then my body adjusted to them. "Fuck, I need you to move." My pussy milked Cade in response to my words.

"As you wish." Cade pumped me hard as Huxley took a more relaxed pace behind me. Cade's mouth found mine, and he didn't miss a beat. His tongue fucked my mouth just as hard as his cock did. I moaned as I felt my muscles clench.

"Kiss him. Let him know how much you like what he's doing to that little ass of yours," Cade demanded, his hand wrapping around my throat as I turned to meet Huxley's mouth with mine. His kiss was soft at first, slipping his tongue between my lips. He traced my lower lip with his tongue before sucking it into his mouth. I gasped. He bit my lip, and I exploded. I clenched around both of them as they fucked me through my throbbing orgasm.

"Fuck," Huxley cursed. I felt him tense behind me, his cock still thrusting. I reached my arm back to grip his hair.

"Come for me. I want to see you lose control." There was nothing sexier than the idea of the dark fae letting go with me. I turned my head to the side. His lips met mine in a messy, brutal assault as his cock stilled. I felt his pulse, and his mouth dropped. "Mmm, good boy." He shuddered again. His hands gripped my arms as he spilled all of himself inside my ass.

I turned my head to meet Cade. His rhythm had slowed while Huxley and I both enjoyed our release. A wicked smile crept up my lips. I grabbed his neck and pulled him towards me. He sped, his cock impaling me at a brutal pace. I gripped his hair and forced his eyes to meet mine.

"Your pussy is mine." Cade gripped my thighs. I could feel how close he was. His thrusts staggering.

"I want to feel you come. Give it all to me." His eyes darkened as I made him stare back at me. He wanted to see me come. Now, it was my turn. I would break this man.

He kept thrusting, slowing. "No," he growled. "We come together. We're completing the bond tonight." He gripped me hard against him. He moved me slightly, so I felt him against my G-spot.

"What?" Huxley gasped behind me. Cade hadn't let him in on this plan, either. Cade was a reckless fool, and I was here for it. He kept rubbing me in just the right way to make me squirm. My pleasure spiked with each thrust.

"Holy fuck." I gripped his shoulders, my nails digging in as another climax built deep within me. He smiled at me, the satisfaction in his eyes evident as he gazed at me. I was so fucking close. His finger dipped between us, flicking against my sensitive clit. Once, twice, a third time, I screamed. He held my head and roared as his own climax hit him. Our eyes stayed steady as we both shook. Huxley braced himself against my back, probably keeping both of us from hitting the floor. Something in my chest heated. I felt the bond as my core clenched around him. He stilled, his cock still buried deep within me. I saw a spark of white in his irises, and I knew he was feeling the same.

"Fuck, Kitten. I like the feel of you around me. I might never leave." He gripped my ass as his cock slid against me.

"Not that I'm complaining, but we have some shit to get to." I heard the pop of a cap before Huxley's hands were soaping up my back. He slid his slick fingers in my ass, and I squeaked. Cade was still inside me, which had me wanting to ask questions. I should know by now these two were experts at what should be impossible. Not that I minded. Cade's tongue was amazing. I wouldn't mind a repeat performance. Maybe two. It's not like any of us need to sleep.

Cade finally pulled out, dropping my legs. "Always the reasonable one, Huxley. If you play your cards right, she might just let you at that sweet pussy. You know you want to bond as much as I did."

"You two don't even know what's going to happen. Don't you think that whoever fucked with us wants us to bond? Did you think something bad might happen if we give in?" Huxley continued to rub his hands over my body. He was careful, running his hands over every inch of me. It was interesting. I turned to face him. His face was level with my pussy as he soaped my legs. A lover hadn't cleaned me before. I didn't mind it.

"I don't care. We'll stop them either way." I looked down at him. I wanted this feeling with him, too. I needed it. It pushed me to take him. My pussy clenched at the thought of coming again. I pulled him up to my mouth.

He kissed me slowly, not letting me take control. "I'm not doing this right now." He rested his forehead against mine. He held my shoulders. "I want to. Damn, I fucking want to. But I think we should find out what happens with you and Cade before you bond with anyone else."

I knew he was speaking reason, but my heart sank in my chest. "What's this?" I rubbed my hand over my chest. It hurt. I didn't like it.

"Rejection, Kitten. It's not a fun experience." Cade stepped closer, his arms wrapping around me and pulling me into his chest.

"Why does it feel so physical?" I rested a hand on his chest. It surprised me that Cade would be the one comforting me. Huxley seemed more like the gentle one. Cade was more controlling.

"That's what happens. Haven't you been rejected before?" Cade's brows furrowed, looking down into my eyes.

"Obviously not."

"I'm sorry." Huxley looked down at me. "I just don't think it's a good idea. I didn't say we would never do it. I didn't know that Cade planned to complete the bond. Neither of you know what that means. It was reckless." His voice was low, his eyes staring at the stone floor. "I guess you two are the rebellious type. Act first, consequences be damned." He shook his head.

I took his chin, forcing him to look me in the eye. "Don't deny me again. The next time I ask, you won't reject me." My voice came from the pit of my soul. My devil didn't like being rejected by anyone. I didn't care about the reason.

He nodded. He went back to soaping himself before standing under the showerhead, further from me. He rinsed himself and stepped out without another word.

"Kitten." Cade brushed my hair behind my ear. "This isn't a bad thing. It's a sign of trust. He wants you to be sure. He wants his time with you. To treasure you."

"I'm not some girl who needs to be doted on. I'm the fucking devil. He should give me what I want." I looked up at Cade.

There was a different smile on his face. Not the mischievous one, but something else. "Of course, you don't need that. But maybe he does. We don't get to be here very long. We've all had our share of heartbreak. It may be about him, not you." He kissed the top of my head. I was still staring out where Huxley had left. I needed to get over it, but I was shellshocked. I hadn't been rejected before. Not by anyone. No one dared. Why did this feel so hurtful? Why did it feel like I was ripping in two over a man I'd known less than a day? What the hell was wrong with me?

"I'll give you a few minutes alone." He placed a soft kiss on my lips before exiting the shower. He placed a towel for me on the counter before he slipped out of the bathroom door. How did he know I needed some time to myself? The bond, he would know everything I was feeling now. Maybe Huxley was right. Completing the bond was reckless. I would do it again in a heartbeat. I could feel my connection to Cade like a living piece of myself. He was a part of me, as I was a part of him. It was an incredible connection. One that I wanted to cherish. How could something that felt so right be bad? I've never felt such wholeness within myself. I never wanted to let this feeling go. To think I could have three more.

I walked out of the bathroom with my towel wrapped around me. Huxley stood in front of the mirror, sliding a coat over his stark-white shirt. I didn't want to look at him. He wanted me to regret what Cade and I'd done. I wouldn't do that. I was a woman who took what she wanted. At that moment, I wanted him. Cade stood to the side, a towel wrapped around his waist.

"It's not that I don't like it. I don't think I look very good in your clothes." Huxley pulled at the jacket sleeves that were a little too short. The whole suit looked just a little too small on him. He was certainly more robust than Cade. I was surprised he even agreed to wear his clothes.

I wrapped the towel tighter around myself. I glanced back to the bathroom, realizing the only thing I had to wear was on the bathroom floor. Shit. There was no way I was putting that back on.

"That's why you have your own closet," Cade replied as he pulled down a gray pair of slacks and a white shirt from the closet. He looked damn fine in the towel. I wouldn't mind if he wore that for the rest of the day.

Huxley looked at me, and I swear he could read me like a book. "I'm heading back to the club. I need some answers." His jaw tightened. "You think you'll be all right here? Obviously, someone is targeting you. I don't know that you'll be safe as long as you pose a threat." His eyes met mine before he looked away. I knew he needed space from me, but it was stupid. He had just fucked my ass, and now he needed space. I closed my eyes, inhaling deeply.

"You know she'll recognize you as a horseman. We both spoke with her last night."

"I plan on altering my appearance. It's a gift of being a fae. I can glamour myself to appear as someone else." Huxley still hadn't met my eyes. I wasn't sure how I felt about him going back to Lydia's sex club.

"Whatever." I flicked my hand and turned away from him. I didn't want him to see how much this bothered me. I'd known the guy for a day. I needed to get my shit together before I turned into one of those sappy girls.

I knew the minute he left the room. Cade stepped behind me. "I could probably keep you distracted while he's gone." His lips bent to kiss my bare shoulder.

"I don't know. I think we should find out more about this bonding thing. See if anything's changed." His teeth rested on my shoulder. He scraped down, causing a flutter to go through my belly.

"I think we can find out right here in this bedroom." He turned me around to face him, yanking my towel off me in one fell swoop. "Now, that's much better. I don't think I'm done with my little devil yet." He yanked me against him, his cock hard and ready.

"How?" I couldn't believe some of the stuff he'd been able to do.

"Another one of the perks of being a horseman, although I haven't been able to use this power in quite some time." A playful grin split his lips. "I think I'll be finding out just how much my power has changed right now— with you." His lips crashed into mine, and despite how sensitive I already was, my body hummed for his. Maybe saving the world could wait a few more hours. He nipped my lip, and his finger circled my clit. Or days, I could save the world in a couple of days. I mean, what's the worst that could happen?

Chapter 11

Luci

A formless black cloud drifted across the mouth of the cave. A chill ran through my body that I'd been trying to ignore. Huxley wasn't there. I couldn't breathe, and I was sure it was because the blackness was coming for me. I didn't know how I knew it was coming for me, but I did. My heart pounded so loudly that I was sure everyone could hear it. I turned to see the spot Huxley had once occupied. The black cloud formed a shape, a person, and now stood behind me. It was him. I knew it. I could feel him. This was the creature that was hunting me. I could feel it, feel him. He wasn't a man but a monster. I could feel the longing to be free inside the dark depths of his soul. If you could count what he had as a soul. It felt different from the ones I'd encountered in Hell. There was something more to him. The cloud coalesced into long hair, sharp cheekbones, and inhuman green eyes. The eyes of the creature stood out. I'd never seen this man before. His green eyes swirled in their depths. There was something haunting about him. Something I felt I should remember. His eyes darkened from jade to a dark emerald. He felt wrong. Every part of my body hummed with how wrong all of this felt.

"Ah, the little devil came to visit me in my pit. How lovely." His voice grated against my chest. What the hell was this? Who had power over a dream like this?

"I didn't choose to come here." I winced as the words tore from my throat. I wasn't supposed to be here. Wherever here was.

"I know. I brought you here. I can find anyone anywhere through their minds. You're fast asleep in the arms of your bonded. Do you feel safe, little devil?" His words hurt, and I wasn't sure how I could feel each syllable like a drum against my temple. What the hell was this? Who was this? "All in good time, all in good time."

I felt my arm being shaken. I blinked my eyes open. Cade was leaning over me, concern etched on his face. "Luci, Luci, are you all right?"

"Yeah . . . no . . . I don't know." I closed my eyes. The pounding in my head followed me from my dream. Cade's hand smoothed down my face.

"You were screaming. I couldn't get you to wake up at first. What happened?" He kept his hand against my cheek. I wondered if he was checking for a fever or something. Like the devil could get a fever. Fucking hell, why was I able to feel the pain?

"It was a dream, I guess." I flopped my arm over my eyes.

"If it were any dream, I would have been able to rouse you sooner. Tell me what you saw." Cade was all business.

"A green-eyed man, long hair. He said he was in some kind of pit. It's not my pit, though. He formed into a man from black smoke. It was wrong. Everything about it felt wrong." I rubbed my eyes. "How could he pull me to him while sleeping? On second thought, how could I get a headache from a dream?" The pounding hadn't subsided.

"What else do you remember? Anything may help."

"I don't know. I felt like I should remember something, but I don't know what. His words hurt. Every time he spoke, I felt pain."

"You said everything hurts?" He searched my face. Maybe he was looking for an answer I didn't have.

"Yeah, why?" I wasn't sure why that detail struck him.

"I need to do some more research. I think that may help, but I'm not sure yet." He paused. "I'm sorry, Luci." He pulled me up and sat me against his chest. He kept a hand on my head and started talking. His words were soft and soothing, coaxing me into a half-sleep state. "We'll figure this out. It's too coincidental that you would dream of this now."

"I don't know what I should have remembered." I don't know why that feeling stuck with me, but it did. That and the disorienting pain.

"I'll be in the shower." I put on my clothes from the night before and headed to the bathroom. This is something I won't forget. My intention was for this figure to be locked up. He needed to be punished for what he did.

The scalding water from the shower felt good. It washed away any remnants of the dream. It also helped the pounding in my head. I couldn't believe I was getting a headache from a dream. It was just a dream, right?

I stepped out of the shower and wrapped a towel around my body. I was looking around for a hairbrush when there was a knock at the door. It was weird how everything I'd needed appeared. I knew Cade was responsible, and I appreciated it. "Yeah, come in."

He stepped into the room with a broad smile spreading across his face. "I made breakfast. I hope you brought an appetite." His dimples winked at me. How could I have forgotten how stunning Cade was? How much I needed him?

"I could eat." I moved towards him, wrapping my arms around his neck. I pressed my lips to his. Having him close helped shake away the dream. It was probably some weird bond thing, but I would take it as long as it made me feel better. Lydia hadn't been wrong. Something in my life was missing. I didn't want to think about her having access to my deepest desires, but she wasn't wrong.

He brushed a lock of hair behind my ear. "What's going on in that pretty head of yours, Kitten?"

My heart raced erratically, a lingering sense of unease coursing through my veins like a relentless tempest. "Nothing," I stammered, my voice betraying the turmoil inside me. The dream, if that's what it truly was, had left an indelible mark on my soul, and I grappled with its elusive meaning.

I couldn't bring myself to confide in him about Lydia's uncanny intuition. How could she have seen through the walls I so carefully erected around my desires? I yearned for a partner to connect on a level that transcended the mundane, but vulnerability scared me. It was an admission I wasn't prepared to make to these strangers, no matter how intriguing they seemed.

All I craved at that moment was to find Lydia once more, to unravel the enigmatic threads that bound us. But it had to be a clandestine meeting, away from the prying eyes and probing questions. My secrets were mine to guard, hidden beneath layers of self-preservation.

The allure of physical intimacy beckoned, yet I resolved to guard my mind and heart fiercely. I would savor the pleasure offered by these men, but I wouldn't surrender my innermost self to them. In a world where vulnerability was a liability, I vowed to remain the master of my emotions, even as my heart yearned to break free.

He kissed my head. "All right, keep your secrets."

I furrowed my brow as I looked at him. How could he possibly know? "What?"

"It's okay, Kitten. I know you don't want to tell me everything you're thinking. You don't trust me. I haven't exactly given you a reason to, considering you came here to stop me from fulfilling my very purpose." He waved a hand out. "But I know you're not telling me something important. I hope you'll trust me enough to share soon. Especially if our lives are at stake."

"I'll tell you if I feel the need. Until then, you don't get access to my every thought. A devil must have her secrets." I winked as I strode past him and out the door. "Did you say something about breakfast?"

He caught up to me quickly in the hall. "A woman after my own heart. Yes, please, I would love nothing more than to feed my mate until she's well-satisfied." He winked.

"Oh, is that actually a mate thing?" I turned, not sure if he was serious. Cade was hard to read. One minute, he was being the cocky, albeit charismatic, player. The next, he was whispering sweet words into my ear to calm me down. It was hard to keep up with him.

Cade's laughter resonated through the air, a confident and charming cadence that sent a thrill down my spine. "Taking care of one's mate is an essential duty," he quipped, his voice as alluring as a siren's call. His response was a subtle admission that set my senses ablaze, confirming what I had suspected all along. This man was no stranger to seduction, and he exuded the aura of a seasoned player well-versed in the art of wooing.

His polished exterior— that of a refined gentleman— concealed a deeper allure, a magnetic charisma that undoubtedly drew others into his web. I could imagine him skillfully employing this charm to navigate the waters of desire, leaving a trail of enamored hearts in his wake.

But I wasn't one to easily fall prey to such tactics. Oh no, I could see through his smooth veneer, and I knew better than to be ensnared so effortlessly. While others might succumb to his advances, I was determined to maintain my guard, to keep my heart well protected from his beguiling ways. His intentions might be masked with charm, but I wasn't about to be just another conquest in his pursuit of pleasure.

"Well, I won't argue with that." I laughed at his obvious attempt to be charming. "Besides, it doesn't exactly hurt for your mate to get properly fed, does it?"

"No, it certainly does not." He pulled me into a gentle kiss. It was strange. Kissing him was like the kiss of a man on fire. His lips were cool and smooth, but his body was on fire. I melted into the feel of his mouth on mine. As quickly as the kiss began, it ended. He smiled at me. "Now, come on, you need to eat."

"And you need to behave," I chided playfully. The mischievous glint in Cade's eyes reminded me of a child exploring a treasure trove of sweets. It was a side of Cade I hadn't witnessed before—genuine, unguarded, and utterly refreshing. In my mind, the horsemen had always been enigmatic figures, veiled in an aura of aloofness. Yet this candid moment, where Cade let his guard down, felt like an extraordinary revelation.

The warmth that surged through me as I observed this unguarded version of him surprised me. It was as if I had glimpsed the inner workings of his soul, the vulnerable humanity that lay beneath the formidable exterior. I couldn't help but feel drawn to him in a way I hadn't anticipated. But I couldn't ignore the nagging realization that moments like these were fleeting, and the barriers would eventually return.

Deep down, I knew this captivating glimpse of Cade's true self would be temporary, like a fleeting comet streaking across the night sky. And as much as I wanted it to linger, the practical side of me understood that the unyielding realities of his life would soon reclaim him.

Questions filled my mind as I pondered his intentions. Was he trying to distract me from something, using this endearing façade as a shield? He urged me not to divulge my secrets, but what about his? Were there hidden truths he held close, buried within the recesses of his heart?

The enigmatic dance between us deepened as I grappled with these thoughts. I yearned for a connection that transcended the superficial, yet I was keenly aware that Cade, like me, was a keeper of guarded truths. The intricacies of our entwined lives were becoming more apparent, and I couldn't help but wonder how much of ourselves we were truly willing to reveal.

"Or what?" He raised an eyebrow as he pulled out a chair for me to sit. "Drink your coffee, and I'll get you something to eat."

I sat at the modern table. Everything in his place was sleek and modern. He slid pancakes with berries and whipped cream in front of me. "If you're lucky, I may get creative with this after breakfast." He set the whipped cream can between us.

"I think we've wasted enough time, don't you?" Grabbing the syrup, I was ready to dig in. There were three kinds. I selected the berry one. The first bite was pure heaven on my tongue. I moaned.

"I disagree, especially when you moan like that over pancakes. It reminds me of the other sounds I like to hear you make." He licked the syrup off his bottom lip.

Damn, I was going to have a hard time focusing with him around. Apparently, whoever did this knew exactly what they were doing. "Focus, you said you needed to do research."

"Ah, yes, I'll need to get in touch with Thane. He knows more of the celestial history than I do. Tracking him down today shouldn't be a problem." He was so proper while he ate. It made me feel like a bit of a fiend as I shoveled the dripping piles of goodness into my mouth. I didn't care. This was too damn good to slow down.

"Should I go with you? I would like to meet Thane a bit more formally than before."

"No," Cade said so fast I paused. Syrup dripped onto my plate as I stared back at him.

"Why don't you want me to meet him?" I lowered my fork.

"He's not exactly civil. I don't think you should meet him just yet."

"You know I'm here to stop all of you. The sooner I meet him, the faster we stop the apocalypse." I didn't like that he was already hindering my mission.

"You'll meet him in due time. I believe you should check in with Huxley. He may have learned something from the club last night." His voice honeyed into the charismatic man who easily hid things from me. Maybe I should follow him today?

"Like how to make another woman come. I'm not so sure I want to see the aftermath of the sex club." I rolled my eyes. I hadn't exactly liked knowing one of my men was going to a sex club. He wasn't really mine, considering Lydia had fucked everything up. It didn't change how I felt about them. They were mine. Something deep within me didn't like Huxley leaving me last night. Shaking the mating bond wasn't something I could do lightly. It was hard-wired into my emotions. Nothing changed that.

"Jealous?" Cade's brow rose.

"No, he can do what he likes. We met yesterday. I have no real claim on him." Pushing the empty plate away, I didn't want to talk anymore about Huxley.

"Liar." Cade shook his head. "Make yourself at home. I know you have an assistant who's probably worried to death about you. She was a demanding little thing, if I remember correctly. I'll be in touch." He walked around the table to kiss my cheek. "Don't get into any trouble without me." His words were a whispered breath against my ear.

He wasn't wrong. Kesa was probably freaking out that I'd been gone so long. She knew I was on a mission, though, and could go days without speaking to her. Still, I could try to be courteous. Shit. I hadn't even thought about my phone when I went into the lake.

I stood, bringing my plate to the sink. On the table was my phone, with a note next to it.

I took the liberty of fixing this for you. It's as good as new. -Cade

Of course, he did. I picked it up, checking for anything I missed. Cade was right. I had over twenty missed calls from Kesa. Had he checked before breakfast? I dialed Kesa.

She picked up immediately. "Where the hell are you?"

"With the horsemen, as planned. Why?"

"Izzy's been looking for you. Did you confront a Virtue last night?" I didn't like her accusatory tone.

"Yes, she's the brains behind bonding me with the horsemen." I could strangle her, although I didn't want to take another swim in the lake.

"Well, the Elites heard about it. Your brother heard, too. No one in Hell is happy. They're demanding you come back now before you piss off anyone else in the hierarchy." Her words were rushed and demanding. It grated on my nerves to hear one of my people trying to order me around. I wouldn't tolerate it.

"Careful, Kesa. Remember who you're talking to." I paused, letting the threat have the desired effect. "I have a job to do, and I'm not going back until I find out what the hell is going on. They're just going to have to deal with it." I hated having to talk to Kesa like she was the bad guy. "I know you're just the messenger. Should I go talk to my brother? I learned a few things he may find interesting." Not like I wanted to, but if I could alleviate his worry, I would at least make the trip.

"No, I can talk to him. That's what I'm here for, right?" She didn't exactly sound happy. "Can I at least tell him about Lydia being responsible for the bonding? He may be a bit more understanding."

"No, I want to keep that under wraps. Right now, only you, Lydia, and the men know. I would like to keep it that way." I sighed. "Tell him we had a little disagreement at her club. He won't ask more after that."

"Wait, you went to Lydia's club without me?" The sting in her tone caught me off guard.

"I was investigating who was behind my bonds. I'm about to head back there if you want to go with me. One of the horsemen went there last night to blow off some steam. I intend to join him." I wasn't exactly telling her everything. It was weird because I trusted Kesa completely, but something told me not to share everything with her. Izzy warned me not to trust anyone. I hated that I'd included my best friend on that list.

"Oh! Yes!"

"I'll see you in ten." I hung up the phone and glanced down at myself. I hadn't exactly dressed to go to a sex club. I needed something else. I wanted to remind Huxley who he belonged to, or at least what he was missing. A pang of jealousy went through me at the thought of him fucking anyone else last night. He'd been with me. I didn't care if we didn't officially bond. He was mine.

I blinked into the house Kesa rented for us. My black dress clung to my body. I smoothed down the fabric that barely covered my thighs. I'd slipped on my kitten heels just for Cade. I wouldn't see him until later, but he'd enjoy the reference either way.

"Damn, who are you trying to impress?" Kesa knew me a little too well.

"Huxley ditched me for the club last night. He said he was going to see what he could find out, but I took it as a personal affront. I plan on showing him exactly what he missed out on." The corner of my mouth quirked up.

She clapped her hands together. "Yes, are we going to partake in all the fun? You know, it's been so long since we went wild. I think it's about time we did."

"Kesa, we had an orgy two nights before we left Hell. Wait, was it you who had two men chained to the wall?" I cocked my head, looking at her.

"Okay, well, it's been too long. We should have fun. I mean, we're only young once."

"That saying is for humans. We're immortal."

"Will you quit raining on my parade? We're going to a sex club. I want to have some fun. I know you're all sexually frustrated just by looking at you. I take it you're still not enjoying the horsemen as you should." She shook her head. "I know if I were you, I'd be riding those cocks all day. Shit, I wouldn't be going to a sex club. You have your own personal entourage ready to beg for you. What's not to love about that?"

I laughed. "Come on, let's get you to the club." I took her hand and whisked us into the same back room I'd come in before.

"You know, one of these days, you should try the front door. Maybe you wouldn't have Virtues so mad at you for just popping in unannounced." Kesa wobbled on her feet for a second before gaining her balance. I thought she'd be used to transporting by now.

"You okay?" I rested a hand on her arm.

"Yeah, just a bit queasy. I never get used to that." She ran her hands down her dress. Looking around the room, her nose scrunched. "This is Lydia's club? She could really use an interior designer."

I surveyed the room with a critical eye. "It sure is a far cry from the luxurious red room I'm used to."

Kesa wrinkled her nose at me. "This looks like the kind of place someone would get tortured in, not have fun in."

"Don't tempt me." I chuckled and walked over to the center of the floor. Hanging from the ceiling was some sort of contraption with a ridiculous number of hooks attached to it. Looking around, I saw chains hung from every wall.

"Well, this certainly isn't what I expected," she said, arms crossed as if guarding herself against whatever might come out from one of these dark corners.

"Yeah, it's definitely different," I said, though I couldn't help but feel intrigued by all that this place had to offer. Maybe this would be just what we needed for our night of fun. I walked over to one of the walls and ran my fingers through the chains. Feeling their cool metal against my skin gave me a thrill that only intensified as Kesa stepped closer behind me.

"What do you think?" she asked nervously as her own fingers wrapped around one of the chains.

"I think we should have some fun," I said with a wicked grin before turning back to face her, taking her hand in mine. "Let's see what this club has in store for us."

"I thought we were looking for Huxley?" Her brows furrowed as we entered the hallway of the second floor. There was a balcony around the entire second floor so patrons could watch what was happening below. Voyeurism never went out of style. I was usually the one being watched. I liked the feel of all the eyes on me as various men worshiped me like I deserved. I wouldn't settle for anything less.

"We are. I can see everything happening on the main floor. I doubt Huxley would hide away in a private room when he's supposed to be scouting for information. He'd want to be in the center of the action." I scanned the floor below, looking for the mate who'd rejected our bond last night. I could feel the subtle hum of him in my chest.

That was one hell of a perk. The bond was like a tracker for my mates, even though we hadn't completed the bond. Maybe Lydia deserved some gratitude. She certainly made my mission here easier and a lot more fun.

I pointed down at the leather-clad bar. Huxley was milking his drink as he hunched slightly over the bar, his arms resting on the rail. The place smelled of booze, sweat, and the masculine musk of men. I could tell the crew worked to mask it with flowery cleaners and bleach. The clack of heels caught my attention behind me before a man in a toga approached.

"Can I get you beautiful ladies something from the bar, or are you more interested in what our private rooms have to offer?" His white teeth glimmered against the rotating lights from the stage.

"I wouldn't mind seeing exactly what you have to offer." Kesa's voice turned silky smooth as she ogled the bare-chested man.

"I'm not available for another two hours, but I would make an exception if you were both willing to play." The scandalous look he gave me said everything I needed to know. My power was in full swing right now. I was the epitome of lust and desire. The toga-clad man wasn't supernatural. I was surprised that Lydia would allow humans in her club. I wondered if it was so she could manipulate her workers into doing whatever was asked of them.

My eyes blazed as I looked at the man before me. "How about if you fetch us some drinks, and we'll see how the night goes?" I smiled at him.

He gulped. "Yes, ma'am." He turned, hurrying down to the bar.

"Ugh, you didn't even tell him what kind of drinks." Kesa rolled her eyes.

"Don't worry, he'll be down there, making everything imaginable to bring to us." I shook my head. "Lydia hires humans. Although, I don't mind the display. I'm not exactly sure a human man can satisfy my needs right now." My eyes were fixed on my mate at the bar. At my words, he looked over at me. I figured he felt it the moment I'd transported here, but I wanted to be certain.

"Oh, so you came here to fuck the horseman? I get it. Should I make myself scarce in one of the private rooms, or are you going to spend at least a few minutes with me before you go with him?" She shifted in her annoyance.

Her snark made me laugh. "I promised you a girls' night. I plan on having one. Besides, I wouldn't mind reminding him what exactly he's missing."

"Oh? Why? I thought you'd already hooked up with him."

"We were together, but he decided to leave the party a little early last night." I pressed my lips together. I hadn't exactly planned on sharing that information with Kesa or anyone beyond my bonded. Kesa was my friend. There was a long relationship of trust between us. She would die before betraying my confidence.

Kesa's eyes widened, filled with a mix of awe and intrigue, as she stepped into the pulsating heart of the sex club. "This is amazing."

The air crackled with a heady blend of anticipation and desire, a palpable electricity that sent shivers down my spine. My senses were instantly overwhelmed by the sight, sounds, and scents enveloping the space.

I watched as Kesa's gaze swept across the expansive room, drinking in the opulent yet provocative décor. The bar, draped in rich, supple leather, exuded an air of dark sensuality. Its sleek surface glimmered under the ambient lighting, inviting patrons to rest their hands and desires upon its inviting façade. The dimly lit atmosphere enhanced the mystique of the club, casting shadows that whispered secrets and fueled fantasies.

Every inch of the club seemed purposefully designed to ignite the senses. Intricate patterns adorned the walls, their details enticing the eyes to wander, while soft, velvet curtains framed intimate corners that promised tantalizing encounters. Neon lights flickered and danced, casting vibrant hues across the dance floor, where bodies moved with an uninhibited grace.

The symphony of sounds enveloped me, blending into a captivating crescendo. The rhythmic pulse of the music reverberated through my veins, coaxing my body to sway in harmony with the seductive beats. Laughter, whispered conversations, and the occasional moan mingled in the air, creating a symphony of desire that elevated the club to an oasis of unapologetic pleasure.

The intoxicating blend of excitement and curiosity swirled within the atmosphere, fueling a desire to immerse myself fully in the experience. In this realm of temptation and exploration, the club breathed with a life force all its own, a sanctuary where inhibitions were shed and fantasies were unapologetically unleashed. I wanted to devour every second of the lust I felt pulsating around me. It fueled me like nothing else could.

"Lydia certainly has created quite the club. Not my style exactly, but it'll do."

"Oh, I love it. Can we dance a little before we take part in any of the main floor action? I love this DJ." She swayed her hips to the upbeat song.

"Oh yes, let's." I grabbed her hand again and hurried around the people and onto the dance floor. There were several men and women dancing naked in suspended cages. Most of the people on the dance floor were scantily dressed.

Seizing Kesa's hands, I pulled her close, our bodies becoming one with the infectious rhythm that reverberated through the air. Laughter escaped our lips, intermingling with the vibrant energy of the club. Around us, the world faded into a blur as we twirled, our movements an intimate dance defying the existence of anyone else at that moment. The music enveloped us, infusing our beings with pure, unadulterated joy as we surrendered ourselves to its pulsating cadence.

The tempo shifted, seamlessly guiding our bodies through a kaleidoscope of beats. Nevertheless, we continued our animated dance. It was a whirlwind of motion, a testament to our carefree spirits as we moved in synchrony, oblivious to the outside world. But as the euphoria lingered, a sharp pang resonated from my feet, a reminder of the earthly limits I had long forgotten. In hell, such discomfort was unheard of.

With a gentle exhale, I gazed up at Kesa, her joyous bopping oblivious to the discomfort gnawing at me. Our connection remained unbroken, the music still playing its enchanting melody, but the ache in my feet nudged me to seek relief. "Shall we get our drinks?"

She nodded, smiling widely. "Sure!" We got up off the dance floor and made our way over to a table where two glasses of champagne were waiting for us, accompanied by a card with Lydia's signature on it. These weren't exactly what we'd ordered. I'd prefer my whiskey.

I hope you're more polite in my club tonight. -Lydia

We picked up our drinks, clinking them together before downing them quickly in unison. The cold liquid felt so refreshing going down my throat after the dance. The warning didn't go unnoticed, but I planned to be on my best behavior tonight. Lydia had a club like no other, and I wanted to enjoy myself. I also had no intention of ending up in Lake Mead when I was done.

I felt Huxley's eyes on me before I glanced over to where he perched at the bar. His thumb skimmed over his bottom lip as he took in my body. I could feel the desire radiating off him. Good, it was about time he showed me the appreciation I deserved. "So, are you ready for some real fun?" I said the words as I kept my eyes glued to Huxley's. This show was about to be for him.

"Oh God, yes!" She licked her lips in anticipation. This wasn't our first time enjoying lovers together, and it certainly wouldn't be our last. "I've been scouting the available merchandise. I think you may be interested in the vampire in the corner over there. He was watching you dance earlier. I know you said you weren't up for a human tonight, so I went for the supernatural with the most stamina for you."

God, I loved this woman. "You certainly know how to multitask, don't you?" I should have known. Kesa's position was to anticipate anything I needed before I knew I needed it. There should have been zero doubt that transferred to anywhere we went together.

"My role doesn't end at Hell's gates. You know that." She winked.

"Why don't we take a gander at some of the rooms upstairs? I hear there's a room for each sin and every fantasy you could imagine. The building doesn't look big enough for that, but you know Lydia has some magic up her sleeve." I heard the soft purr of her behind me.

"Did someone say my name?" Lydia stood behind me.

"Speak of the devil." I smiled, resting my hand over my heart. "I promise I am on my best behavior. I'm only here to enjoy your fine establishment."

"I believe that's your role, being the devil and all." She laughed as if her joke was the funniest thing in the world. I tried to throw back my head and laugh with her, but I wasn't all that great at faking it. "I know you will be well-behaved since our last encounter. Or at least, as behaved as my club requires of its patrons." She winked.

"You really have a nice club," Kesa cut in. She could certainly sense the tension.

"Thank you, Darling." She rested her hand on her chest. "I see you've already broken the heart of one of your boys." She pointed her finger to Huxley, who was still milking that same drink. Why did he even bother?

"He wasn't willing to meet my every demand. You know me. I have a low tolerance for that sort of thing." I smiled. "I believe your tolerance is equivalent to mine." I couldn't help the jibe.

"I believe you may be correct. Although, I did have a little fun with your horseman this morning. You left him awfully distraught. I felt it was my duty to comfort him. You understand." Her tone was smooth as silk.

I pressed my lips together, trying to calm my racing heart. She knew exactly what she was doing, and there was no way Huxley would have left me to be with her. "That's why I'm here. I'm looking for someone who's up to my high standards. I hear you have some specialties here that I won't find anywhere else, on Earth, that is. We certainly have our fair share of fantasies in Hell, of course." Another rub. Bitch better not make another mention of being with one of my mates. There wouldn't be much stopping me from attempting to kill her where she stands. Divine plan be damned.

"Why yes, I do. I'm not sure it will be anything like what you're used to, but I like to make sure my visitors leave more than satisfied. Come, let me show you around the rooms for our VIP guests." She snapped a finger, and two men flanked her. When she got to the stairs, they lifted her and carried her up to them. Damn, she brought the full-service game to a whole new level.

As I followed her up the stairs, I couldn't help but feel intrigued. Lydia had always been known for her extravagant taste. It seemed that even her club was a living embodiment of that. The walls were painted a deep crimson, and the floors were made of polished black marble that shone under the dim lighting. My mind raced with thoughts of what kind of debauchery awaited me behind each door. The walls were adorned with erotic paintings of what I guessed happened behind each door. They were expertly painted with the kind of attention to detail I admired.

As we walked, Lydia pointed out various rooms, each one more opulent than the last. There was a room filled with plush cushions and silk sheets where couples were locked in passionate embraces. Another room was decorated like a jungle, with vines and exotic flowers hanging from the ceiling. In one room, there was a woman suspended from the ceiling by ropes, writhing in pleasure as her partner teased her with a feather as another's head moved between her thighs.

Lydia smiled as she watched my reaction to each room. "I have a feeling you'll find something to your liking here," she said. "I take pride in providing the best experience possible for my guests."

"I can see that," I said, feeling a twinge of envy. I had my own club back in Hell, but after seeing this place, I had all kinds of remodeling ideas. Lydia had truly outdone herself.

Lydia led me down a dimly lit hallway. The sound of moans and whispers grew louder as we continued the personal tour. I doubted she offered this to just anyone. I was lucky she'd forgiven me for last night. Lydia's eyes sparked with each sound of pleasure coming from the surrounding rooms. You'd think she was the one fueled by lust instead of me.

We finally came to a stop in front of a door that stood out from the rest. Unlike the others, it was made entirely of tempered glass, giving an obscured view of what was inside.

"Now, my darling, this is one of our most popular rooms," she said, her voice a seductive whisper. "But I must warn you, it's not for the faint of heart."

I raised an eyebrow, intrigued. "Oh really? Do tell."

Lydia smirked before pushing open the door. My eyes widened as I took in the scene before me. A couple was tied to a large, ornate bed. A man stood over them, a whip in his hand. He turned to face us, a wicked grin spreading across his face.

"Lydia, my love." He stepped forward, offering her a kiss on both cheeks. "And a new guest. Perfect timing," he said, his voice deep and smooth like velvet. "Would you care to join?"

I felt a surge of desire pulse through me at the thought. But I couldn't let myself get too carried away. I had to maintain control. Still, I couldn't resist indulging in a little fun. I stepped forward, my eyes locking with the man's.

"What do you have in mind?" I purred, my voice laced with seduction. "You're going to have to make it damn good to lure me," I smirked.

"Oh, Lydia, did you bring me a special guest?" The man smiled widely.

"I have. This is Lucifer, but here she goes by Luci, the devil in the flesh." She held her arm out, indicating to me. "I'm sure you could find something that's up to her standards." Lydia winked. "Come, Kesa, I have just the room for you." She whisked my friend away.

The muscled man stood before me with a flogger in his hand. Something about him felt vaguely familiar, and the hum in my chest vibrated just below the surface. It was hard to tell with the thick sunglasses he wore in the dimly lit room. "Would you like to punish them before I dismiss them?"

"No, I do enough of that in my day job."

"As you wish." He snapped his fingers, and the cuffs to the chains unclasped from their wrists. "You're dismissed," he commanded, and the two hurried away from the bed. The woman wobbled a little when her feet hit the floor, but the man helped her before they both scurried away. I could appreciate the fear behind their eyes. He'd done an excellent job with them.

I turned back to face him, wondering what exactly was so special about him that Lydia would leave me here. Her expectation was that I would get exactly what I desired. I'd come to this club to have a good time with my friend. "Color me impressed. Those two were punished well. Too bad you're going to need something a little more than a puny flogger to get me aroused."

The man chuckled before gesturing to the bed. "Please make yourself at home."

I narrowed my eyes at him. "Comfortable? Okay, what exactly are your plans?" I motioned to the bed. I wasn't one to just hop on a bed I'd just seen a couple vacate. I liked my small luxuries.

In an instant, the bed was different. New red satin sheets, a square frame with poles at each end, and a metal headboard took the place of the plain one that'd been there a moment ago. "Is that more to your liking?" he asked.

I glanced at him, confused. "How did you know?"

"I have a special gift. I can read your deepest, darkest fantasies." He paused, his eyes lowering to look at me through his lashes. "Yes, even yours, little devil. You have a creative yet suspicious mind. I have to say, I'm quite fascinated by you."

"Okay, that explains the magic trick. What's so special about the room?" I glanced around. It didn't look any different beyond the new bed.

"The room gives you exactly what you desire while increasing pleasure or pain tenfold." He stopped, taking a few steps closer to me. I could feel the heat of his body on my back as I took in the charged atmosphere. Even the paintings changed to the ones I'd admired in the hallway. His fingers brushed my hair back from my neck. "You're used to getting everything you want," he whispered. "But that's not what you truly desire, now is it, Butterfly?"

"What? Of course, I want everyone to do what I want. Who wouldn't?" I felt instantly defensive. My hands clenched, and the desire to flee struck me. I didn't like this guy rooting around in my thoughts. Something felt off in the same way my dream had.

"Oh, my dearest Lucifer, that's not what you truly desire. Sure, you like being worshiped by your lovers, but you want something else. You don't like having to do your job as the devil. You don't want anyone to know who you truly are at your very core, now do you?" His breath skimmed across my neck as his lips brushed my skin lightly.

"Why should I care if they know?" What was he doing to me? I felt breathless, and he'd barely touched me.

"Oh, but you do care. You care very much. It's why you're here now. What would happen if they knew Lucifer? What would happen to the world if they knew you cared about all of it? Down to every last living being on this earth. You want to save all of them. You want someone to be by your side as you fight those who would disagree with saving your souls. You want someone who's devoted but will also stand against you as well as by your side when it counts." He kissed my neck. I felt the swipe of his tongue all the way down to my toes. Damn, this room was fucking magical. "You want the challenge of an equal and a partner in crime. You can have it, my dear. You can have everything you desire. Let me show you." He wrapped his arms around me, picking me up and placing me softly onto the bed.

"How?" I didn't know how he would change my entire existence in this bed, but I was willing to let him do whatever he wanted to me as long as his touches continued to feel this fucking good. Every nerve ending in my body was just waiting for the slightest touch of his fingers, mouth, fuck, anything. I wanted all of him.

"Oh, my Love, you'll have me. You'll have everything you desire." His nails dug into my hips as his mouth explored mine. I never wanted to leave this bed, this room, him. He was right. I could have everything I desired— right here, right now.

Chapter 12

Huxley

I'd done the impossible. I'd left my bonded without finalizing our bond. The look in her eyes and the darkest part of her demanding me called to my soul. Yet here I was. Sitting at the bar, drinking whiskey, not bonded. I'd been happily drowning my sorrows in a glass of whiskey. Until I felt her enter the club. Fuck, what the hell was she doing here?

I couldn't move from my seat. My desire to return to her was so overwhelming; it took every ounce of strength I had to stay seated and not go upstairs to find her, hear her sultry voice, feel her touch on my skin, and fuck, taste every part of her. Hell, even her temper was a turn-on. Any woman would be lucky to have Lucifer as their immortal partner. The memory of fucking her flooded my mind, making me ache all the more.

As I took another gulp of whiskey, the bartender next to me turned.

"Hey dude, you okay?" he asked in response to my silence.

"I'm good." I blew a breath in an attempt to keep my cool as the memories stole a piece of my soul, as well as broke my heart.

"You look like shit." He touched my hand when he went for my glass.

I didn't like being touched by a stranger. "Fuck off."

"Sorry, man. I only meant to touch what looked like broken glass." He whispered behind his hand with a frown on his face, "You know, human compassion for another."

"You don't want compassion from someone like me." Great, now this guy thought I was some big bad demon beast running around killing everything in sight after I just told him I wasn't dangerous.

"Trust me, you're right about that one man." He sighed, shaking his head. He turned back around to tend to his customers as they walked up, looking for something stronger than coffee this early in the morning. I left last night to get away from my mate. I couldn't bond with her. Not while Cade had just fucked her. I wanted our time together to mean something. Cade wanted to tie her to him for purely selfish reasons. I couldn't be that guy. I wanted more.

I felt her eyes on me from above. I wouldn't look at her. I wasn't sure what game she was playing, but I wouldn't give in to it. Hearing every word that fell from her plump lips was a curse. I watched as she went to the dance floor. Every part of me screamed to turn away from her. I couldn't. The devil captivated me. My cock stretched against the fabric of my pants. Turning towards the bar, I took another drink. This woman would be the death of me.

Earlier that night, Lydia tempted me into taking part in one of the rooms. I wasn't up for it. I wanted information from her, but I knew she wouldn't be the one with me. It was pointless if I didn't get information. That was my goal here. I'd watched every patron

Lydia showed any interest in. So far, they'd been the run-of-the-mill supernaturals. No one was powerful enough to open our world. It felt like a lost cause. I doubted a woman as smart as Lydia would be doing business here, anyway.

When Luci came, I knew things were about to get interesting.

Even though I got a taste of her last night, I couldn't take my eyes off her. She was wearing a tight black dress that barely covered the top of her thighs. Those thighs, fuck, I could feel them, feel her. I was lucky I left when I did last night. I didn't trust myself with this much desire for her affecting every thought and action.

She was an exquisite creature that challenged me at every turn. Strong-willed, determined, and stubborn; nothing would get in her way. I smiled, realizing how completely opposite we were and how perfect it was. In a perfect world, I could be her husband and love her every day. Who wouldn't want that?

I took another gulp of whiskey, ignoring the burn as it slid down my throat. That pain was nothing compared to the wound on my soul caused by not returning to her last night. Fuck, I hated that Cade acted without thinking through the consequences. What if he kept her to himself and didn't let anyone else bond with her? My selfish ass walked away from that beauty. *I'm a jackass!* When he approached the bar a few minutes after I did, I felt it before he spoke.

"Hey, Hux." He never looked at me as he ordered his mid-morning drink with the young bartender, who made him something wickedly sweet smelling—fucking hell. Even his drink had a scent associated with it!

He turned towards me with a smile on his face. It was pretty fucking genuine, as far as I could tell. "You need to get over the past, Brother. This time isn't like before."

"Yeah, sure. This time, we get to stay on Earth and live happily ever after with Lucifer. Not a fucking chance! What the hell have you been smoking?"

He turned to watch her. She hadn't noticed Cade. I doubted he had any intention of letting her see him here. "Fine, sulk in your misery. I plan on making the most of every second we're here."

"Just like every other time. Maybe I'm sick of the whole dance." I shook my head, looking down into my glass. "You didn't think. You have no idea the consequences of what you've done. As usual, we'll be the ones cleaning up the mess. Fucking Cade! Can you just leave me to my day?"

"Fine, but you need to figure your shit out. She won't tolerate the next rejection. Did you see her?" Cade downed the glass in one gulp.

"Yeah, I saw." I pressed my lips together. It was fucking impossible not to. She lit my heart on fire with a few simple words.

"Good. Now quit sulking and take what's yours. We have more important matters. You fucking the devil shouldn't be one of them." With that, he disappeared just as he'd come. Cade had no problem using his power whenever he wanted. At least the club was filled with supernaturals with their own power.

Lydia approached Luci and her friend. My hands clenched when Luci accepted her offer. Not that I had a right to be jealous. I'd been the one to walk away last night. I watched her as she spoke with Lydia, and well, I just wanted to drink her in. Every ounce of power in me wanted to claim her. There wasn't an inch of me that didn't want it. The woman was driving me insane, but she was also here to send me back to a black world with no one but my brothers for company. Being here almost felt like a trap, and I was fanning the flames ever closer to being swallowed up by the inferno. Cade was a fool. She wanted us gone. The sooner, the better. Bonding meant nothing to her. It was a step to getting rid of us. I couldn't have my heart ripped from my chest again. I wouldn't let it happen again.

Lydia took them upstairs. I tried to focus on anything else. Quite the feat, considering I was in a sex club. Every noise and smell brought me back to the woman walking around the balcony. She was interested in every detail Lydia showed her about this club. Luci surely had her own little sex dungeon in Hell. I was certain of it now that I knew just a little about her. I intended to find out more about our devil. I didn't have a reason to pay much attention before. Now, I needed to know every detail. My fucking life, and possibly hers, depended on it.

Luci stepped down a few times during their tour but quickly returned to Lydia's side. I paid special attention to anything she commented on. All I wanted was the chance to breathe in her scent one more time and be near her like I was last night. I felt the power coming from the last door Lydia showed Luci. Fuck, what the hell was that? My heart clenched. There was something about that room. I heard the couple stagger out and collapse on the floor before their heart stopped. What the hell?

I darted up the stairs after her. Something was wrong. I could feel it. Lydia escorted Kesa out of the room, leaving Luci with whatever supernatural creature was in there. The two bodies who'd been there a moment before had vanished into ash. Why couldn't I feel the being's power until the door opened? Where had Lydia taken Luci? It wasn't only the danger that sped me forward. There was no way I would let another man have a chance at her. Lydia had shown Luci every corner of this building with fear in her eyes. The owner knew something that made her leery of every man passing through these walls. What would have Lydia frightened? She was a virtue with more power than most. Although her power dealt with the fates of others, she'd certainly shown us what she was capable of last night. Her being spooked was a serious red flag.

I stopped at the door where Lydia had led Luci. When I opened it, the room was empty. What the fuck? I turned. Lydia hadn't made it far down the hall. I spun her around to face me. "Where is she?" I demanded.

"I left her to her fun. Why?" There was a spark of mischief behind her swirling blue eyes.

"No, you left her with someone powerful. Take me to my bonded now!" My demand mixed with fear. I wouldn't lose her. Not when I'd just found her.

Kesa's brow furrowed. "We left her in that room. Just go check it out." Kesa pointed to the door I'd just left.

I marched back to open it. Kesa flanked me. There was a dark room with a bed in the center, but not a soul was present. "Where is she?" I turned on Lydia. The fear was back in her eyes as her fingers trembled slightly at her sides, the only movement giving her away. I couldn't imagine what she'd be afraid of in her own club.

"He wanted her. She should have never come back to investigate what was going on. She should have left it alone." Lydia shook her head. I didn't like that look in her eyes. Like she'd already known she was dead.

"Who wanted her?" My words were clipped and demanding.

"Don't take that tone with me. I will boot you like I did last night." She rolled her eyes. "You're not exactly here for my club. You think you'll find out what's really happening by staking me out?" She paused, taking me in like it was a disappointment. I wasn't here for her club. "You won't find anything. That room was a portal. Luci isn't in our world anymore." The self-satisfaction in her words grated on me. I needed her help to get Lucifer back.

"Where did it lead? Can you send me through?" I knew I sounded as desperate as I felt. It didn't matter. I needed to get her out of there. I was the damn reason she'd come back here in the first place.

"You expect me to just send you through?" She let out a perilous laugh.

"What do you want?" I ground out.

"Hmm . . . the possibilities . . ." She tapped her finger to her lips as she took me in.

"Lydia, we're losing time. I saw what happened to the couple when they left that room. I won't let that happen to Luci." I hated to admit I was at a disadvantage here. I would do whatever she asked.

"I want a favor to be collected later. One I can call on at any time without limit." She smirked. Favor trading was a big deal among supernaturals. I didn't want to agree to just anything, but I was losing precious time. Who knew what was happening to Luci while we negotiated terms?

Kesa gasped. "No, you can't."

"Done. Now open the portal to her, now."

"I'm going to need more than your word on this. I'm going to need your blood." Lydia smirked. An athame appeared in her hand. After sliding it carefully across her palm, she held the athame to me. "Time to seal the deal."

Every part of me knew this was a horrible idea. I held my hand out to take hers. She took it and spoke the words. "If either of us should break our pact, as it was done to you, it shall be magnified ten times ten in retribution upon you."

"As will you." I paused, taking a beat for the magic to burn the cut in my palm closed. "Now, open the portal."

Lydia snapped her fingers, and the door opened. "Once you pass, though, you will find her. Although, you may not be happy about what you find. I do believe she's having quite an enjoyable time with him."

Her words hung in the air, an unsettling promise of what awaited me on the other side—a revelation that churned a mix of worry and jealousy within me. "How do we get back?" I asked, my voice tinged with desperation. "Will this door remain open?"

Her response dripped with wicked amusement. "You only asked to go to her, nothing about coming back," she retorted with a malevolent glint in her eyes. With a swift wave of her hand, she propelled me forward, and the door slammed shut behind me, sealing my fate.

A rush of anxiety surged through my veins as the scene unfolded before me, completely different from the empty room Lydia had used as a launching point. My heart sank at the sight of Luci spread out on the bed, her wrists and legs cruelly shackled to the posts. I couldn't fathom why she would willingly subject herself to such restraints. My perception of her as the one in control shattered, replaced by a disturbing image of vulnerability.

A man stood beside the bed, wielding a flogger with an unsettling air of dominance. My blood boiled at the thought of him daring to lay a hand on Luci. She couldn't have been here long, yet her flushed cheeks betrayed the pleasure she found in this captivity. Rage surged within me, igniting a fire that blinded me to reason.

"Why is she shackled?" I snarled, my fingers crackling with vehement energy as they sliced through the air, shattering the chains that dared to bind her. The clasps crumbled, granting her a momentary reprieve from the sinister hold they had over her spirit.

"Ah, the Horseman of Famine. To what do I owe the pleasure?" I sensed the potent power emanating from the man before me. His swirling gray eyes betrayed the might that swirled within, a dangerous force that demanded respect.

"Who are you? What have you done to her?" Rage surged beneath my skin, my muscles tensing with primal fury. Luci lay unconscious, her vulnerability gnawing at me as she remained trapped in this compromising position.

"She's fine, I assure you. She's enjoying the best sex of her life," he sneered, taunting me with her flushed cheeks and the chains that now ensnared her legs once more. A guttural growl escaped me at the sight of her restraints, fueling my fury.

"Wake her up, now. She doesn't know about the power drain. She's an unwilling participant in this. Let her go. I'm not asking again." My words tumbled out in a torrent, driven by my burning desire to protect her from this treacherous deception. She deserved the truth, not this vile manipulation.

He chuckled, a mocking glint in his eye. "She agreed to all of it. Would you like to join her? I can feel the lust you have for our little devil," he taunted, using that possessive "our" that grated on my nerves. The surge of jealousy fueled my next move, and I lunged forward, slamming him against the wall. My hand found its way to his throat, clutching with a vice-like grip.

He merely grinned in the face of my fury. "Jealous? Good, I can use that. I thought hers would be enough, but having both of you here is quite the opportunity. I'm not one to turn down such a prosperous position," he snarled, arrogance oozing from every word. With a snap of his fingers, darkness engulfed me, and consciousness slipped away.

When I awoke, I found Luci in a compromising position, a man's head between her legs on the bed. The room had changed, and the sounds of moans filled the air as she writhed against the chains. Rage surged within me, knowing she wasn't consenting to this. That was my mate, and I wouldn't let anyone defile her in such a way. Gripping the man's hair, I hurled him away, but he vanished in an instant.

"Hey, what the fuck, Huxley?" Luci's glare pierced through my rage, her confusion palpable, but I had to make her understand the truth in this nightmarish haze.

"This isn't what you think it is," I pleaded, my desperation seeping into each word, my heart aching for her to grasp the danger surrounding us.

"I think you're jealous of anyone else being with me, even though you refused to bond with me last night." Her hands clenched, the shackles restraining her trembling under her forceful yanks. "You have no right to keep me from desire if you don't plan on giving it to me."

"No, Luci, you don't understand. This is an illusion. You're being drained of your power, but the distraction masks it," I declared, waving my hand where the man had vanished, emphasizing the deceit woven into this twisted charade. With a snap of my fingers, the shackles released her from the bed, her wrists still bearing the marks of her captivity.

She rubbed her wrists, disbelieving. "What? No way, Lydia wanted me to enjoy her club," she protested, her voice ringing with uncertainty, but I needed to convince her of the sinister truth lurking beneath the surface.

"Think about it. Why would she change her mind so quickly? This is a trap. We need to get the hell out of here before you're drained completely," I urged, reaching out for her hand on the bed, desperate to anchor her to reality.

She glanced from my hand to my eyes, searching for any deceit. "This isn't because you're jealous?"

"Well, I am, but that's not important. We need to get out of here," I admitted, my emotions turned into chaos, torn between my love for her and the danger that loomed around us.

She rolled her eyes, her playful pout at odds with the gravity of our situation. "Are you sure you don't want to just join me? We're alone here now, and I didn't finish," she teased, reminding me of my desire to bond with her, a desire that now clashed with the very real threat to our lives. Would I tempt death to be with her? That was a question for another day.

"Although I would love nothing more than to taste you. We can't. Both of our powers will be drained, and I think we'll need them to get the fuck out of here." The room appeared unchanged, but I couldn't trust my eyes. The deceptive simplicity tempted me to open the door, but experience warned that nothing was ever that easy. A lurking sense of foreboding crept up my spine, urging caution.

"You came here without an exit strategy? What kind of warrior are you?"

"I'm Famine. Strategy is not my forte. That's War's job." I yanked her up from the bed. With a snap of my fingers, she was back in her black dress. Her eyes didn't leave mine as she slipped on those impossibly sexy heels. Fuck, if I didn't want to devour every inch of her beautiful body right now. Focus. Once we were safe, I could indulge my fantasies.

"So, what's the plan?" she asked expectantly.

"I don't really have one. I had to trade a favor with Lydia to get here to save you. I hadn't thought beyond much else." My eyes scanned the room, looking for what might be different from the other, some flaw in the illusion. There had to be some flaw I could capitalize on in the deception. My fae magic should easily break the visual as soon as I found one thread, unlike the others.

"You did what?" Her accusation forced its way into my heart.

"You didn't know what was happening. I don't know who the guy who had you was or what he was capable of, but now, we're at least together." I squeezed her hand.

"Perfect. I've always wanted to die with the only man who's ever rejected me," she snarked. Her arms crossed over her chest. If we weren't in danger, I'd think her tirade was adorable. As it was, if I didn't unravel this mirage, we'd both be dead.

I rolled my eyes at her. "He was using your power. He considered my presence a gift so he could claim both of our powers. I've never felt a supernatural like him, and I'm fae. Death will be our only companion if we don't figure our way out of here."

"Okay, I'll play along." Closing her eyes, I heard the hum of her power. Before I knew what she was doing, I saw it. The foundation of our deception. My magic whisked out of me, dismantling the surrounding image. Relief rushed out of me in a hard breath. A door stood in front of us, an open invitation.

As I hesitantly pushed open the door, an ominous darkness swallowed me, enveloping my senses like an icy shroud. The musty scent of damp earth filled my nostrils, and the air felt heavy and suffocating. The narrow space of the cave seemed to stretch endlessly; its mysterious depths were shrouded in impenetrable blackness.

Each step forward brought an eerie echo that bounced off the rough stone walls, whispering secrets that sent shivers down my spine. The void-like darkness seemed to drink in every ounce of light, leaving me feeling vulnerable and exposed in its suffocating embrace. This was no ordinary cave; it was a realm of unknown peril and hidden enigmas, where every sound, every breath, seemed to echo with an otherworldly intensity. Pulling my magic, a green light emanated from my open palm. Luci gasped at the unexpected light.

As the cave echoed with a sinister chuckle, the green eyes of our adversary blazed like fiery emeralds against the inky darkness. His hand rose, crackling with unleashed power that sent shivers down my spine. He had caught wind of our escape attempt, and his malevolent intent was evident.

Without warning, a bolt of searing energy struck me, propelling my body backward with ferocious force. My back collided with the unforgiving wall, pain searing through my bones. Luci gasped at the shockwave, her eyes narrowing with fierce determination as she prepared to face this formidable opponent.

Her stance shifted, her every movement a dance of deadly grace. The air crackled with electric energy, and the anticipation of the impending clash pulsed in my veins. She was a force of nature, a tempest of power and fury, and the atmosphere seemed to hum with her unyielding resolve. "We were having such a good time. Now, you think you can throw my mate around?" The man narrowed his eyes at her taunting words.

With lightning reflexes, she lunged at him, her fists a blur of motion. Their blows clashed, the cavern walls echoing with the thunderous impact of their battle. Each strike was a symphony of strength and skill, weaving a lethal dance of combat. The cave seemed to tremble under the weight of their ferocity, the very ground beneath them quaking with the force of their clash.

They circled each other, like predators sizing up their prey, the air thick with tension. The darkness seemed to feed their power, amplifying their prowess with every move. It was a mesmerizing spectacle, a display of raw strength and determination that left me in awe.

Luci's eyes blazed with unyielding fire, her will unbreakable. With a primal roar, she unleashed a torrent of power, driving her adversary backward. He staggered, momentarily thrown off balance, but quickly regained his footing with a wicked grin.

Their duel intensified, the clash of their powers illuminating the cave with dazzling bursts of light. Their movements were a blur of motion, a dance of combat defying reason. In this brutal ballet, every punch and kick was a symphony of violence and tenacity.

As the battle raged on, I could feel the energy surging through the cave, each blow vibrating with palpable intensity. My heart pounded in my chest, my breath quickened, and I felt as if I were part of this electrifying struggle. Yet, I couldn't move.

It was a fight like no other, a battle that would be etched in my memory forever. The cave bore witness to this epic confrontation, its walls a testament to the power and resilience of these fierce combatants.

A long, red-haired woman with a gorgeous hourglass figure stepped into the cave silently. The two were forced apart by her magic. She kept them suspended against the wall. Luci was the first to break the hold and dropped to the floor in an ambitious crouch. It was obvious she was ready to take on whoever thought they could defy the natural order. There was obviously a reason she'd been chosen by her father as the ruler of Hell. She fought with such unyielding tenacity. It set my heart on fire.

The woman loosened her hold on the man. "I'm not ready for them yet. Put them back where you found them." Her voice, like liquid silk, tantalized my senses as she glided behind us, leading us into what appeared to be a replica of a bedroom. Her smooth, delicate skin brushed against mine, sending a shiver down my spine as she unlocked a concealed panel in the wall. The hidden exit revealed an escape route, tempting my curiosity with its secrets.

Turning to the man, she kissed him passionately, cupping his cheek in her hand, before striding away without a single backward glance. It was as if we were mere pawns in her enigmatic game, mere playthings on display for her amusement.

Enthralled by her bewitching presence and her captivating allure, I felt powerless to resist her charms. Her very essence exuded a mesmerizing power, and I found myself entranced, losing sight of my bond with Luci, who was still back in the cave.

Ignoring caution, I followed her out, unable to resist the allure of the unknown. As I stepped out of the room and into the cave, the memories of my bond with Luci faded into obscurity, replaced by an overwhelming sense of fascination and enthrallment.

Suddenly, my surroundings shifted, and I blinked back to consciousness, my head throbbing painfully. I found myself lying on the floor of Lydia's club's bedroom, disoriented and confused. Luci was on the bed, her wrists free from the shackles that had held her before. She moaned and swayed slightly as she sat up. Her hand held her head as if trying to shake off the remnants of a potent spell.

Struggling to my feet, I felt unsteady and dizzy, my sense of reality shaken by the illusion I had just experienced. It was all a mirage, a wicked ruse that had ensnared my senses. I had been bewitched by Lydia's deceit, and I couldn't help but wonder what other illusions lay in wait, waiting to ensnare the unwary.

"Are you fucking serious?" Luci accused. Her eyes bore into mine. "You leave me behind for a pretty piece of ass." Luci still held her head, but her glare was fierce.

"She was more than that. Didn't you feel it?" I was awed at the woman's presence. Who was she? I wanted more than anything to know, to please her in any way I could. I shook my head. What the hell was I thinking? Please her? Who the fuck was she to have me simping for her after a single look?

Luci snapped her fingers in front of my face. "Yes, I felt it. You just met Lilith. If she's involved with this, we're all fucked."

Chapter 13

Luci

We awoke inside the wretched club, our memories a tangled mess of confusion and disarray. A relentless throbbing pounded like a war drum behind my eyeballs, threatening to split my skull wide open. Immortality be damned. I cursed the very existence that allowed me to endure this torturous pain on Earth. All I wanted to do was sleep for days. It wasn't fair that I was an immortal who experienced pain while I was on this lovely Earth.

Back in that accursed place, anger gnawed at me like a relentless beast. The thought of being ensnared by that treacherous bitch, Lydia, filled me with fury. Yet leaving Kesa behind was out of the question. I knew that Lydia, the conniving wench, was in cahoots with the wicked Lilith, and that couldn't bode well for anyone.

Lilith, that deceitful demon, had enjoyed centuries of my infernal work. I thought our relationship was more solid than the stones of Hell itself. But she had betrayed me, and I couldn't let her diabolical schemes come to fruition. Hell breaking loose on Earth was the last thing we needed.

I had granted Lilith a place among the damned, but her insatiable thirst for power had led her to stab me in the back. Now, I had to untangle this web of deception and confront the demoness before chaos consumed us all. The stakes were high, and there was no room for complacency.

"What are you doing?" Huxley grabbed my arm to halt me.

"Finding Kesa. Then we're going to find out what the hell Lilith has been up to." I shook my head. I couldn't believe her role in the deception. I wanted to piece together our latest interaction, but I couldn't while we were in this wretched club. The man I'd fought obeyed Lilith's command. He was probably a demon. Although he seemed stronger than your run-of-the-mill demon. He wasn't any of the Princes of Hell. I knew each of them biblically, so to speak. Lilith hadn't minded me going through each of her sons. What had her meddling in my life now?

"You think Kesa's still here? She was concerned about what happened to you. She told me not to make the deal with Lydia. Why would she stay?" Huxley followed as I busted through each of the doors. I didn't give a fuck about ruining Lydia's club. That conniving bitch deserved it after deceiving me. Damn, I needed to find a soul to punish before I took my rage out on one of these unsuspecting supernaturals.

"I can feel her." I raised my hand and slammed it against the door that Kesa should have been behind. I punched my fist through, and cracks formed in its wake. I pulled my hand out, turning it as I watched blood drip down my knuckles.

"Are you okay?" Huxley spun me to look at my bleeding hand.

Blood dribbled down my wrists, glistening in the dim light, turning an even darker shade as it mingled with the dirt from the cave. I wasn't sure how I'd gotten dirty, but the evidence was all over my hands. It took the attention away from my pounding head. Kesa was behind that door. I would break it down piece by piece if I had to.

The joy of finding Kesa was snatched away as soon as I stepped into the room. The sound of two people getting hot and heavy with each other wiped my mind clean. In the far corner, the vampire from earlier was chained against the wall. Kesa was on all fours in front of him, her head bobbing up and down, while another supernatural man slammed into her from behind, making sure she felt every inch of his cock as it stroked her inside. He came as I watched them. Kesa's motions became erratic as she and the vampire came apart together. Her legs shook before she sat back on her knees, wiping her mouth as she did.

The room shook as I pulled power from all around me. I couldn't fucking believe her. "You better bloody well be under a spell. If not, I'm going to strike you while you kneel before me." My eyes blazed red as I took in the scene. How could she? Kesa knew they trapped me. Yet, here she was, getting off in the bitch's club like nothing was happening. My fucking best friend. The betrayal ripped through me.

"What took you so long, Darlin'?" The man behind her licked his lips and wiped a hand down his filthy beard. That was a dark contrast to Kesa's delicate features.

"Asmodeus? What the hell are you doing here?" My hands clenched at my sides. Lilith and a Prince of Hell in one day. Not a coincidence.

"Enjoying some earthly pleasures. Although, considering I'm enjoying them with your little demon assistant here, you might call it having a little Hell on Earth." His mouth curved into a villainous smile. His humor was usually endearing. Today, I wanted to sew his lips shut.

"Kesa, what the hell? You knew they trapped me, and you decided to, what, have a threesome in my absence?" I glared at the woman who was supposed to be my best friend.

"What? I knew he'd save you." She pointed at Huxley, who stood to my right. "It'd be one hell of a waste of a favor if he didn't. Besides, it was supposed to be a girls' night. You left me to do whatever was behind door number one, so I'd say that's the pot calling the kettle black. How was I supposed to know it was a trap? You're the powerful one here." She shrugged.

Dammit, she wasn't wrong. She'd done exactly what we came here to do. She even went and found the vampire she'd picked for me. It still grated on me that she continued after knowing they trapped me.

"You couldn't have known he'd save me."

"Well, actually, I figured you'd save yourself. Not like you need me to come rescue you, Luci." She rolled her eyes. "You're usually the one who people need rescuing from. I had all the confidence in the world in you. He just had to tell you what was really going on. I knew you'd burn it all down and get out of there. Wherever there was, of course." She was far too casual as she spoke. It didn't help that her cheeks were flushed and her body nude as she went on like it was no big deal. I couldn't blame her for getting off while waiting. It was exactly what I would have done in her place.

"Where did you pick up this asshat?" I held my hand out to indicate Asmodeus.

"I resent that." He held his hand to his chest in mock hurt.

"Lydia mentioned he was here. I figured I'd say hi to an old friend. It was his idea to include the vampire." She shrugged. "He knows me too well." She bit her lip while her eyes went skyward. He knew her well. They'd certainly spent enough time together in Hell.

"Fuckin' A, Kesa. I don't even know what to do with you right now." I shook my head. "I'm going back to the house. Do you want to hitch a ride with us, or are you going to stick around here?" I didn't like the idea of leaving her, but I also knew Asmodeus wouldn't let anything happen to her under his watch. I wondered if she was his favorite of all those in Hell.

"I kinda like it here. I can find my way back." Her eyes went back to the two very naked men in the room. I understood why she'd picked the vampire. He was damn fine. Even under the club lights, I could see the attraction. Plus, the stamina of vampires was unmatched.

"Fine, just don't get caught up in whatever the hell Lydia is doing. I don't want to find you later. She trapped me. She'll go after you, too." I pressed my lips together. I didn't actually like the idea of leaving her here, but Lydia didn't seem all that interested in Kesa, only me.

I glanced back to Huxley. "Come on, let's go."

He blinked. "That's it. You're just going to leave her here. A moment ago, you were about to take down the building to find her." His mouth hung open.

"Yeah, I really need to get a handle on my temper. Don't worry, I'm in therapy." I waved it off as I transported us both back to my rented house. Although I could go back to Cade's, I wanted some space for contemplation first. Talking to Huxley about what Cade and I discovered seemed important, considering he'd risked his life to save me.

"You know, you guys could do something else besides acting out your anger through sex. You know, try to talk to one another." Huxley batted his eyes at me as we stood in the foyer.

"You think Asmodeus is my therapist?" I burst out laughing.

"What? You just said you were in therapy. I figured it was some kind of sex thing, you know since you all seemed so familiar. I assumed . . ." Huxley trailed off. His innocent look had me bending over hysterically, laughing, unable to control myself. I gripped my stomach, unable to stop. Tears streamed down my cheeks before I finally tried to get a hold of myself. Huxley's brows furrowed as he watched me lose it. That only fueled my hysterics.

"You assumed we had sex therapy." I gripped my stomach, trying to catch my breath between words. "That's just . . . fuck, I don't know . . . damn, my stomach hurts."

"Well, what kind of therapy do you go to then?" He looked so confused. It took me a minute to remember that he wasn't from this world. What would a horseman know about therapy?

"The regular kind. You know where you sit on the couch, and someone helps you process life events and gives you ways to cope with emotions like anger." He was so naïve it was almost adorable.

"You need to talk about your anger instead of bottling it all up. Makes sense. I'm sure you have a lot to get angry about in your position." He moved forward, reaching out to hold my hand in his. "You know," his pitch lowered to a whisper, "that some of the best sex can work out anger."

"All right, smartass, weren't you just telling me to do the opposite?" I glared, my mind replaying the rejection from last night. It grated on me today as much as it had then. "So, let's see if I have this right. Instead of fucking me and bonding last night because, according to you, we were with Cade, and you wanted it to be between us." I used air quotes around his bullshit excuse. "You'd rather have a threesome with Kesa and Asmodeus from Club Naughty?" I gave him a sideways glance. For someone who acted like he knew little about this world, he sure knew how to hit all the wrong buttons. I wanted to pummel him like I had the man in the cave. How dare he?

"First off, there's no way in hell I'm bonding with you until we know the consequences . . ." He stared at me to see if I would challenge him. "Second off," he went on, "Kesa doesn't do it for me like you do."

My heart skipped a beat at his words. I was still pissed. Stupid bond bullshit had me ready to forgive him for a little nicety. "Whatever. I never knew a man to be so afraid of a little sex. In my experience, they'd do just about anything for it. Especially with me, the epitome of lust and desire."

To my surprise, he shrugged and turned away from me towards the vacant living room. "I'm not willing to risk it."

"Seriously, you're rejecting me again?" My mouth hung agape at the gall of this man.

"No, there wasn't a formal invitation, and I'm nothing if not a gentleman." He disappeared from the room, using his teleportation powers to leave me gaping after him.

"What the fuck? He is such a fucking tease." I shook my head in shock after the damn horseman who'd turned me down twice. It made sense that he was the horseman of famine. He sure was leaving me wanting. The payback for his actions would be brutal. When he finally gave in to me, he'd regret every damn time he left me wanting more. I hadn't gotten the chance to tell him what Cade was investigating. I guess they'll have to discuss that themselves. I certainly wasn't going running after Huxley. He could come groveling back to me.

"Izzy, I need you," I called out through my mind. Again, one of the perks of being the devil. She appeared before me in mere seconds.

"Yeah, boss, I was kinda busy with something." She pulled down the hem of her top.

"It was an emergency. I have some news." I walked over to sit on the couch, unsure of where exactly to start with everything that happened. I should have taken a minute to process before calling on her.

"Oh yeah, what's up?" She followed me and sat in one of the adjacent chairs.

"I ran into Lilith today. Certainly wasn't expecting that one. I think she actually helped me, but I'm not sure exactly how or why. I was trapped in some kind of illusion by a man with swirling green eyes living in a cave. Unless that was an illusion, too." I tapped my finger on my lips. I realized I was processing aloud and explaining what happened to Izzy at the same time. "I've seen him twice now. He pulled me into his pit, so he called it, in a dream last night. When I was in the dream, I felt an immense amount of pain, which I shouldn't feel in a dream state. Only in my human form have I ever felt pain. But this . . . this was excruciating. Every word he spoke pounded in my head like a jackhammer. I couldn't stop it, and I couldn't get myself out of there." I stopped, pressing my lips together. "I need to find out who the hell this guy is and why Lilith is working with him."

"Holy shit, that's a lot to take in. I haven't seen Lilith in a while. I didn't actually think she was even bothering with her demons anymore. I guess she's been scheming something behind our backs." Izzy shook her head. "Anything else?"

"Lydia was afraid to give us any idea who the guy is that she's been helping. She bonded me to the horseman. She tried to make it sound like it was what I wanted." I shook my head. "Like I would ever want to settle. Psh."

I felt Izzy's eyes studying me, but I didn't want to meet her gaze. I knew she was probably seeing right through the bullshit of that statement. I didn't want to be called on it.

"Okay, few would spook Lydia, so that might narrow our focus." She nodded as though she were taking mental note of everything I'd said.

"I also left Kesa with Asmodeus. His timing of showing up while Lydia trapped me and whoever this guy was made me suspicious. Can you find out what all of them have been up to for the last few months? It can't be a coincidence that he showed up at Lydia's club at the same time I was tricked. Something feels off about the whole thing." I stopped, looking Izzy in the eyes. "There are no coincidences."

"Damn, Girl. Any other bombs you want to drop on me?" She paused. "Wait, you left Kesa with him even though you're suspicious of him?" The accusation was clear.

"He has a soft spot for her. He'd give his own life before he'd harm her. Besides, she was having way more fun, and I wasn't about to stop that party." Kesa and Asmodeus had been together many times in Hell. I know him well enough to trust her with him. I'd seen him obliterate demons who spoke out of line towards her. You didn't do that for someone you didn't care about. Even if you are a Prince of Hell.

"Oh, yeah? Girls' night without me, I see. You know, if you would take me on these outings, you probably wouldn't have been trapped with any swirling-eyed dude. I would have seen right past the bull-shit and saved you from yourself." Her tone had me laughing.

"Well, shit, I guess I'll have to take you on every outing from now on." I couldn't help it. The idea that she wouldn't be off fucking some dude while I was trapped had me laughing hard. She scowled at me. Based on the club the other night, she'd been off in Marcus' office for a long time. We would have left her if I hadn't called her back to us before leaving.

"I'm entirely serious." She rested her fist on her hip, glaring at me.

"I know you are. Can you go digging? Time isn't exactly on our side right now. I feel like I'm behind on everything. I don't like playing catch-up. Not with something this dire."

I stood at the precipice of an abyss, my mind whirling with uncertainty and responsibility. The weight of the world pressed heavily on my shoulders, a burden I had never asked for, yet one I couldn't ignore. I despised the gnawing feeling of not knowing, for knowledge was my currency, and now, the fate of humanity hung in the balance.

In the not-so-distant past, I had been concerned with a single soul, an insignificant speck in the vast cosmic landscape. How triv-ial that worry seemed now, with the entire world teetering on the edge of oblivion. Time has become a slippery eel, slipping through my grasp as the days blurred into an indistinct haze.

I had never sought the role of the devil, never sought the mantle of responsibility that came with it. Yet, I knew I couldn't stand idly by while the world crumbled around me. There was no room for reluctance, no room for hesitation. The world needed me, and I wouldn't let them down.

A storm raged within me, a tempest of determination and fury, as I vowed to unveil the malevolent forces at play. Someone out there sought to unleash chaos upon the Earth, and they would pay dearly for their audacity.

My heart pounded like a relentless drum, my eyes ablaze with fierce determination. There was no denying that I grew tired of my role as the devil, and I was also no savior. I had never been one to wear a halo, but I couldn't allow the world to succumb to whatever darkness they had planned, either.

As the night wore on, my mind became a battlefield waging war against the unknown enemy. The future of humanity hung in the balance, and I was their last line of defense. But who was the puppeteer pulling the strings, and what nefarious plans did they have in store for Earth?

I scoffed at my nonchalant thoughts, my lips curling into a sardonic smile.

No big deal? Right?

Little did I know that the sinister puppeteer was already one step ahead, lurking in the shadows, waiting to unleash an unimaginable evil upon the world. The night was far from over, and the final showdown loomed ever closer. The fate of the world hung in the balance, and my resolve would be tested like never before. Would I emerge victorious, or would darkness swallow the world whole? Only time would tell, and the clock was ticking.

Chapter 14

Cade

"Thane, I know you're here." I strode out of the elevator into Death's sleek apartment. His home always reminded me of a panther ready to strike. All its features were sharp, like the tips of a panther's claws. Every piece of furniture was aligned in perfectly straight lines. It was as straight and narrow as his personality. He was Death, after all. Death was inevitable. I walked into the living room. Thane was standing, looking at the pictures. He had his arms crossed over his chest and his lips pressed into a hard line. When he heard me enter the room, he turned to look at me.

"Cade, what do I owe the pleasure?" His smirk let me know he was more than aware of my most recent activities. Thane had always been the one to keep the group in line by any means necessary.

"I hold in my possession some information, knowledge that I knew would pique your interest," I began cautiously, fully aware of Thane's unwavering focus when it came to matters that engaged him. His single-minded determination could be both a boon and a challenge, as he seldom paused to question the circumstances that led us to our current situation. To him, the task at hand took precedence over all else, and he'd fulfill his duties without hesitation.

Yet I knew that rushing to reveal everything I knew would be unwise. Thane's inquisitive nature could be harnessed for our benefit, but only if he saw the reasoning behind my actions. So, before I disclosed the extent of my knowledge, I needed to navigate the intricacies of his mind and ensure he comprehended the bigger picture.

It was a delicate balance, like a dance on a tightrope, seeking the perfect moment to unravel the truth before him. I couldn't risk his impulsivity clouding our judgment, but at the same time, I couldn't afford to underestimate his intelligence. Thane was sharp, and he deserved my complete trust.

The gravity of our circumstances weighed heavily on my shoulders, and as I prepared to share my insights with him, I understood that every word I chose could determine the course of our journey. I braced myself, aware that once the information was revealed, there would be no turning back. This was a pivotal moment in our shared destiny, one that would shape the path ahead and bind our fates together.

"Should I assume you mated with the devil?"

Damn, straight to the quick. I shouldn't have expected any less. "That isn't what's important. Do you know who can cause pain in the dream realm? Someone with green swirling eyes, tall, lives in some kind of pit." I figured since he'd gotten to the point, I could, too.

"I disagree with the importance of you mating with the devil. You'd struck a deal affecting all of us without batting an eye." There was a tick in his jaw when he spoke. When I'd made the deal, he stood silent. Now, I would experience his true feelings on the matter.

"Fine, get whatever you have to say off your chest. I know you won't move past it until you do." I rolled my eyes. Thane could be so temperamental about certain things.

"You agreed not to mate with her. Yet, when the opportunity for a bit of information presented itself, you made a deal without consulting any of us." His eyes narrowed.

"We had the same goal. It's not like you were offering anything to get what we needed." I turned away from him. "I did what was needed to continue our mission. You cannot deny that you'd do the same. Although you had the opportunity, I was the one to seize it—as I've always been the one in our group willing to burden myself with the risks no one else will take. You should consider it a gift. I was willing to make the deal when you shied away from it.

"The notion of this being a gift for all of us is hardly convincing, especially when it's apparent that you stand to gain the most from it. Your intentions to defy us were clear from the start, and now, you conveniently exploit it for your own advantage. It's disheartening, Brother, for I know you too well. And to think you've allied yourself with the very person striving to thwart our endeavors, how can we possibly trust you?" The words slipped from my lips, laden with both disappointment and suspicion.

As I observed Thane's countenance, a rare display of emotion flickered in his eyes, betraying the pain that he, too, felt. Unlike the rest of us, Thane was never one to wear his heart on his sleeve, but his eyes spoke volumes, revealing a soul grappling with inner turmoil.

His guarded demeanor had always made it challenging to gauge his feelings, yet at that moment, I glimpsed the raw vulnerability he tried so hard to conceal. It struck me, like a sudden gust of wind on a cold winter's night, how much we had changed over the years and how difficult it was to truly know the hearts of those we once believed were kindred spirits.

Uncertainty clouded the air, and a heavy silence enveloped us. The bonds we once shared were now frayed, and the foundation of trust we had built seemed on the verge of crumbling. I yearned for the connection we once had, but the path ahead felt treacherous, shrouded in shadows of doubt.

In that fleeting moment, as Thane's emotions played across his face, I wondered if redemption was still within reach. Could we mend the rift between us and find solace in the strength of our brotherhood once more? Or had the sands of time irreparably eroded the ties that once bound us together? Only time would tell as we navigated the murky waters of our uncertain future.

I sighed, knowing that I would have to be careful with my words again. "It's not about trusting me, Thane. It's about the bigger picture. Our world is in danger, and Lucifer may be the key to stopping it." I paused. "You didn't notice that this time was different. She's not lying about us being released by someone other than the Almighty. Don't you find that even a little curious?" Thane had always been the seeker of wisdom. He'd filed away the events of all human history. He'd studied humans more than any other in our group. I was certain he would consider this another mystery to solve.

Thane remained silent for a few moments before finally speaking up. "And why do you think I would want to help you figure any of this out after what you've done? Curiosity is your thing, not mine." I blinked at his lie. When had Thane ever lied to me? I couldn't think of a single instance.

"We're brothers, Thane. We've fought side by side for centuries. We need to look past our personal issues and protect the sanctity of what this world represents to everyone." I sounded like a sap, but it was our role to protect the sanctity of the balance of this world.

He pursed his lips, considering my words. "Fine. What do you need me to do?"

I hadn't expected him to give in so quickly. It took me a moment to gather my thoughts. "I need you to find out everything you can about this person who can cause pain in the dream realm. I haven't heard of such a being, but I know you've studied much more than I have. He's most likely the dark one who's being spoken of around the supernatural community. We need to know everything about him. He'll be coming after us soon enough."

Thane nodded slowly. "I'll see what I can do."

"No arguing? You're just going to do it?"

"Have you met with Izzy to receive the information from her side of your deal? I'd hate for your risk to be fruitless." I could read the sarcasm in his tone.

"I already have what we need. As soon as the bonding was complete, an object appeared in my bedroom. There was a note that read this will lead you to the box. Happy Hunting- Iz. She kept her end of the bargain."

"Excellent. When should we depart?" Thane was eager.

"I have a few things to take care of first." As I turned to leave, I couldn't help but feel a sense of relief wash over me. Despite our differences and personal grudges, Thane was still willing to help me when it mattered most. Now, all we needed was to find out who this mysterious man was and put a stop to him before he could cause any more harm. "Find out what you can in the meantime. I'll be back as soon as I can." I stopped in front of the elevator, waiting. When the doors opened, Huxley was standing there. "What are you doing here?"

"Where's Thane? We need to talk." Huxley rushed past me into Thane's apartment. "Call in Ryder too. We've got a fucking problem."

"What's going on?" I followed him back into Thane's apartment.

Huxley was the last of us to be rattled by anything. He was obviously angry about something. "Call Ryder. I'll tell you when we're all here."

"Fine." I pulled out my phone. Ryder answered on the second ring. Gunshots rang out through the speaker. "Ryder, we have an emergency."

The growled response was all I got as he hung up the phone. Ryder stood in front of the three of us in an instant. "This better be important."

"Why? What could you have possibly been doing?" I hated how Ryder made it seem like every single thing he did was important.

"Monitoring the situation and battles in a few key countries. I'm making sure the bigger players get involved, and soon." He glared at me. I was surprised he even answered me. Usually, he blew me off whenever I questioned him about anything.

"You take the fun out of coming here, you know that. Can't you slow down a little so we can spend more than seven years here?" I shook my head. "You're always so quick to rush into war. Would it kill you to have some patience?" War was usually the reason we had to leave Earth. He sped things along, starting these monumental wars that hurried along with the champion. For once, I would like to spend a little more time here. Especially now that we have a mate to play with while we're here. I always enjoyed my escapades with women, but our little devil was next-level sublime. I wanted much more time to cherish her.

"We're here to complete a mission, or have you forgotten that already? Don't think we all don't know how you betrayed us. We felt you bond with her. Traitors don't last in my world." He took a step closer, getting directly in my face. "If we didn't need you, I'd kill you on the spot for your betrayal."

"Okay, you both need to calm down." Thane put an arm between us. It took Ryder a minute, but he stepped back and went to the decanter on the counter. Thane turned to Huxley. "All right, Hux, you got us all here. What's the emergency?"

Huxley took a deep breath before speaking. "Lydia lured Luci into a trap at the club. She was taken to an underground cave. It sounds like it was something she'd seen before. The man who took her was trying to siphon her powers. Lilith intervened. It was the only reason we both survived. At least, I think it is. I'm not sure what they have planned, but she said she wasn't ready for us yet. Whatever that means."

"What do you mean, trap? How was Lydia able to pull that off?" I asked, feeling a sense of foreboding settle in my gut. How had I not felt her distress? As her mate, I should have felt it.

"Lydia is the reason we're bonded to her. She knew about her desire for connection. I don't know how they're doing it, but they know enough to lure her. She walked right into the trap without suspecting a thing. He seemed to have a personal grudge against her," Huxley replied grimly. "It also seemed like she may have seen him before today."

I shared a knowing glance with Thane. "How? When? I didn't feel a thing."

"Did Lilith say anything else we can use?" Ryder asked, his eyes narrowing with suspicion. He was always on a mission. He would dig through her words, looking for motive or weakness. It was who he was at his core. It didn't seem to matter that we'd been seeing her and hadn't told him about any of it. I was intrigued by the fact he could feel me bond with her. How was Lydia able to manipulate something inside of us so easily? We've always been a separate entity, not on either side. We were the epitome of balance. Not anymore. Someone was tipping the scales on both sides to rock the entire grand design. I wasn't sure I liked how deep this was going. I certainly didn't like not knowing all the players involved. I would need to make amends with Ryder so we could discuss this together.

"No, but it seemed like Lilith was using this guy. I don't know why he would have stopped at her command without some kind of controlling relationship between the two. They both have something more planned for all of us." Huxley walked over to the counter, pouring his own glass of bourbon.

Silence descended over the room as we all processed this new information. The fact Luci had encountered someone who could trap her was alarming enough, but the fact he seemed to have some kind of hold over her was even more concerning. If he could control an archangel, his power was certainly above our level. We needed to find out who this man was and what his intentions were before it was too late.

"I'll see what I can find out," Thane finally spoke up, breaking the silence. "In the meantime, we need to keep an eye on Lucifer. We don't know why this power is targeting us after mating us to her, but we need to all stay together in this fight. Without her, we won't get the information we need about what's really going on here."

I blinked. Thane certainly changed his tune from a few moments ago.

"Agreed." Ryder nodded. I was surprised that Ryder had been the first one to say it. He hadn't even spent time with her like Huxley and I had.

I nodded along with the others, feeling a sense of unease settle over me. We were dealing with something new and unknown, and it made me feel vulnerable and exposed.

Thane turned his attention to me. "Care to fill them in on why you chose to visit me today?" His eyes sparkled. I hated him for calling me out like that.

Damn him. I sighed. "Fine. Luci had a dream about the guy last night. It's probably why she recognized him." I looked away from all of them. I wasn't keeping secrets exactly, but I also wouldn't give them any additional information. I was already a traitor for having sex with her. It didn't matter that Thane knew exactly why I'd bonded to her. It was to get what we needed to find Pandora's box and break the fifth seal.

"What? Why didn't you say something this morning?" Huxley looked at me accusingly.

"When? After you'd run off like a scared little boy?" I knew it was a low blow.

Huxley charged. Thane stopped him. "Cade, we don't need your smart mouth right now. We need to work together. Everyone needs to be informed about everything for our plan to work. We're brothers. We can't afford to keep things from each other."

I rolled my eyes. Like he wasn't keeping things from the group. He wasn't wrong, though. We already knew far too much about each other. Now, we were expected to share a mate. Ha. "It wasn't my information to share; it was hers. The dream she had was after she'd fallen asleep last night. If you'd stuck around longer, maybe you would have known about it." Huxley wasn't the type to fuck and run, but he had been a coward last night, and he knew it.

"That's bullshit, and you know it." Huxley pointed a finger at me. Thane was still planted between him and me. Not that we'd actually physically fight. That was Ryder's forte.

"No, what you told Luci last night was bullshit. You lied when you said you chose not to bond with her because you're worried about the consequences, and we both know it." I turned away from them all. "I'm going back to check on our mate. If they targeted her once, they'll do it again. In the meantime, you need to get your shit together. Figure out what each of you is going to do about her because one thing is for sure— the bond won't go away. You each need to decide what you'll do about it. I've already made my decision. You all need to do the same."

I transported out of the room. I was sick of always being the one they blamed for everything. It wasn't my fault they didn't have the balls to act on their desires. I see something I want, I take it. No hesitation. They were all cowards. I planned to live every second I was here. Besides, it wasn't like the consequences of our actions would get us killed. We were the damn horsemen. We'd just go back to our world until we were released for the next cycle.

Why wouldn't we want to live out the time we had here to the fullest? That was always their mistake. They were too fucking cautious. The mission to end the world was at the forefront of their thoughts every second. It was ignorant and boring. The quicker we started, the shorter the time we had here. None of them agreed with me. At least Huxley had joined me in some fun a few times, but the others never budged. We were here to complete the mission, nothing more.

Life was a tapestry of fleeting moments, and lately, I'd been acutely aware of its brevity. The devil's arrival in our lives had shaken me to my core, forcing me to confront the impermanence of it all. She'd given me a reason to stick around longer, to embrace the chaotic beauty of existence with an intensity I'd never known before.

But it wasn't just about me. I hoped she could do the same for the guys—Huxley and the rest. Their time here was as precarious as mine, and we couldn't take it for granted. Each second felt more precious now as if the sands of the hourglass were slipping away faster than ever.

Luci's desire to send us back, to protect the humans from our sole purpose, only fueled my determination. I wouldn't let her do it without a fight. I wanted to stay, to savor every thrill, every laugh, and every heart-pounding moment we shared. Life was meant to be lived, to be experienced in all its vibrant hues, and I wouldn't let the sands of time wash away our chance for something extraordinary.

And so, I played my part, making her scream my name, weaving a bond between us that transcended any ulterior motives I may have had. Yes, I bonded with her for information to uncover the mastermind behind this malicious plot. To further the collective purpose of the horsemen. But that didn't negate the feelings that had blossomed between us, the depths of desire that swirled in the depths of my soul.

The stakes had never been higher, yet there was a poetic beauty in it all. Like an explorer venturing into the unknown, I navigated the mysteries of my heart, relishing the journey with every beat of my rebellious spirit.

Life might be short, but it wasn't about the length of our days; it was about the depth of our experiences. I was determined to seize every moment, to dive headfirst into the unknown with an unwavering spirit. As the sands of time continued to fall, I knew I would savor every second with our devil, unraveling the threads of fate that bound us together and discovering the secrets of this cosmic tapestry.

As I approached Luci's place, an eerie stillness hung in the air, enveloping the surroundings like a heavy shroud. The usual hum of life was conspicuously absent, leaving an unsettling silence in its wake. Every fiber of my being tingled with apprehension, sensing something was wrong.

With each step, my heart pounded in my chest, a primal warning of impending danger. My instincts screamed at me to proceed with caution, to be prepared for whatever awaited beyond the threshold.

"Luci," I called out softly, my voice a mere whisper in the hushed atmosphere. I strained to catch any response, any sign that she was all right.

But there was nothing. Just a haunting silence, echoing like a ghostly chorus in the dimly lit corridor.

My hand hovered hesitantly above the doorknob, my fingers trembling with anticipation. I steeled myself for what lay beyond, bracing for the unknown.

With a slow, deliberate turn, the door creaked open, revealing a dim interior that swallowed the light. Shadows danced across the walls, hinting at hidden secrets lurking in the darkness.

I stepped into the room, my senses on high alert, scanning for any sign of movement or disturbance. Every sound seemed magnified in the hush—the soft whisper of my breath, the faint creak of the floorboards beneath my feet.

And then there she was. Luci lay on the couch, an ethereal vision in the dim light. Her eyes were closed, lost in peaceful slumber, yet the vulnerability in her posture struck me like a sharp arrow to the heart.

Without a second thought, I closed the distance in swift strides, drawn to her like a moth to a flame. The softness of her features tugged at my soul, and I couldn't help but reach out to stroke her hair gently.

Her eyelids fluttered open, and I was met with the warmth of her gaze, hazy with sleep. For a fleeting moment, the world faded away, and it was just the two of us in this cocoon of serenity.

In that moment, I felt an unbreakable connection—a thread woven through time and space, binding our souls together in an inexplicable dance of fate. My heart swelled with emotion, and a sense of protectiveness washed over me.

In the stillness of that room, an unspoken understanding passed between us, transcending words. It was as if the universe had conspired to bring us together, even amid the uncertainty and danger surrounding us.

I leaned closer, drawn to her like a sailor to the siren's call, losing myself in the depths of her eyes. There was a secret, a revelation waiting to be unveiled, and I was determined to discover it—to explore the depths of this enigmatic woman who had captured my heart.

As our gazes locked, I knew that whatever lay ahead, we would face it together, hand in hand, navigating the tumultuous waters of fate. The world may be uncertain and treacherous, but in this moment, there was a glimmer of hope, a promise of something extraordinary waiting just beyond the horizon.

"Cade?" she murmured. "What's going on?"

I leaned down and kissed her deeply, unable to contain my desire. She responded eagerly, her body pressing against mine as our tongues tangled in a dance as old as time itself. I never wanted to leave her side again.

When we finally broke apart, gasping for air, Luci gazed at me, and for a moment, I was lost in the depths of her eyes. They were like pools of molten gold, drawing me in and never letting go.

"What are you doing here?" she asked, sitting up on the couch.

"I wanted to make sure you were okay," I answered truthfully. "After what happened . . ."

Her face fell, and she looked away from me. "I'm fine. Did you talk to Huxley?"

I sat on the couch next to her and reached out to pull her to my side. "Yeah, he told us what happened." She probably didn't like all of us knowing what happened, considering we barely knew her. Weakness wasn't something she'd share with another easily. Last night was a rare moment for her.

She nodded, and we sat there in silence. Suddenly, she turned to look at me with fire in her eyes. "Why did you do it?" she asked bluntly.

"Do what?" My head cocked to the side as I looked at her.

"Sleep with me," she clarified, looking at me intently. "Why did you do it when you didn't know the consequences?"

I shrugged nonchalantly, trying to lighten the mood. "Why would I worry about the consequences? I never have before." It was the truth.

She studied me. "That's not an answer. Why did you choose to bond with me? We could have held back the bonding, but you pushed us forward. I need to know why."

Shit, had she found out about my deal with Izzy? I looked away from her, clasping my hands together in my lap. "I don't know. I wanted to have sex with you from the moment I saw you. When I felt the bond, I wanted it, all of it, with you." I closed my eyes. Truth was always the best in such situations. "My history hasn't been the greatest. I fall fast and hard. My heart has been broken so many times. Yet, I never wanted to fear the possibility of love. I never wanted to hold myself back from the greatest gift this world has to give." I paused, shifting my body towards hers, and took her hands in mine. "With you, there was a level of safety knowing we were bonded mates. Once bonded, it'll be harder for you to leave me. I understand you've come here to stop us from our purpose. Yet, I believe there might be a way to hold onto you, even if we have to leave this plane of existence." I sighed. "You're my chance at forever. Leaping didn't even take forethought. I'm here for all of it with you."

Her eyes searched mine. Looking for the lie that wasn't there. She opened her mouth to speak but closed it again. Taking a shaky breath, she looked at me. "I can't stop thinking about you," she breathed. "Ever since last night, I can't get you out of my head."

I smirked, feeling a sense of satisfaction wash over me. "Good," I said as I turned towards her, pulling her into me so that our lips met in a fierce kiss. I wrapped her in my arms, letting the primal need push me forward. I would never tire of claiming her as mine.

She moaned as she melted into me, her hands running through my hair as I explored every inch of her mouth with my tongue. My hand traveled up to cup her breast, thumbing her nipple through the fabric of her shirt. She let out a gasp that was music to my ears.

"We shouldn't do this," she whispered against my lips even as she leaned into me.

I pulled back to look into those hauntingly beautiful eyes of hers, already knowing what I wanted to do next. "Why not?" I asked. "You already know the bond is there between us. Was my confession of undying love not enough? Should I get on bended knee? Ask your father for permission?" I smirked as amusement lit her face.

"How can you be so sure? The Earth's existence depends on you going home. How can you know I won't betray you in the end?" I wondered at her questions. Had she been betrayed so many times, it was the expectation rather than the exception. I stared into her beautiful eyes, hoping that one day, she would let her guard down with me so that I may get the briefest of glimpses into that battered soul of hers. At the same time, I knew she was being betrayed by the closest of friends. I betrayed her by not informing her of the friend's treachery. I was no better.

"I can't. I only hope you'll be a little dismayed by my absence." I brushed my thumb across her cheek.

"So, you're counting on me not to break your heart?" The corner of her mouth lifted.

"You're the only one who could." I pressed my lips lightly to hers. Or at least I meant to kiss her lightly. She claimed me with such surprising force. I matched her ferocity with a fire all my own.

As she lay back on the couch, I found myself caught in a tug-of-war between my desires and the weight of our mission. At that moment, it wasn't just about my own pleasure; it was about securing my place by her side, ensuring our bond grew stronger than any force in the universe.

Her vulnerability beneath me stirred a deep longing, a yearning to leave an indelible mark on her heart and soul. I knew if she wanted me as much as she wanted to save the world, then I had a fighting chance of staying with her, of breaking free from the chains of our former reality.

With a tender touch, I traced my fingers along her skin, memorizing every curve, every freckle, as if etching her essence into my very being. I wanted to brand her with my touch, to make her mine in a way that transcended mere physical pleasure.

But beneath the playful façade, I felt the weight of the responsibility we carried. The world hung in the balance, and every action we took had consequences far beyond our own desires. Our connection was more than just a fleeting moment of passion; it held the power to change the course of history.

In that instant, I made a silent vow to myself. I wouldn't squander this opportunity. I wouldn't let fear or doubt cloud my judgment. I would seize the day, cherish every second, and embrace the enigmatic dance of fate that had brought us together.

This wasn't just about pleasing the devil; it was about embracing the uncertainty, the chaos, and finding our place amid the tumultuous symphony of existence. I wouldn't disappoint, not her, not myself, not the world that desperately needed saving.

As I lost myself in the depths of her eyes, I knew we were bound by something far greater than desire—a cosmic connection defying explanation. In this moment of revelation, I felt a surge of determination, a fierce resolve to forge a future where we could be together, united against the odds.

So, I surrendered to the intoxicating dance of our souls, savoring every touch, every sigh, as if each were a precious gift. I would leave no inch of her body untouched, no corner of her heart unexplored. This was our chance, our shot at freedom, and I wasn't about to let it slip through my fingers.

The world beyond those walls might be waiting, but in this moment, we were the masters of our own destiny. Together, we would face the unknown, leaving behind a legacy of love and courage that would echo through the annals of time.

Chapter 15

Luci

The next morning greeted me with a lingering haze of passion and contentment, my body still humming with the sweet ache of another night spent tangled in Cade's embrace. I stretched, reaching out instinctively for his warmth, but my fingers found only empty sheets. "Cade?" I called out, a flicker of disappointment dancing in my chest. Silence was my only reply, and I reminded myself not to expect him to be at my beck and call every morning.

Shaking off the lingering remnants of slumber, I rose from the bed and padded my way to the bathroom. The water cascaded over my skin, washing away traces of the night. With every droplet that caressed my body, my mind was split between the passion consuming me and the weight of the world resting upon my shoulders.

Emerging from the shower, I dressed with purpose, donning my signature leather jacket and boots. There was no time to dwell on the blissful distractions of desire. The fate of the world demanded my attention.

As I made my way to the kitchen, the aroma of freshly brewed coffee teased my senses. Kesa stood there, toast in one hand and coffee in the other. Her eyes sparkled with a mix of curiosity and amusement as she took in my disheveled appearance.

"Another wild night with Cade, I see," she remarked with a knowing smirk.

I rolled my eyes playfully, trying to conceal the flutter of excitement in my chest. "You could say that."

Kesa leaned against the counter, her posture relaxed but her gaze searching. "You know, while you're busy saving the world, you still deserve a little breakfast in bed now and then."

I chuckled, grateful for her lightheartedness amidst the gravity of our mission. "Maybe I'll put in a request for that next time."

We shared a moment of camaraderie, two souls bound by friendship, and a shared sense of purpose. In the face of impending darkness, we stood strong, ready to challenge fate and forge our own path.

As we sipped our coffee, I couldn't help but savor the bittersweet taste of the moment. The weight of the world may rest upon my shoulders, but in the embrace of love and camaraderie, I found the strength to face whatever challenges lay ahead.

"You should. He's the one who set the expectation on day one."

I laughed. "I'm glad you're back to your normal self. Asmodeus must have shown you a damn good time. What time did you get back?"

"Yeah, I missed him a bit." She had that faraway look, like someone in love. "I got back sometime around two. Not that I slept much with Cade being here." She gave me a pointed look.

"Like you have any room to talk. You spent yesterday doing the same thing." I rolled my eyes. I'd left her with two supernaturals in a sex club.

"True, it's the reason I own earplugs and headphones. When one doesn't drown you out, the other will." She smirked.

"Speaking of Cade, have you seen him?" I shouldn't care that he left, but the unease inside my gut pushed me to find him.

"He said something about having to meet with his brothers. He didn't tell you?" Her eyebrow rose as she looked at me.

"He probably just didn't want to wake me." I shrugged. I went to the fridge to grab something for breakfast. I didn't have to eat, but it felt like a normal ritual to have coffee and breakfast. When in Rome . . .

"He left you some pastry in the bag." She pointed to the white bag on the counter.

"What?" I glanced in the direction she pointed. I peeked in the bag to find three different types of donuts, all looking like sugary heaven. Oh, I could get used to this.

"Yeah, he wasn't sure what you liked, so I gave him some pointers. He's not a bad guy, considering he's the Horseman of Pestilence." She shrugged. It was probably the only compliment about him I would ever hear from her.

"Yeah, we've had a few good nights. I do love how he gets me breakfast. Something about the mating makes him want to keep me well-fed. I don't mind." My heart squeezed at his thoughtfulness. Even though he wouldn't be here, he'd thought to make sure I got something for breakfast. It was a sweet gesture for a guy who didn't strike me as the type. That made it all the more special.

"Don't fall in love with the horseman. I don't care if the sex is phenomenal. We're here to send them back and stop the world from ending. No dick is worth destroying the world." She stood in front of me. "Do you hear me?"

I hated when Kesa went all motherly on me. "Yes, ma'am!" I saluted her.

"No, I'm serious. I see you getting all goo-eyed over there. You will totally forget about why we're here. They have to go back, Luci. They have to."

"Yeah, yeah, I know." I waved her off. I went into the living room to piece together what I would do next. Izzy would let me know what she found as soon as she had something, but I didn't want to wait around for her. I wanted to be taking action.

"So, what do Lilith and Lydia have in common? Who the hell would be able to unite those two?" I threw my feet up on the coffee table as I leaned back on the couch to enjoy my coffee and donut.

"Wait? Lilith was there? How did I miss that?" Kesa blinked.

"Well, to be fair, you were a little preoccupied when I saw you at the club after we'd run into her. I'd be surprised if you remembered anything I said." I took a drink of my coffee. I didn't really want to think about the position Kesa was in when we found her after I'd been tricked. It irked me that she was getting off while I was in danger. I understood her point, but at the same time, she was supposed to be my best friend.

Kesa shook her head. "I don't even remember the last time I saw Lilith. She was probably in Hell. I just don't know where she's been." She lowered herself onto the couch next to me, a concerned look on her face. "But you're right; there has to be something tying those two together. We just need to figure out what it is."

I nodded, finishing off my donut. "We need to figure it out before whoever the asshole is with the swirling green eyes decides he wants me to visit again. I can't say either time has been all that pleasant."

Kesa's phone rang, interrupting our conversation. She glanced at the screen before answering. "Hello?"

I leaned back, giving her some space to talk. A frown crossed her face as she listened to whatever was being said on the other end of the line. Holding the phone against her chest, she turned back to me, worry etched across her features.

"It's Izzy. She found something."

"Why's she calling? Why doesn't she just come here?"

"She can't. Your brother decided she needed to stick around Hell." She held the phone out to me. "She wants to talk to you."

I took the phone in my hand. "Iz, what's going on?"

"Tell your fucking brother that I'm doing important work for you, so he lets me leave Hell. I can't stay. He thinks I'm his damn assistant or something."

I chuckled. Leave it to my brother to decide that everyone in Hell was his personal assistant. "I'll talk to him." I didn't have time to deal with him today, but I guess I would have to make time.

"No, talk to him now. Here." The last word was muffled before my brother was on the line. I pressed my lips together. I could envision the hell she was giving my brother.

"Hello, dear sister. Why can't I use your demon to do the work that needs to be done? I thought I would have full rein while I was covering for you." Sariel was annoying on a good day.

I wanted to correct that Izzy was a fallen, but now may not be the time. "I have Izzy working on the Horsemen thing. I need her with me." I wouldn't argue with my brother, considering he was doing me a favor right now.

"Why are you so insistent on this horsemen fiasco? You know they'll be stopped just like every other time they were released. You never bothered with it. What's changed?" I pressed my lips together, debating on how much I wanted to share with him. Izzy's warning was still fresh in my memory. I would need to give him something to sate him and make him give up Izzy.

"This time is different. They weren't supposed to be released on Earth yet. There's no champion to stop them; no seals have been broken that could be reversed. It's different, and I need to find out why. There can't be this many souls all coming in at once. It will throw off the balance in both Heaven and Hell. If you haven't noticed, it already has." I hoped I gave him enough to back off.

"Are you finding anything out? How would they be out before their time? No one but Father can do that." Sariel sounded as confused as I felt when it came to this situation.

"Obviously, he's not the only one. Otherwise, they wouldn't be on Earth. Listen, I have things to do. Can you send Izzy back to me, please?" I knew I would get more from him by being polite. He was so easy, and I appreciated it.

"Fine, but have her get me a competent replacement before she leaves. How did you even run things around here? The Elites are impossible to deal with at this point. They think everything they do is right." I couldn't blame him for the annoyance, but his words had me more than a little concerned.

"Sariel, you're only supposed to be covering for me. You aren't supposed to be changing anything. What have you been doing that made you annoyed with them?" I was cautious. Sariel knew not to change anything big, but I was nervous.

"Don't worry, this place will be much more efficient when you come back." He paused. "You know me. I can't help but leave things better than I found them. Don't worry so much. Your sanctuary is in good hands." He hung up the phone before I could comment.

"Fuck, he better not screw up Hell while I'm gone. It works exactly how I need it to work." I rolled my eyes. "Can you have someone monitor my brother? I don't trust that he isn't down there changing everything."

"I already have him monitored. I can check in with what he's doing specifically." Her eyes narrowed on me. "Should I be worried?"

"Yes, we both should." She hurried from the room, her fingers racing over her phone. Good, I didn't need to think about the shit show that Sariel may create in Hell. I rested my feet back up on the coffee table. How could I find out information about Lilith? I closed my eyes, running through all the connections to her I knew. My eyes flashed open when I hit one name.

"Kesa?" I called.

"Yeah?" Her phone was held against her chest. "When you're done with whomever, I have a question. It's important." I didn't know who was on the phone, so I wouldn't say anything until we were alone.

"Okay, just give me a second." She dipped back into the kitchen. "Hey, can you take care of that for me? I need to know everything he's doing in a timely manner. Every. Single. Thing. Got it?" She nodded before hanging up.

"What's up? I was checking in on your brother." I detected a little annoyance from her, but I didn't care.

"So, Asmodeus is close to Lilith, right?" It had been a while, but I remembered them being close. They were even rumored to be married.

"They were once. I don't believe that's the case anymore. Why?" Kesa narrowed her eyes on me, and I couldn't blame her. I was about to deliver a big ask, knowing she would do it whether she wanted to or not.

"Can you get close to him to find out for sure?" I glanced over at her.

She bit the side of her lip and looked away from me. She knew exactly what I was asking of her. After a minute, she rolled her eyes. "Fine, I can find out."

"You know I love you, right?" I smiled.

"Yeah, sure." She got up from the couch without looking at me.

"Shit," I whispered. She went back into her bedroom. Most likely to get space from me. She was the one saying I should keep my eyes on the mission. Now, I was asking her to use her sex life to get information. It didn't feel as good when the shoe was on the other foot.

As I sat there contemplating my next steps, the front door to the house burst open. Cade strode in, looking like he owned the place. "Morning, Kitten," he drawled as he made his way over to me.

"Where have you been?" I demanded, irritation seeping into my voice. I didn't like being left in the dark, especially when it came to Cade.

"I had some business to attend to with my brothers," Cade replied smoothly, his hand caressing my arm in a gesture of apology. "But I'm back now and ready to answer to your every whim, my beautiful Queen of Hell." He laid it on thick. It made me suspicious.

Kesa snorted under her breath. "Yeah, I bet you are." I hadn't heard her come back. She knew as well as I did we needed them all on our side.

I glanced up at Cade and saw the sincerity in his eyes. Maybe Kesa was right, and I shouldn't fall for him. It was hard to resist someone who made me feel so good. The charm helped, too. "Okay," I said finally. "What did you find out?"

Cade settled down on the couch next to me. "It seems that Lilith and Lydia both have something we need," he said gravely. "Without it, there's no end to the world."

"And that's a bad thing?" Kesa muttered. "Sounds perfect. We just need to make sure you don't get whatever it is."

"Yeah, someone might stop you before you even get the chance." Cade leaned forward, his elbows on his knees, as his hand ran down his face. He looked defeated.

"What's it you need to stop the world?" I drew a blank. Each of the seals required something to open them. I wasn't sure to which he was referring.

"The box. It opens the fifth seal. Without it, we can't end anything. It was the protection set up by your father, so the end wouldn't happen unless it was truly time."

"Box? As in Pandora's box? Isn't that Greek?" Kesa asked from the doorway.

"It's all the same, really. As you well know, no one has the true story. We need Pandora's Box. Thane believes Lilith or Lydia have it." He hadn't moved from his rigid position.

"How does he know this?"

"Thane is the head of the vampires. He seems to know everything." Evasive, again.

"What aren't you telling me?" I asked.

"Nothing." He got up from the couch and moved towards the door.

I held my hand out, freezing him in place. "Cade, you told me you wouldn't lie to me." My power tightened around his throat. We were mates, but I'd warned him about lying.

He struggled against my hold as his eyes filled with a mixture of hurt and betrayal. "Let me down," he ordered.

I tightened my power again, wrapping coils of it around his legs and arms so he couldn't move. "Tell me what you're hiding from me."

He struggled against the bindings before finally going limp. I watched as his magic snaked out from him in the golden light. It dissipated when it touched my power. His eyes narrowed on me. "We've already established I am more powerful than you. Our bond doesn't change what I came here to do."

He growled. "I'm doing the same."

"And I can't let you end the world, so tell me what you're hiding from me."

"We already have what we need to find the box." His spiteful words came out through clenched teeth. I could feel his pride.

"Oh?" I lessened the hold around his throat.

"Yeah, I made a deal. Bond with you, and I get what I need to find the box." A smile curved his lips.

My chest constricted, and I couldn't pull in air. "What?"

"You're not the only one here on a mission," Cade responded.

In my devastation, I'd dropped my magical hold on him. I lashed out, my body charging at him. Before I could reach him, he transported out of the room. "Fucker!" I screamed. The sound dredged up from my very soul before I dropped to my knees. Kesa was next to me in a second, pulling me against her.

"I got you." She rubbed my arm, holding me tight against her chest.

Chapter 16

Huxley

I clutched my chest. "What the hell?"

I'd been waiting in Cade's penthouse for him to return. Cade appeared in the kitchen, clutching his chest and coughing as though he'd been deprived of air.

"What the hell just happened?" I stopped in front of his hunched form.

"I fucked up, that's what." He pounded on his chest as he pulled air into his lungs.

"Explain."

Thane and Ryder were in the apartment an instant later. "What the fuck, Cade?" They wore matching expressions of accusation.

"You were supposed to stay close to Lucifer. What did you do to her?" Thane stepped closer.

Cade finally stood upright. "I told her." He met Thane's eyes.

"What? Why?" Thane shifted.

"Told her what?" Ryder looked at the two men.

"I'd made a deal to bond with Lucifer to get information on how to locate Pandora's Box so we can open the fifth seal." Cade strode over to his liquor cabinet. He poured himself half a glass of bourbon and downed it in one gulp.

"I ask again, why?" Thane stood across from him at the counter, staring him down with the penetrating gaze that only a vampire could manage.

He sighed. "Look, I know I fucked up. Do I have to relive it?"

"Damn straight." Ryder stood next to Thane.

Cade rolled his eyes. "Fine, she knew I was lying. She used her power to throw me against the wall until I told her." He refilled the glass and downed it again. "Huxley knows how persuasive she can be."

"Fuck, Cade, you told her you wouldn't lie to her again." I shook my head. "Why did you agree to a deal like that?" I didn't understand why he would make a deal.

"I did it so we'd get the box, or have you forgotten why we're here?" He shook his head. "Damn, you haven't even fucked her, and you're dismissing our mission."

"Bullshit, you were going to fuck her anyway, and we all know it." Ryder glared.

"Fine, but I got what we needed in the process." He waved us off.

"How could you?" I knew Cade could be a cold bastard, but this was beyond anything I imagined him capable of doing.

He met my eyes. "I didn't think I would ever tell her. Ryder wasn't wrong. I was going to do it, anyway. I wanted the chance at love without betrayal. I wanted her to have a reason not to send us back. Hell, I wanted a chance at happiness." He hung his head.

"Instead, you betrayed her." I shook my head.

"Pretty much and fucked up any chance I had at her wanting us around." He refilled his glass. "So much for happiness, guys. Looks like it might be death for all of us. I don't know about you, but I welcome it." He downed another glass.

"Fuck, someone needs to stay with him. I'm going to check on Lucifer." I didn't even wait for a response.

As I hurriedly made my way to Luci's place, my heart was weighed down by the burden of my brother's betrayal. How could Cade have made such a reckless deal? The guilt and sorrow threatened to overwhelm me, but I pushed on, determined to be there for Luci, even in the face of his mistakes.

When I finally reached her door, I felt the tension in the air, the remnants of their heated argument still lingering. I hesitated for a moment before knocking softly, not wanting to intrude on her pain. The door opened, and Luci stood before me, her eyes red and swollen, a silent testament to the pain she was enduring.

"Huxley," she said, her voice thick with emotion. "What do you want?"

"I heard what happened," I replied gently. "I came to see if you were okay."

"I'm fine," she snapped, but her eyes betrayed her true emotions. The door slammed in my face. I caught it a second before it hit me. Luci walked away from the door, expecting my absence. Her hands clenched and unclenched at her sides. Pacing, it took her a minute to realize I was still there. "No, you need to fucking leave. I'm not dealing with any of you again." Her power burst from her, throwing me against the door. I wasn't even sure she meant to do it. Her emotions were so raw. I righted myself, taking a step towards her, my hands up in surrender.

"I know you're hurting," I said, taking a slow step closer to her. "And I know you're scared to trust any of us. But not all of us are like Cade."

She looked away, her defenses up, but I saw the glimmer of hope in her eyes. "Sure, you are. Everyone will betray one another to get what they want. You're no different."

"No, my purpose in coming here was to ensure your well-being. My decision not to bond with you was born out of genuine concern and affection. Understand this— I am not Cade, nor will I ever try to be him," I spoke through clenched teeth, the mere mention of his name stoking a fire of anger within me. The pain he had inflicted on her was unbearable as if it echoed in the recesses of my own heart. In just a few fleeting days, he had shattered her, leaving behind a trail of devastation.

The weight of my emotions threatened to overwhelm me, but I refused to let them surface fully. I couldn't let anger cloud my judgment or compassion, for my feelings were a testament to the deep connection I held with her. I loathed witnessing her pain, for it ignited a fierce protectiveness within me. But I had to be strong, for her sake.

As much as it pained me, I knew I couldn't mend her broken heart with vengeance or hollow promises. I wasn't Cade, and I wouldn't pretend to be someone I wasn't. My path was forged with sincerity, and my intent was to heal, to offer solace in a way only I could.

Though he had hurt her, I refused to let her despair consume her entirely. In the face of her vulnerability, I resolved to be a constant source of strength, a steady presence to guide her through the darkness. I was determined to prove that, even without bonding, my care and devotion were unwavering. Time would be the truest testament to my commitment, as I stayed by her side, mending the wounds he had callously inflicted and showing her that love and support could be found, even in the most unexpected places.

"It's what I get for trusting someone. I should have known better." She paced away from me, her thoughts taking her away from me and back into her own mind. I needed to reach beyond her defenses. Not that I thought I could at this moment. She was hurt. I wouldn't make light of her pain.

"No, you can't blame yourself for his actions. He's the asshole who hurt you. For that, he should pay, but your willingness to trust is a beautiful thing. Don't lose it because of one asshole."

She let out a hysterical laugh. "Right, if it's so beautiful, why do I keep getting hurt? Fuck everyone." She paced the floor like a trapped animal. She had so much pent-up energy she needed to expel it somehow.

"Can I take you somewhere?" I asked.

She stopped in her pacing and looked at me, surprised and suspicious. "What? Where?"

"I know what might help you release some of that anger. You can't keep it inside you." I took another tentative step closer to Luci.

"How do I know I can trust you?" she whispered, her vulnerability showing through the cracks in her façade.

"I won't lie to you, Luci," I said firmly. "I won't do anything to hurt you. I'll always come for you when you need me. I promise."

"But how can I believe you?" she asked, her voice breaking. "Every time I let someone in, they hurt me. They leave, or they betray me. Why should you be any different?"

"Because I care about you," I replied, reaching out to gently cup her cheek. "I've seen the pain you've endured, and I want to be there for you. I want to be the one you can rely on, the one who won't let you down."

She closed her eyes, tears spilling down her cheeks. "It's hard to believe that," she admitted, her voice barely a whisper.

"I know," I said softly, wiping away her tears with my thumb. "But I'm willing to prove it to you, Luci. I won't rush you or push you into trusting me. I'll be patient, and I'll show you with my actions that I'm not like Cade."

She opened her eyes, searching mine for any sign of deception. "I want to believe you," she said, her voice wavering. "But it's so hard."

"I know," I repeated, pulling her into a gentle embrace. "And I won't force you to trust me right away. Just know that I'm here for you, no matter what. And I won't let you face this alone."

She clung to me, her tears soaking into my shirt. "I don't know if I can do this," she whispered.

"That's okay," I said, holding her tightly. "We'll take it one step at a time. I won't let anything happen to you. We'll figure this out together."

As I comforted her, I knew that winning her trust wouldn't be easy. She had been hurt before, and her walls were high and fortified. But I was determined to be patient, to show her through my actions I could be trusted. We had a long journey ahead of us, but I was ready to take it on— for her and for us. Together, we could face whatever challenges lay ahead and find a way to heal the wounds of the past. And I would make sure she knew, without a doubt, she wasn't alone.

"Come on, let's go destroy some shit."

She laughed. "What?"

"You need to let go of that anger." Pausing, I said, "Oh! I have the perfect place where you can set all that rage free." Gently, I rubbed her back as she looked up at me with a mixture of hope and wonder in her eyes. I would do my best not to betray that confidence.

"Okay, where are we going?"

"A rage room. You can break all the things you want." I smiled down at her.

"A what?" Her brows furrowed in confusion.

"A rage room. I hear they're all the rage right now, no pun intended." I shrugged. "It seems like the perfect opportunity to check it out."

"Ah, okay, let's go." She wiped her cheeks. "Give me a minute to get cleaned up." She sniffled.

"Take all the time you need." I heard her footsteps as she ran up the stairs.

"Not bad, Horseman, not bad." Kesa came out from the hallway.

"How long have you been there?" I hadn't heard her at all. I was so focused on Luci, I hadn't been alerted to anyone else here.

"Long enough. I'm going to gut your brother Cade." She sipped from her mug like it was an everyday thing to threaten someone's life. As a demon, maybe it was. "You better heed the warning. I don't take betrayal lightly. I will kill for her without a second thought."

"Good to know." I took a step back. Something about her told me she was one hundred percent serious. "I don't have any intention of betraying her."

"Your brother probably didn't either. Yet here we are." She waved her hand out.

"I know." I lowered my head. "Cade can be, well . . . Cade." I wasn't sure how to explain him to anyone else. I was used to his behavior. Every time I thought he'd changed, he proved he hadn't. The way he rushed to bond with her, I should have known. It wasn't

Cade being Cade. There was no way I thought he'd made a deal to bond her to get something we needed to end the world. I wondered if Cade was in on whatever was going on here. Not that he had the power to do anything of this magnitude, but what the hell? I thought he agreed with Lucifer.

Luci hurried down the stairs. Her ripped jeans and leather jacket were sexy as hell. The low cut of her tight red shirt had me hard in an instant. Damn, I couldn't be thinking about that now. She needed a comforting man, not a horny one. She caught my eyes and cocked her head like she knew exactly what I was thinking. Hell, she probably felt it since she was the epitome of lust. I needed to keep that shit under wraps. Being a man of my word, I swore not to harm her.

"You ready?" She slipped the chain of her purse over her shoulder.

"Yeah, you look amazing."

"I know. Now let's go break some shit." She pulled on my hand. I transported us to the front of the building, keeping us glamoured.

As we entered the rage room, Luci's eyes widened with excitement. The room was filled with many objects to break—plates, vases, even old televisions. The sound of shattering glass and ceramic filled the air as we put on our safety gear. Luci grabbed a baseball bat and swung at a stack of dishes, releasing all her pent-up anger and frustration. Luci let out a primal scream as she swung her bat and smashed a vase on the ground.

I watched as she destroyed everything in sight, smiling as she let out screams of frustration with every hit. It was like watching a wild animal tearing into its prey, but instead of blood and guts, there were just broken pieces of glass flying everywhere.

"You're not going to join me?" Luci asked between swings, taking a moment to catch her breath.

I chuckled. "Oh, I will. Just wanted to let you have fun for a bit."

She nodded and continued smashing things with a newfound vigor. And then I heard a shuffling sound coming from outside the door. I motioned for her to be quiet and listened closely. There were definitely footsteps coming down the hallway.

"Luci," I whispered urgently. "We have to go now."

"What? Why?"

I felt the surge of supernatural energy coming down the hallway. I wasn't sure what breed they were, but their strength had the hairs on the back of my neck standing at attention.

"Just trust me." I took her hand and pulled her towards the back door.

We got out just in time as the door burst open, and several men stormed in, armed with guns. One of them sent out some kind of magical force, testing for our power specifically. What the hell was going on?

"Shit," I muttered under my breath. "I should've known this was too good to be true." I blocked her view, standing between her and the looming threat.

"What's going on?" I felt her hand on my shoulder as she attempted to see around me. I wasn't sure if she could feel their magic and power like I could. It was one gift of being a fae. I could feel others' energy. There's was dark with sinister intentions. I didn't like it. I needed to get Luci out of here.

"We need to get out of here now." I gripped her hand and glamoured us before transporting us to my fae realm.

"Did they bring guns?" Luci let out a laugh. "They thought they could go after us with guns?" Hysterics took over, and she laughed whole-heartedly.

"Those were tranquilizers, not your typical guns. They were packing some major magical signatures. I don't know what they were, but we weren't ready to fight them."

"What? I could have used a good brawl. Let's go back." She held her hand out to take mine.

"You can't just go in blind not knowing what you're up against." I shook my head. I wouldn't let her go back.

"You know who I am, right?" She narrowed her eyes at me. "That's kinda what I do."

"No wonder you got along so well with Cade." I looked to the ground, then to her, realizing my mistake.

"Excuse me?" She glared at me. In an instant, she was gone.

"Shit, shit, shit." I transported back to the rage room. Luci literally stood in the center of the room. At least six gun lasers were trained on her. "Do you have some kind of death wish, woman?" I gaped.

She motioned for them to come hither. Not one of them moved. Why would they? She was surrounded. Why would she put herself in harm's way like that? She wasn't invincible.

I watched, frozen, as Luci continued to taunt and provoke the gunmen. They trained their weapons on her, but she didn't seem to care. Her eyes glinted with a fierce determination that I had never seen before. It was as if she was daring them to take her down.

"Luci," I whispered, "what the hell are you doing?"

She smirked at me over her shoulder. "Seeing which of them has the biggest balls. Come now, which of you is it?"

I could feel my heart hammering in my chest as the tension in the room escalated to unbearable levels. These men were clearly not here for a friendly chat.

Suddenly, one of them raised his weapon and fired.

Everything seemed to happen in slow motion after that. I saw Luci twist out of the way with supernatural speed, her eyes glowing with a fierce intensity. She darted towards one gunman and grabbed his wrist, twisting it until he cried out in pain and dropped his weapon.

The others hesitated for a moment, stunned by her sudden attack. But Luci didn't give them a chance to recover. She moved like lightning, taking them out one by one with quick, precise strikes.

I couldn't believe what I was seeing. Luci was like a force of nature, unstoppable and unbreakable. And as much as I wanted to help her, I knew she didn't need my help.

When the last gunman lay writhing on the ground in pain, Luci turned to look at me with a triumphant grin on her face.

"Told you I could handle myself," she said with a shrug.

I couldn't help but smile back at her. She was magnificent. "I guess you were right."

"Now, let's see who sent them."

Luci strode towards the fallen gunman, her expression unyielding and cold. I followed her lead, staying a few steps behind her in case of any further attacks. The man groaned in pain as she knelt next to him, her eyes locked onto his with an intense stare.

"Who sent you?" Her tone was hard and unyielding, a stark contrast to the playful flirtation she had used moments before.

The man spat at her feet, glaring up at her with open hatred. "Like I'll tell you anything."

Luci didn't even flinch. She simply reached out and grabbed the man's hand, twisting it until he cried out in renewed agony.

"I think you will," she said softly, almost calmly. "Unless you thought today was a good day to experience the worst pain of your life. Did the person who sent you tell you I'm the punisher in the flesh? No, of course not. You wouldn't be here." Yanking back on his hand until every bone in his wrist broke, she dropped it. The man's piercing scream echoed in the warehouse room.

I watched in silent awe as Luci interrogated the man with ruthless efficiency. Luci picked up a piece of broken glass and walked around each of the men. "Now, boys, the one of you who talks first will gain my favor." She kicked the boot of one of them as she walked. "The rest of you will experience pain like none you've experienced before. Now, who wants to tell me who sent you?"

"She'll kill us," one man spat towards Luci.

That snapped my attention. My thorns drew up from the ground beneath him, wrapping him in a torturous embrace. Each of the thorns pierced his flesh, and I sighed in pleasure at the taste of my enemy's blood. Luci smiled widely at me.

"Damn, that's sexy." She beamed at me.

"Well, if I'd known sooner that impaling your enemies was the way to your heart, I would have gotten on it immediately." My thorns wrapped around his neck, and in an instant, his neck snapped. I would let no one treat Luci like that. Not on my watch.

"So, who's ready to talk?" Scanning the room, she waited. Stepping into the broken glass added to her threats. Everything in this room was destroyed from our time here.

I drew up more vines, wrapping the rest of the men. "Maybe they just need a bit of motivation," I smirked.

One of the men's eyes widened. He was next to the man whose neck I snapped earlier. "Lilith, Lilith sent us," he blabbered.

In an instant, he was burning. "We tried to tell you. She'll kill us." A second later, they were all burning.

"What the hell?" Luci stared around at the men, who were now all piles of ash.

"Apparently, she still wasn't ready for us."

Chapter 17

Luci

"Fucking Lilith." I clenched my hands at my sides. I took us back to my house. "Kesa," I called out. No answer. What the hell? Where was she? "Kesa," I called again.

"Do you have her working on something?" Huxley asked.

"Shit, yeah. I guess I sent her to find out what Lilith was up to. I guess she started right away." I pulled out a stool in the kitchen and sat.

"Would you expect anything less?" Huxley smirked at me.

I rolled my eyes. "No, but she's supposed to be here when I need her."

"Well, you get me instead." He pulled out the stool next to me.

"Yeah, but you're not getting the information I need." I grabbed my phone from my purse. I dialed Kesa. It went straight to voicemail. "What the hell? She should have service everywhere." I dropped the phone on the counter.

"Izzy," I called out, letting my power reach out to her.

She materialized in the kitchen, swaying as she materialized. She brushed down her shirt before she turned a scathing glare on me. "Lucifer, we talked about this. Could you at least warn a girl before you just pop me wherever you are?" Her scathing look softened when she looked at me. "Oh, babe, what's wrong? What's going on? Did this bastard hurt you? I'll punish him for you." Her glare turned to Huxley sitting next to me. He held his hands up in surrender.

"I wouldn't." He muttered.

"Where's Lilith?" I asked.

"What? Why?" She looked more than a little confused.

"Just tell me where she is?"

"You haven't given me enough time. I haven't gotten enough information on her location," Izzy complained. Her hesitation was uncharacteristic.

"Bullshit, Izzy, tell me where she is now." I knew when someone was lying to me. Izzy lied. I don't know why, but she did. I would dig into that later. For now, I needed to confront Lilith.

She narrowed her eyes at me before shaking her head and closing her eyes. "Fine, but you're not ready for what's in store for you when you see her."

"What the hell does that mean, Iz?" I stood, jumping over the counter to stand in front of her. "What are you not telling me, Izzy?" I grabbed her shirt in my hands and held her firm.

Her eyes widened. "Um, Lilith has been busy. Remember, you're not one to kill the messenger."

"Start talking." I gripped her tighter.

"I heard rumors that Lilith has been working with an ancient demon, one who hasn't been seen in centuries. He's powerful, Luci. More powerful than any of us can imagine," Izzy explained, her voice shaking with fear. "I don't even know if he's real, but the whispers are getting louder."

I released my grip on Izzy and took a step back, my mind reeling with the implications. An ancient demon? Working with Lilith? What could she possibly want with him?

"We need to find out more about this demon," Huxley said, his voice firm and resolute. "We can't go blindly into a confrontation with them."

"Agreed," I said, nodding. "But first things first—we need to find Lilith."

"That's not all." Izzy swallowed hard.

"There's more?" I waited.

"Lilith has made a deal with someone powerful," Izzy said with a shaky breath. "Someone who can give her what she wants in exchange for something equally valuable."

"What does Lilith want?" Huxley asked, leaning forward to listen intently.

"I'm not sure," Izzy admitted, looking down at her hands. "But I heard whispers that she wants to overthrow you, Lucifer, and claim the throne of Hell for herself."

My heart rate quickened. Lilith was always ambitious, but this was on another level. "We need to stop her," I declared firmly. "Whatever it takes."

"Agreed," Huxley said, his eyes burning with determination.

"But how?" Izzy asked, looking up at me with concern. "She's powerful, and she'll have demons on her side, your demons."

"Certainly, not all of them have aligned with her," I said, my mind racing with the possibilities. "If so, I still have friends who are loyal to me. And if worse comes to worst, I'll fight to protect what's mine."

Izzy nodded slowly, looking relieved. "Okay."

"Good," Huxley said, standing and stretching his arms. "Then let's get started. We have work to do."

"Time to find Lilith and bring the fight to her. Where is she, Iz?" I stared at her. Let's see if she was being honest.

"Luci, you have no idea what you're walking into. I know you're not a fool."

My power whipped out so fast Izzy was against the refrigerator. "What did you say?" I growled.

Her desperate fingers clawed at my invisible power as she pleaded, "I didn't mean it. I'm your friend, and I worry about you." In a moment of decision, I let her go.

"Don't call me a fool again."

"Noted." Izzy rubbed her neck. "You need to find a new schtick." She held her hands up when I darted my eyes in her direction.

"Why, that one works?" I shrugged.

"Fair enough," Izzy followed me into the living room.

Huxley halted in the kitchen. "I should call my brothers. They'll be interested to know what's going on."

"Why, so they can get the box before I have a chance? No." I glared at him.

"I'll only mention how we were attacked. I'm going to tell them we're lying low for now. You know, what smart people who valued their lives would do." I wanted to punch him for the dig, but he wasn't exactly wrong. I hadn't batted an eye at the prospect of taking on a demon that may be more powerful than me. It was laughable that they were more powerful, but I hear miracles happen every day.

When Izzy and I were in the living room, I turned on her. "Where's Lilith, Izzy? I'm not asking again."

"Ugh, fine." She sighed. "She's living in a mansion on the hill in Sin City. You won't miss it. She's done the place up to look very dark and ominous. Very Lilith-esque, if you will." She smirked. "Black metal gates and a garden filled with midnight blue and deep purple flowers. Including the ones that only bloom at midnight." She paused. "There's even a greenhouse at the top. How long do you think she's been living up here? I haven't heard about her in years." Izzy's eyes widened as she realized the ramifications of what she was saying. It was part of her job to know what everyone was up to for me.

"You're slipping, Izzy. Do better." I closed my eyes and focused on what Izzy described. Of course, she'd take up residence in Sin City.

The image of Lilith's mansion formed in my mind's eye, and I felt a surge of anger and determination coursing through me. She had hidden herself away for years, and now she was back with a vengeance, scheming and plotting to overthrow me and claim the throne of Hell. After all this time, I provided her refuge for her demons. I did all that I could to make them feel welcome in my home. Now, she betrayed me. I would put an end to whatever plan she'd concocted to take my home. The only way that would happen was over my dead body.

"Izzy, I need you to stay here," I said, my voice firm. "Monitor things, and if anything happens, contact me immediately."

"But Luci, I want to help you," she protested.

"I know you do, and I appreciate it," I replied, placing a reassuring hand on her shoulder. "But I can't risk losing you. You're my best friend, and I need you here. I need you to tell my brothers if something goes wrong."

She hesitated for a moment before nodding reluctantly. "Okay, but you better come back in one piece, got it?"

"I promise," I said, giving her a small smile.

Huxley stepped forward, his expression serious. "I'll go with you, Luci. I won't let you face this alone."

I appreciated his offer, but I shook my head. "No, Huxley. You need to stay here as well. You and Izzy can watch each other's backs. I'll be okay."

"Luci, we don't know what we're walking into," he argued. "You need all the help you can get."

"I know, but I can't risk it," I said, my voice tinged with emotion. "I won't be able to focus on the task at hand if I'm constantly worrying about your safety."

Huxley hesitated. "Not a chance. You aren't going into this alone. I won't allow it. We may not have bonded yet, but I will protect you with my life."

I shook my head. I couldn't tell him I didn't trust him after what Cade did. Although, he'd had my back in the rage room. He was damn sexy when he used his powers. I closed my eyes. "Fine, you can come with me. But you aren't telling your brothers. Izzy will notify them of anything if she needs to. Okay?" I didn't want any surprises. I'd had enough for one day.

The night was dark and filled with an eerie silence, and I could feel the weight of the impending confrontation pressing down on me.

As I made my way towards Lilith's mansion, I couldn't help but feel a mix of fear and determination. This was a dangerous path I was treading, but I had to stop Lilith before she could bring about any more chaos and destruction.

I stared up at the black iron gates, a smirk plastered on my face. "Iron, nice touch."

"Not really." Huxley took a step back.

"What?" I turned to look at him. He was shrinking back from the iron.

"I can't go through the gates. Being near them burns, Luci. I can't follow you." The desperation in his voice cut deep.

"I'll be okay," I reassured him.

"No, stop. You can't go in there alone." Huxley took a step towards me before jumping back again, wincing. "Fuck." He rubbed his arms.

"I have little of a choice, do I?" I pressed my lips together, pulling what determination I had within me to go forward alone.

I reached out to the imposing black metal gates of the mansion and pushed them open with a surge of power. The air was deathly silent. The only sound we heard was the wind passing through the leaves of the trees and the crows announcing my arrival from the treetops. Crickets chirped; a lone owl hooted in the distance. A sound I wouldn't expect to hear in the day's light, but there was something different about this place.

The garden was indeed filled with midnight blue and deep purple flowers, their petals shimmering in the moonlight. I felt the dark energy emanating from the place, a clear sign that Lilith had made herself at home here. The flowers were masterfully picked, and their sweet scent wafted through the air, masking the rot in the soil underneath.

The earth rose from the ground and crawled up the walls of the mansion. The cobblestone walkway led to the grand front doors, ten feet high, and windows just as large. The front door itself was pitch black and seemed to swallow any light that hit it. This place was a living, breathing organism. It screamed at Lilith's presence, a city lived in and loved by a demon goddess.

Taking a deep breath, I walked towards the mansion's entrance, my heart pounding in my chest. I knew that the next moments would be crucial, and I had to be prepared for anything. I couldn't let fear cloud my judgment, not when so much was at stake.

I entered the mansion, the air thick with tension. Every step I took felt like a battle, and I had to remind myself to stay focused and vigilant. I couldn't afford to let my guard down, not even for a moment.

As I made my way through the mansion, I couldn't help but think about Huxley and Izzy waiting for me. But I knew I had to face this challenge head-on. Lilith had to be stopped, and I was the only one who could do it. It was a burden I had to bear, but I wouldn't back down from the fight. I would protect my loved ones and the world, no matter the cost.

With determination in my heart, I continued on my path, ready to confront Lilith and put an end to her wicked plans once and for all. Whatever happened next, I knew I wouldn't be alone. I had the strength and support of my friends behind me, and that was enough to give me the courage to face whatever lay ahead.

Chapter 18

Cade

I had been drinking heavily all night and had found myself in a strange state of mind. I was swaying in time to the soft jazz music filtering through the air, my thoughts drifting towards nothing and everything at once. In the corner of my eye, a flash of movement caught my attention, and a sudden sense of dread coursed through me. Slowly, I turned my head and saw my phone buzzing next to it.

"Cade, you need to get your ass here now. Luci went in to confront Lilith alone." Huxley had me blinking out of my drunk stupor in a second.

"What? Why aren't you with her?"

"The gates and fence are iron. I can't cross it." His panicked words hit me like a punch to the gut.

Sobering, I tapped into the mate bond. I felt her heart pounding from fear and anticipation, as well as my own. "Where are you?"

"A mansion outside of Vegas. You need to get here. She's going to kill me for calling after everything you did to her." He stopped, irritation and rage mixing into a guttural sound deep in his throat. "If you ever cared for her at all, you'll get here now." He hung up the phone.

Glancing around my bedroom, I must have passed out at some point. I didn't actually remember getting to the bedroom. Flopped down on my stomach, my suit was a wrinkled mess around me. At least I'd taken off my jacket at some point. A pain at having to leave looking like this hit me before I felt Luci's fear again. Whatever I was worried about was gone. I needed to get to Luci. I couldn't let her go in alone.

Gathering my courage, I rolled out of bed and hurdled to my feet. With quick movements, I grabbed a few weapons and stuffed them into my pocket before heading towards the door. I had to get to Luci as soon as possible. Huxley paced about a hundred feet from the gates. His shoes clicked a rhythm along the black pavement, echoing in the stillness of the night. His shoulders stiffened, and the tension in his face showed the worry he held.

Sighing as soon as his eyes hit mine. "Thank, Fuck, Cade, she's in there alone. She wouldn't even let Izzy go in with her." Relief and fear mingled on Huxley's face.

"It's probably good Izzy isn't with her. She's the one who made a deal with me." I glanced up to take in what was ahead of me. The mansion was grand but foreboding, with a dark aura that sent shivers down my spine.

"What? You left that part out of what you told us." Huxley's eyes were wide.

"Yeah, I wasn't trying to share more than I had to at the time."

"You didn't tell Luci?" It was a statement more than a question.

"Yeah, hit her with betrayals at once. I think I've done enough damage, don't you?" I took a step towards the gates.

"Wait, are you going to tell her? She needs to know that her friend is working against her." He backed up. The gates would hurt him, even as far away as he was. Fae couldn't be this close to iron. It amazed me at his ability to walk around the city. Not that many used straight iron anymore. It still amazed me.

"It's not my news to tell. Now, do you want me to go find Luci, or are we going to continue this chat?" I gave him a pointed look.

"Oh yeah, go," He waved me forward. "And Cade."

"Yeah?"

"Don't fuck this up."

"I'll do my best," I smirked. "What excellent parting words," I murmured.

The air around me was thick with tension as I stepped through the gates. My heart hammered in my chest, and my stomach felt like it was filled with lead. I had no idea what to expect, but I knew that it wouldn't be good. The crunch of gravel beneath my feet sounded overly loud in the stillness of the night, and I felt a bead of sweat trickle down my back.

I felt the weight of the iron gates as soon as I approached them, but I focused past it, pushing through with my powers. The gates creaked loudly as they opened, and I knew it wouldn't be long before Lilith was alerted to my presence. As scared as I was, something inside me kept me going forward—something that told me this was something I had to do for Luci.

The mansion loomed in front of me like a beacon of evil. An aura of darkness seemed to waft from its windows and doors, sending chills racing down my spine. A part of me wanted to turn around and run away—go back home where it was safe—but another part urged me forward, urging me to find Luci before it was too late. Taking a deep breath, I forced myself onward up the stairs and towards the door.

I made my way through the garden, careful not to touch any of the flowers clearly tainted with dark magic. The mansion itself was even more ominous than the outside, with twisted vines creeping up the walls and shadows lurking around every corner. I felt Luci's fear like a beacon, guiding me towards her.

As I approached the mansion, I felt all the dark magic surrounding the entire place. It was a trap. Every single part of this place was tinged with magic. It was good that Huxley had called me. Neither Thane nor Ryder could sense this level of sorcery. There weren't many on the planet who could perform spells quite like this. I broke the wards I'd come across on the lawn. I hadn't even made it up to the door before the magic halted my progress.

How had Lucifer made it inside already?

I had to get to her. I worked as fast as possible to clear the wards that were obviously placed around the perimeter for magic users. Lucifer may not have even flinched when she'd walked through them. I, on the other hand, needed to break them before even attempting any forward progress. The wards coiled tightly around me, a formidable obstacle. One wrong move, and I'd be dust. Lilith had sensed my alliance with Luci; she was always one step ahead. My deal with Izzy to mate with her weighed heavily, and I knew I had betrayed Luci. But deep down, I craved that bond despite the regret.

For that, I was a selfish bastard.

Maybe I'd get lucky, and she wouldn't kill me on sight.

Finally, I'd broken down the wards enough so I could go through the front door. I blew out a sigh of relief before I noticed what lay ahead. Demons, a hallway filled with demons.

"Fuck me."

CHAPTER 19

LUCI

My heart pounded in my chest as I stepped further into Lilith's mansion, my senses on high alert. The stench of sulfur and dark magic filled the air, a clear sign that demons lurked nearby. I tightened my grip on the trident I conjured in my hand, its prongs crackling with electric energy. Poseidon ain't got nothing on me.

As I turned a corner, I came face to face with a group of snarling demons, their eyes glowing with malice. Without hesitation, I swung my trident, unleashing bolts of lightning that sizzled through the air and struck the demons down one by one. But more of them came, drawn to the clash of powers like moths to a flame.

I was surrounded, but I refused to back down. With a wave of my hand, I conjured a wall of fire, forcing the demons to keep their distance. But they weren't easily deterred. With a collective growl, they lunged at me again, and I focused my power, sending shockwaves through the ground that knocked them off their feet.

The battle was fierce and unrelenting, and sweat trickled down my forehead. I knew I had to find Lilith and put an end to her schemes before more demons descended upon me. With fierce determination, I fought my way through the mansion, leaving a trail of defeated foes in my wake.

I felt a familiar presence behind me. It was Cade. Perfect, I'd love to take down all my enemies at once. "Cade." I gritted my teeth, not turning to look at him.

"At your service," he mocked.

I whirled around, my eyes blazing with fury. "You," I spat. "What are you doing here?" Rage coursed through my body. His features shifted as though he were in pain before he schooled his features. Damn poker face. I hoped he could feel my hatred for him. He deserved to know every facet of the pain he put me through.

"I couldn't let you go in alone," Cade held his hands up in surrender. "I'm here to help."

"I don't need your help," I snapped, not wanting to let my guard down around him.

He stepped closer, readying to join me in the fight against the demons. "I know you don't trust me, and I understand why. But I can't just stand by and watch you fight alone."

I wanted to tell him to leave, to go back to his brothers and his destruction of the world, but I couldn't deny the truth in his words. I needed all the help I could get. With a nod, I acknowledged his presence, but I still couldn't bring myself to look at him directly.

Cade's hand snapped out, and a surge of blue light cast out from his hands. A demon dropped behind me with a thud. "See, you need me."

"Don't push it. I'll kill you where you stand."

"You say the most romantic things," Cade smirked before sending another blast into a spider demon. Damn, I hated those things. All the legs were disturbing, to say the least. I also hated the camaraderie I felt as Cade and I fought side by side.

Together, we battled our way through Lilith's minions, each of us using our unique powers to dispatch the demons with deadly precision. Cade used his resourcefulness and adaptability to complement my raw power and authority. I would never admit that we made a good pair. It helped that we could sense the other on a level I'd never imagined. I knew what he would do an instant before he did it. I could send warnings to him without a single word. It came in handy in battle. We'd made our way down the hall. A large, peaked door stood before us. Lilith, ever the pompous one. Of course, her room would be the most ornamented. Who even makes doors this large?

"Are you sure about this?" Cade asked. His eyes took in the large doors before us.

I nodded, my jaw set. "I need to know what's going on."

With that, I pushed open the door and strode inside. The inside of the room was just as beautiful as the outside—and just as sinister. The air was thick with magic, and I felt Lilith's presence all around me.

"Lilith!" I yelled, my voice echoing against the walls. I couldn't see her, but I knew she was there. "Show yourself!"

There was no answer— only silence. It was unnerving, to say the least. Suddenly, there was a rustling sound from behind the desk. The adrenaline pumping through my veins was enough to make me feel invincible. I felt the power within me growing stronger. It was like a fire igniting deep in my core, ready to be unleashed. This was my birthright, my destiny. No one would stand in my way. Especially not Lilith. The sound of Lilith's perilous laugh had me gripping my trident.

The sound of laughter hit me again. I felt a wave of anger wash over me. How dare she act so casually when she was trying to take over my kingdom? Another laugh came from a corner of the room.

"Oh, little devil, you can't even find me." I exchanged a look with Cade.

"Magic," he whispered.

"Can you break through it?"

He nodded. "It's going to take a minute and all my focus. Think you can watch my back, or are you going to stab it while I'm working?"

I glared. "I'm not sure. How about you take down the ward, and I'll contemplate not killing you?" I clenched the trident in my hand.

"Again, such a romantic." He waved his hands. A second later, it looked like he was pulling at a string of lighted magic. He worked, weaving it into something else entirely. I was mesmerized by the careful way he worked the delicate strands.

Finally, he pulled at the last bit, and a door appeared before us. I blinked. That hadn't been there before; I was sure of it. Since when couldn't I see through illusions. Magic had never affected me before. What changed? I didn't have time to contemplate that further. Cade reached out, and the doorknob didn't budge.

I yanked on it with no luck. All this, and I would be stalled by a damn lock. Nope, not a chance. I gritted my teeth, and Cade took a step back as though he knew what I was about to do. Steeling myself, I kicked the door down, sending it flying open and into splinters around the room. The sound echoed through the house as I stepped inside. The smell of incense filled my nostrils as I scanned the room.

There she was, lounging on her chaise like some kind of queen. Asmodeus behind her, his hands working dexterously, massaging her shoulders as another man massaged her feet.

"Well, well, well," she purred, "what do we have here?"

"Lilith, what the hell is going on?" I glared at the woman. She waved her hand, dismissing the man at her feet. He stood, bowed, and left the room through a door in the far corner. I should be surprised that he was naked, but I wasn't. This was Lilith's house, after all.

Lilith laughed, a sound that sent chills down my spine. "You really have no idea what you're getting yourself into, do you?" she said, standing up from her lounge. Asmodeus stood just behind her, never staying more than a hand's distance away. It was good Kesa wasn't here. She didn't deserve this betrayal. Only one of us could be emotionally destroyed at a time. His presence had me thinking. Was he only at the club to get information or to keep my friend occupied while Lilith had me where she wanted me? But then why did she let me go at all? Whoever the guy was, he wanted me to stay in his damn cave. Why did she insist I leave with Huxley? What game was she playing?

"I know enough," I replied, summoning all the power within me. "And I'm not leaving until you tell me everything."

Lilith smirked and launched herself at me with supernatural speed. I held my hand out and watched as her momentum slammed against my power, stopping her in her tracks. I felt Cade at my back, ready to protect me if needed. I didn't need him to protect me. I could handle this bitch.

Her eyes narrowed at me, and when she stopped her forward attempts, I let my power go. "Ugh." She smoothed down her dress. "You can be so insufferable sometimes."

"Why do you even bother?" I asked. "You know I'm more powerful than you."

She glared at me. "You aren't as strong as you think you are." She turned away, flipping her hair back over her shoulder, and took her place back on the lounge. Asmodeus followed like a good little minion.

I didn't waste any more time with pleasantries. "Where's the box?" I demanded, my voice low and dangerous.

Lilith arched an eyebrow. "What makes you think I'll just hand it over to you?"

I smiled coldly. "Because if you don't, I'll make your life hell. I think you forget who's been housing you and your demon for the last, what, thousand years or so." I looked down at my nails, feigning boredom.

"You think you're so generous, Lucifer," she growled.

"No one else would take you. So, what is 'it you think you're doing, Lilith? There's no way you'll be able to take Hell from me. Why don't you put everything back to the way it was, and I'll think about letting your demons stay in Hell."

"Ha, you think it's going to be that easy."

"I do."

Before anyone could move, I snapped my fingers, and a burst of energy shot out from my hand, hitting Lilith square in the chest. She fell back against the chair, her hand gripping where I'd just struck. "You're such a bitch, Lucifer. You know that." She rubbed at the spot for a few minutes. I tapped my foot as my impatience wore on.

"I am aware. Now, let's start again. Where's the box? Who the hell was that guy yesterday? Why do you think you have a chance in hell at taking over Hell?" I ran through each question as her glare turned into a smirk.

"God, your ignorance is such a pleasure to me."

I moved my hand again, but this time, it hit a wall. "Don't hurt her again," Asmodeus growled behind her. I shouldn't have doubted he wouldn't let me get in another strike.

"I won't as long as she tells me what I want to know." I looked between the two. "Lilith, start talking."

She rolled her eyes. "First of all, I don't actually have the box you're referring to. You think I'd be holding something that valuable when I know you're looking for me. Besides, I'm simply the messenger in all this." She paused, glancing back at Asmodeus. "What's that saying? Don't kill the messenger. I'm simply helping out a friend." She reached her hand back to take Asmodeus'.

"Oh? Who's your friend?"

"Now, I wouldn't be a very good friend if I told you that, now would I?"

"Lilith, don't make me ask again." I clenched my hands at my sides. Both Lydia and Lilith were in on this, but neither of them would tell me who the hell this guy was. What did he want with me, or the end of the world? It was getting annoying.

She smiled. "Don't worry. I wouldn't want our little devil to worry. Isn't that what he calls you?" She motioned behind me to Cade. "Or is that what the other one calls you? The one you looked quite cozy with yesterday?" She shook her head. "Poor bastard, he goes to all that trouble to try to save you, and you haven't given him a second thought." She released a sigh. "Such a stupid horseman. Did he tell you about the arrangement he made to get the box?"

"I'm well aware of the deal. Why did you want me to bond so badly? You thought having lovers would keep me from doing my job?" I furrowed my brows. "It never had before. Why would it now?"

Lilith chuckled darkly, her eyes dancing with malicious delight. "Oh, my dear Lucifer, it's not about keeping you from your job. It's about keeping you distracted. You see, while you were playing house with the horsemen, my friend was busy finding what he needed, hidden away in the depths of Hell."

My heart pounded as the realization hit me. "He's in Hell?" I whispered, my mind racing to think of who could be powerful enough to navigate the treacherous depths of my domain without my knowledge.

Lilith smirked, confirming my suspicions. "Yes, he's been quite intrigued by you, Lucifer. And when he told me about his little plan, I couldn't resist getting involved."

"Who is he?" I demanded, my voice quivering with anger and fear. I wanted to know who was toying with me, using the horsemen and the end of the world as a means to achieve their own sinister goals.

"Ah, ah, ah." Lilith wagged her finger mockingly. "I can't reveal that little secret. He'd be quite cross with me if I did."

I clenched my fists, trying to keep my composure. "Tell me everything you know. Why does he want the box? Why did he release the horsemen? What does he plan to do now that everything is in motion?"

"He wants to harness the power of the box," Lilith said, her eyes gleaming with wicked delight. "It's said to contain a force unlike anything the world has ever seen. And with that power, he plans to reshape reality to his liking."

"Reshape reality?" I repeated, my mind reeling at the implications. Pandora's box was dangerous enough, but in the hands of someone with such nefarious intentions, it could bring about catastrophic consequences.

"Yes, my dear. He aims to bring about an apocalypse of his own making, one that will plunge the world into chaos and destruction. And he's chosen you, Lucifer, as his key to unlocking that power."

I felt a chill run down my spine. The thought of being manipulated and used like a pawn in someone else's twisted game was infuriating. "I won't let him succeed," I vowed, my voice laced with determination.

Lilith laughed as her eyes locked onto mine. "Oh, how I love your spirit, Lucifer. But do be careful. This friend of mine is not to be underestimated. He's cunning and powerful, and he has an army of demons at his command."

I took a deep breath, steadying myself. "I'll face whatever challenges come my way. I won't let him or anyone else destroy the world."

"Such bravado," Lilith purred, stepping closer to me. "It'll be such a pleasure to watch you try."

Before I could respond, Lilith vanished, leaving only a cloud of black smoke in her wake. I clenched my fists, my mind racing with thoughts of who this mysterious figure could be and what I needed to do to stop him.

"Luci, are you okay?" Cade's voice brought me back to the present, and I turned to look at him. Anger and hurt still lingered between us, but for now, we had a common enemy to face.

"I'm fine," I said, my voice determined. "We need to go to Hell. There's someone I need to talk to."

Cade raised an eyebrow. "Hell? Are you sure that's a good idea?"

"I don't have a choice," I replied, my heart heavy with the weight of responsibility. "I need answers, and I know just the person to give them to me. Let's go."

Chapter 20

Luci

I thought about everything that had happened thus far and who would benefit most from both Earth and Hell being in turmoil. Why was it paramount that I be distracted from Hell?

I closed my eyes and listened to my kingdom.

The screams of tortured souls filled my ears. The sounds used to be like a sweet lullaby, familiar and comforting, but now, they grated on my nerves. Something wasn't right. The usual order and routine of my demons seemed to be off balance. I tried to focus on the swirl of emotions running through me, but it was impossible with the chaos in my kingdom. I decided to take a stroll, hoping that moving around would ease the restlessness inside me. As I walked past barred doors of demons, some of them malevolent, others just resigned to their fate. I couldn't help but think about the last few days.

Cade. He fought by my side even though I could have killed him for his betrayal. I wasn't sure what to do with that. His betrayal cut so deep, but why? I'd only known him a few days. It wasn't like one could fall in love in a few short days. The bond had to be clouding my judgment. There was no other explanation for how fast I'd been willing to bond with him. I couldn't help but think it was my fault I'd acted so harshly. It wasn't fair to him that I'd blamed everything on him. We were both being manipulated. I knew exactly who he was. He told me he was here to complete his mission just as I was. It was naïve to think he would stop trying to end the world after sex with me. Well, damn good sex, but still. I wasn't being fair. Maybe I'd just rake him over the coals for a few years to make him think about what he'd done.

As I continued my walk, I noticed red eyes in the darkness watching me. It wasn't uncommon for demons to follow me around, seeking attention or favor, but these felt different. They were more furtive and secretive—like they were hiding something from me. I decided to follow them and see where they led me.

The group of demons led me to one of the deepest parts of Hell, where even stronger and more dangerous demons resided. Baal stood tall and imposing, his presence commanding the attention of all who dared approach him. He had two demons restrained at his side, their powers weakened by his dominance.

"What are you doing here?" I asked, drawing closer.

"I'm surprised you didn't figure it out already." He smirked at me. "I'm here on business . . ." He paused. " . . . and pleasure. It's my little corner of Hell, after all."

I, with a cold and determined expression, stepped forward, acknowledging Baal's power. "Funny. I'm here on business too," I stated with a subtle hint of challenge in my voice.

Baal, his voice thundering like the storm surrounding him, responded, "Ah, Lucifer, the fallen one. What business brings you to my realm?" A wicked smile curled on his lips. I knew very well Baal would be privy to whatever Lilith was doing on Earth. There was no way none of this escaped his attention.

My gaze locked with Baal's, our eyes reflecting ancient enmity. "I know your allegiance lies with Lilith. I know this is a mere distraction, a plot to set the wheels of the apocalypse in motion. But I won't let either of you destroy the world, Baal."

Baal's laughter echoed through the storm, blending with the thunderous rumble. "The apocalypse? Oh, how delightful it will be to witness the end of all things. But worry not, Lucifer, I have other interests at hand. Fertility, crops, and the balance of nature. I seek to disrupt the bountiful harvests, to instigate chaos in the natural order. It is through this disruption that Lilith's true plans shall unfurl." He couldn't be the one working with Lilith. She made it seem like her partner was more powerful than me. Baal wasn't more powerful. So, what tied him to all this?

My face contorted with a mix of anger and disbelief. "You are but a puppet, Baal, blinded by your desires. By denying our own demons, we become complicit in their twisted desires. I won't let you or Lilith succeed."

"You have no choice. The wheels are already in motion." He gestured towards the two restrained demons beside him. "You don't recognize them, do you, Lucifer?"

"I know every one of my people on sight. These two aren't mine." I rolled my eyes. I didn't know what game Baal was playing this time, but I'd had enough bullshit this week to last a lifetime.

"You don't claim them?" he asked, his pitch rising.

This felt like some kind of trick. "What are you playing at, Baal? They aren't mine."

His voice boomed. "Do you hear that, my children? Lucifer has denied her own." His wicked laughter echoed in the chamber, and the screams and cries of the demons throughout the realm intensified in my ears. What was this?

"Baal, what have you done?" I held my hands to my ears as the screams and cries became so intense I couldn't stand. My body buckled under the weight.

"You, Lucifer, have denied your own demon and fallen refuge as you swore an oath to do." Baal waved a hand, and the two figures changed. One was Izzy, and the other was Kesa. Their faces contorted in horror as shadows of dark clouds swirled around them. "You are cast from this realm and stripped of the title to which your father once bestowed upon you."

Shadows and tormented screams filled the cavern.

I watched in horror as the demons in shadow lunged for my friends. I clenched my jaw, fighting against the torment in my own head. I had to get out of here. I had to get us all out of here. I ran full speed, my arms outstretched. When I felt their skin touch mine, I transported all of us to Earth.

When we caught our breath in the safety of the rented house, I looked at the two. "What the hell just happened?" Kesa blurted.

Izzy glared at me. "Luci just lost her power over Hell. I'd call that Check and Mate."

* * *

Don't forget, if you liked this book please leave a review. To an author, it's like a hug. (Unless you hated it, then, not so much.)

Review here

Continue the Ditching Hell Series in book two, .

dorablume.net

* * *

Newsletter

About the Author

Dora Blume is a high school English teacher by day, writer by night. She tends to write books with spunky, bad-ass female characters, random movie quotes from the 90's, and page-turning adventure. She lives just outside of Minneapolis with her two dogs, Jack and Bailey. Reading is her life's passion. She even gets paid to share a love of reading with others. Fat girl problems is her blog, check it out if you want a good laugh, or cry, could go either way. Check out one of her paranormal books today!

Read More from Dora Blume

https://www.facebook.com/groups/747878828927862

Milton Keynes UK
Ingram Content Group UK Ltd.
UKHW040653191023
430917UK00001B/72